ACCLAIM

ACCLAIM

"A delicious murder mystery take on *Phantom of the Opera*! Seeing *Phantom* in a modern context with such enjoyable characters was so fresh! A must read for all of those who enjoy this haunting classic!

—AJ SKELLY, bestselling author of The Wolves of Rock Falls series and *Murder at Mistlethwaite Manor*

Angels Wept Tonight

Angels Wept Tonight

Quill & Flame
PUBLISHING HOUSE

Hope Bolinger

Quill & Flame
PUBLISHING HOUSE

To all my theater besties, past and present. Shout out to Sarah, Julie, James, Jess, Tyler, Atlas, Rosie, and Ava. And, of course, to the casts of 60+ shows who made performing a worthy endeavor.

Also By

You can find a full list of Hope's other books at her website:

www.hopebolinger.com

CHAPTER 1

If I have to commit a crime today, it might as well be at a 1920s mansion.

Grabbing folds of my A-line dress, I swish the fabric back and forth and grin at the camera lens. "Raph, it's a good thing I'm wearing a red dress, eh? Red is the color of crime."

I spot him roll an eye behind the lens before the shutter clicks. Blinking into the sunlight, I swipe a stray curl from my face. Hairspray does little in this humidity, and when my hair spent a good two hours pinned with bobby pins to get the perfect ringlets—I expect those, instead of my usual, frizzy, ramen-noodle strands.

Sweat collects on my upper lip and on my legs. Despite the breeziness of the skirt, the underskirt traps warmth. Not to mention, May in Ohio can get into the upper eighties or nineties, and when I checked my weather app in the parking lot, it read eighty-five in bright white letters.

Eighty-eight, with the heat index.

Raphael lowers the lens and wicks off his upper lip with his knuckle. Sweat stains his white oxford at the pits, and I imagine his legs aren't doing all that well in the khaki pants.

"For the last time, Tina." He kneels on the grass, before the sprawling brick building behind him. "We're not committing a crime today." He reaches into the bag and digs out a different lens. As he digs, perspiration drips from his dark hair.

No matter what his tan skin would tell you, he spends most of his time in a dark room, editing photos. I glance at my own pale arms and cringe at the redness spreading on them. Us Angelo's—Mom, Tina, Azriel, and Malachi—all come in two shades. Lobster and mayo.

And let's just say our mayo sandwich is feeling a little lobster-y today.

I perch a hand on my hip and fan my face with the other. By now, the red lipstick has to be smearing down my lip like blood on a vampire.

"The website was very clear, Raph—"

He rolls his eyes once more and claps the lens onto the camera. "Of course *you* read the website, Miss I-Must-Treat-Everything-Like-A-Detective."

I lift a pointer finger.

"The Giry-Reyer Estate does not allow for professional photographers to shoot on the premises without written permission. Email info@giryreyerestate.com for more info."

"You memorized the email? Yeesh, Tina, you need to get a hobby."

I do...detective-ing. That counts as a hobby, right?

"All to say that unless we're snapping selfies in front of the flowers in the garden over there..." I motion to a large plot of land, consumed by the brightest bulbs. We'd taken a few photos by some of the red roses earlier. Raph liked how it matched the dress. "We're technically not allowed to do this."

"Listen, Tina—"

He clicks buttons on the camera, likely adjusting the settings. Although he's shot several of the members of my co-op and the community theater I participate in, when it comes to pictures with me, he wants to get everything just right. The power of besties, I guess.

"—if you want to pay a hefty fee for them to allow us to shoot your senior photos on the grounds, you be my guest. But for all you know, they could tell you no anyway. Especially if there's an event or something going on."

I move my neon yellow wristband up and down my arm in a nervous motion. They *had* mentioned something about an event at the check-in desk, hadn't they?

Squeezing my eyes shut, I replay the scene.

A woman in a green vest greeted us with a smile. A small fan, hooked to the glass screen that protected her from us, whirred.

"You must be here for the Daaé Reunion." She motioned to our wedding-ready outfits. I noticed how a couple nearby, bedecked in a similar fashion, lingered in the corner, scanning through a brochure about the grounds.

I, too, had picked up one of those and perused it as the woman spoke to us.

Scanning through my near photographic memory—it was fuzzy for things like math tests, because, of course it was—I recall the introductory paragraph.

Welcome to the Giry-Reyer Estate. Built in 1923, the estate was the home to the influential Giry-Reyer family. Throughout the years, the Giry-Reyers hosted several events within the home for women's clubs, operas, and other social gatherings. A gem in the northeast Ohio area, the Giry-Reyers left a legacy of a beautiful haven for all. Read more about our events below, such as our Shakespeare Summer outdoor performances, Christmas light expo, and the unveiling of our spring garden.

Although lovely, that didn't matter. What *mattered* was that nine years ago, Dad and I spent a day here. Clomping through the echoey stone halls of the house, admiring the bedecked Christmas trees in every corner of the home.

Our last time together, before the chemo treatments got bad. Before his body sunk into itself, and never recovered again. Before the ladies from church clasped my shoulder and told me that I would need to be a "good little helper" for my widowed mother. Before I played mom number two, since the age of nine.

If we would take senior pictures anywhere, it would be here. Nowhere else meant nearly as much.

In my periphery, at the checkout desk, Raph gave me a long, hard stare. Then he glanced up at the woman.

"Yes, ma'am, we're here for that reunion."

Ice spiked my blood. Could she sniff through the lie? Did we even look like a Daaé, whomever they were?

"I thought so. Well, seeing the camera attached to you, you must be one of the event photographers."

Raph's shoulders jutted up until they shielded his ears. Would he have to prove himself somehow?

"No worries, young man. Antonia said she had everything handled on that end." The woman tore off something on her desk below, hidden from our sight. Her hand popped up, moments later, in the hole in the glass window. Two wristbands, highlighter-yellow, perched in her grip. "Go ahead and put those on. We're only allowing event guests to enter the grounds today. Tours are self-guided if you want to take a look at the grounds before the event."

Heartbeat throbbing in my ears, I bolted out of the room as I unpeeled the sticky part of the wristband. Raphael and I helped each other affix them and snapped photos for the next twenty minutes or so.

"You're positive we're not going to get arrested, Raph?"

He lifts himself with a groan. From the bruises I spotted on his knees last time he shot someone for their senior pictures, he collected quite a few scrapes and blotches from all the up and down he had to do with camera work.

I promised him payment for these senior photos. He refused.

Which was probably for the best, considering I played babysitter most of the time for Mom, and I think I have maybe twenty-five dollars to my name.

"Unless you want to take them at that dingy old theater, we're criminals today. Okay?"

I snicker. No chance we could take it in the community theater that smelled of dust and plywood. Moths chewed holes into the curtains. The board of directors claimed we were about ten years away from getting enough funds for a renovation.

"Fine, Bonnie and Clyde. Except for the married part, of course."

He wrinkles his nose. "Gross."

We dissolve into giggles. Most people pegged us as a couple.

He snaps a few test photos and gestures at a swooping white trellis. What looks like origami swans hang from the slats on thin, transparent strings.

"Go stand under that and smile for me."

I do so. He tells me to relax my mouth, says I hold a lot of tension in my lips. After a few fake-laughing photos, he frowns at the pictures he just took.

"Still holding tension?" My fingertips massage the corners of my mouth.

He shakes his head. "Sunlight's too bright. Photos are overexposed."

Pursing my lips, I squint at the back of the estate. Trees from a forest behind shield the back area with shade. "I think I remember seeing a map on one of the pamphlets. Maybe we go to the Japanese garden back there?"

For a few seconds, he squints in thought. Then all of him brightens. "Great idea. Know if there's a pagoda?"

My thoughts drift back to the social media pages I scanned of the estate, under my mother's watchful eye. She doesn't let us onto any of those types of apps all that much. Says she goes easier on us than some of the other homeschool moms. I doubt it.

Midway through my mind scroll, an image of a sloped garden building pops into my mind. "Yes, they have one. I think it's life-sized too." Shade sounds like heaven right now.

"Let's go, then."

As he collects his equipment, scattered on the grass before him, I make headway toward the back area. Heels click on a stone patio as I spy blue wisteria in the distance.

Glancing back, I wait for him. Probably shouldn't stray too far without my cameraman. This deep scarlet dress catches the sunlight in such a way that I could never blend into any surrounding without getting caught. Best not let a worker spot me and usher me into that family reunion.

A scream pierces my ear.

Pulse racing, I stand frozen in my place as I crane my neck to the right, trying to locate the source of the noise.

Moments later, a beautiful girl in a lacy pantsuit rushes up the hillside. She must've just emerged from the Japanese garden because a pink camellia bush shakes in her wake. The girl had to have trounced right through it, in an escape from something.

What's she running away from?

She catches my eye and raises herself to her full height. Gosh dang, this woman must tower above me by six inches. Not a hard task, considering I don't go past 5'5" on most measurement scales.

I glimpse her collarbone first. It juts out so much that I fear if someone pinches it, it'll crack right in half. Someone, please give this girl a sandwich.

Her piercing blue eyes clock my dress, and then her gaze roves back to the house, and then behind her at the Japanese garden.

"You here for the gathering? You don't look like a Daaé."

"I—uh." Although I spent years acting in community theater, Raph says I have yet to master the art of lying. Frost stills the blood that roars in my ears. What will she do if she finds out?

"You one of the people who auditioned then?" She must've doused herself in one too many spritzes of a summery perfume. My nostrils feel attacked. "Uh." I flick a glance backward.

Raph, did you scatter all of your equipment? Where are you?

She scoffs, nose sneering. "Good luck, then." Shoving her hands into her pantsuit pockets, she marches off in Raph's direction. Her heels poke holes into the grass. Halfway through her walk, she kicks them off and holds them by the straps.

Instinctually, I swivel my chin back toward the garden. Whatever she sprinted away from decided not to make an appearance.

Wait a moment. I spot something. A figure paces back and forth between two bushes, head stooped. Making a catalog of whatever features I can—dark skin, dark hair, lean frame—

Hold on. He turns as he doubles back to continue his stooped march. Is that a...mask? On half of his face?

Like the *Phantom of the Opera*?

Did the Daaé family plan to have some sort of performance today involving that opera?

Panting prickles my ears. Raph sidles up next to me and pats the bag strapped to his shoulders. "Thought I forget a lens back in the car. Took me a minute to find it. What's up with you?"

Before I can recount what happened in the garden, a worker in a green vest advances toward us, arms pumping. He looks to be college-aged. With a frantic sweep of the arm, he gestures at the double doors that lead into the back end of the mansion. "They're about to get started."

Shoot.

Raph and I share a glance.

We don't have a choice, do we?

Heaving a sigh, we amble up the hill and I check over my shoulder at the garden. Now at a topside view, we can take in all the cherry trees and hostas below. The man in the mask disappeared.

Maybe he got the memo about the event starting.

"Seriously, Tina. You've gone all white. Did'ya see a ghost?" Raph waggles his eyebrows, smothering us in humor to hide his nervousness as we approach the doors.

Conversation stings my ears. A room full of beautiful people in dresses and tuxes fills my line of vision. My mind races for an escape plan.

"Not a ghost, I think." My voice gets drowned out as we enter into the din. "A phantom."

CHAPTER 2

Introversion 101.

Best way to avoid conversation? Plug as much food into your mouth as possible.

I pop a devilled egg and shroud myself in a corner between two tapestries. In the large ballroom, the piano nestled in the corner first snags my attention.

Memories surge to nine years ago when Dad and I traversed this very room, my hand laced in his as I pointed at various trees that bedecked the room. Each of the trees had a theme from a famous Christmas movie. I especially loved the one from *It's a Wonderful Life.*

Angel ornaments clung to each branch. Old-fashioned bulbs, the large ones, wove circles around the tree.

"That one's for you, my little Tina." Dad's grin had disappeared into his salt-and-pepper beard. "For you, my little angel."

Rocks get caught in my chest. I swallow the egg and massage my skin until the tightness ebbs. Even years later, moisture brims my bottom lids. The man who taught me to sing, who told me to practice arias from his favorite operas—the ghost of him still lingers, always.

I can feel him. When I trill through the Queen of the Night's high notes from the *Magic Flute*. When my fingers on the dusty old piano in our family room flicker through the songs in *Madame Butterfly*.

He's always there. My angel of music.

With a clear, plastic plate hoisted in his hand like a server, Raph hovers next to me. He crunches on a macaron and swallows. "Tina, bad news."

"What?"

"I was trying to figure out where I heard the word Daaé from."

The name rings no bells in my head.

"Go on."

I keep my gaze pressed on the ornate Persian rug on the floor below us. Introversion 102: a lack of eye contact makes most people avoid you.

"They're that famous opera family, you know." His voice lowers to a hiss. "The ones with the sketchy history."

"Opera family?"

Thanks to Mom monitoring our internet time, and putting plenty of parent blocks on various websites, I can't dedicate much time to keeping up with the latest opera news. I live in music through the librettos Dad kept from his past performances.

"You know, the ones who didn't let people know about their son until he—"

Conversation dies in his throat. When my chin lifts, I see why. Two figures approach us. A girl with the most gorgeous dark skin and large curly hair, and a larger man with thick eyebrows and a scraggly beard.

"Someone didn't get the memo." The girl giggles, teeth all white in her smile. A manicured hand motions to my skirt.

Silver glitter sparkles on the girl's sleeve. The man wears a black striped suit and bowtie. A quick glimpse around the room tells me one thing that makes my face go hot and body go cold at the same time.

Everyone has opted for grays, whites, and blacks. This red dress sticks out like an acne scar.

Lumps form in my throat when I return to giggle-girl-slash-woman, who has extended her hand.

"Meg," she says. "I don't believe we've met."

"Tina."

A firm grasp squeezes my fingertips. Meg releases and gestures to the man beside her. I don't fail to notice the sparkling diamond on her left ring finger.

"Karim."

This time Raph lunges forward and claps his hand in the other man's. From Raph's wince at the shake, Karim must've crushed his bones too. Everything about this family is intense.

My eyebrows narrow. "You two engaged?"

"Yes." Meg's smile doesn't quite reach her eyes, but she holds up the ring. This girl must've repeated this gesture a million times before for curious onlookers. She can't be past twenty at best.

Who am I to judge, though? In my homeschool co-op, plenty of girls graduated with summer wedding plans. People get married early in the Midwest.

Meg tugs at a dangle earring. I notice how the two of them don't hold hands. Maybe they're not one of those all-over-each-other-all-the-time types of couples. Still, every girl I know to have a ring on her finger often clasps her hands in someone else's.

"Karim was one of the people to audition for a leading role last year."

Raphael lights up beside me. "*Le Nozze Di Figaro?*"

A group of people loitering nearby sip on champagne glasses full of bubbles. Once again, I spy the hanging tapestries and wonder if I can hide this dress behind one of them.

Meg taps her finger against her nose. "That's the one."

If I didn't spot the bags under her eyes and her tired expression, I'd say that she carried energy with her everywhere she went.

I wonder if she used to have a spark, and what happened to it.

"Anyway." Meg clasps her elbow with a laced glove. Did I miss another memo about fancy handwear? "Karim swept the stage with his stunning performance, and well," she squeezes his shoulder, face scrunching, "swept a *certain* mezzo off her feet."

Dimples bore into his cheeks. But again, the smile doesn't go that far.

Why aren't they happy?

Maybe I'm reading too much into this. Raph tells me I've gotten too obsessed with novels like *One of Us Is Lying* and *A Good Girl's*

Guide to Murder. Claims I spot clues everywhere, even when they don't exist in the first place.

"Speaking of auditions." Meg clears her throat. "Where's the diva? I'm dying to meet this year's prima donna."

I frown. "Diva?"

From what little I can tell from "divas" I met in community theater—especially the director's daughter—most people didn't seem eager to meet them.

"Oops." Meg covers her mouth in a giggle. This time, her grin appears genuine. It stretches much farther across her cheeks. "Opera terms. Basically, the lead soprano of the show. We're doing *The Pirates of Penzance* for the first portion of our countrywide tour and she's our Mabel."

Oh, duh. How could I forget that term? Dad often mentioned it back in the day.

Again, I did only have sheet music to operate off of all these years. Community theater offered little in the terms of the world of opera, except for the one year they put on *Les Mis.*

"Pantsuit?" I gesture at my skirt and remember that, today, I am not wearing pants. Whoops. "Lacy. Really skinny?"

"I believe that's the one," Karim speaks with the slightest hint of an accent. "Saw her on social media. Supposedly a prodigy. Twenty, graduated early from Julliard. Our manager practically begged Antonia to put her up for the lead role."

"She, umm." I wince. "I think she ran away."

In brief, I explain spotting her stalking off from the Japanese Garden.

"Hmm." Karim scratches at his beard. "That's not good."

"It's not."

Meg grabs a glass off of a platter and knocks back a swig. Okay, maybe she is slightly older than twenty, but not by much.

"What's the matter?" Raph crunches into a celery stick. "If she's out of the show, don't you have an understudy?"

"Yes." Meg sighs. "Me, but I've been looking to scale back considering—"

She pales and glances back at Karim. He springs into action and frees a chair from the wall. Although I'm pretty sure on our guided tour years ago, they mentioned no one could sit on the furniture.

Fluffing out her skirt, Meg breathes a deep sigh. "Thanks, Karim. My body can't take too much more. And considering most of the lead roles go out to those within the Daaé family, they're really picky about replacing them with...outsiders."

Man, and I thought nepotism got bad in community theater circles. Did most of the lead roles really go to Daaé family only?

Why didn't they let outsiders in much? They certainly allowed in someone like Karim, but what did they have to hide to prevent more from entering their circles?

"It's a shame that you guys couldn't take on someone like Tina." My blood spikes as Raph swirls a square carrot in a glob of dip on his plate. "Because she's really good."

"Stop it." I hiss at him, elbowing him in the side. I beam at the other two. "Really not great. I would never think of comparing myself to—"

"Seriously, listen to her sing *Queen of the Night* right here. I can guarantee you haven't seen a better—*oof*."

This time my elbow aims into his gut. I hold up a pointer finger.

"Excuse us for one moment."

Tugging his arm, I pull him next to a tapestry underneath a swoop of scarlet curtains. Maybe I can climb up there and blend into those. "Are you crazy?"

"What? Talking up my best friend?"

Well, I can't really blame him. He always does this. Chats up my singing ability with people at the local theater, in church choirs, you name it. "You *know* I appreciate it, but you also know I haven't gotten leads. And I really don't want to embarrass myself in front of this famous opera family."

He jabs a finger close to my nose. "You *know* the only reason why you haven't gotten a lead is because the director always has to cast his daughter, Matilda. You blow her away in auditions every time. I would know."

Tone-deaf, Raph serves as the cameraman for the local theater. But he once sat in on auditions to *prove* to me that I could out sing the diva Matilda in that theater every day.

Diva in the non-opera sense.

My tone relaxes, almost to a wimpy pleading. "This is different. They are insanely good. I just don't want to have to put myself out—"

Dings from a knife hitting a glass cut off my final words.

A skinny woman with dark hair and pale eyes lifts herself onto a staged platform. Like the diva who ran off, her collarbone sticks out. Next to her sits the piano. And on her other side—

My stomach squeezes. *The phantom.*

He wears a suit and crooked tie, almost like he didn't quite know how to tie it on straight. Playing with some translucent buttons on his oxford, he keeps his head stooped. Just like in the garden, as though something sad or shameful took place.

Why did the girl run away from him?

"Good afternoon." The woman's voice projects. Clear, crisp. As though she'd spent years in dictation classes, making sure to hit every consonant. "My name is Antonia, and it is my delight to welcome you to the annual gathering of the Daaé family."

A sweeping arm gestures in the direction of Karim. The glow of his phone absorbs his attention. Something tells me he spends a great deal of time online.

I buckle into myself, shielding my chest with my arms. The more I can hide behind the crowd of bodies in front of me, the better.

"I would especially love to thank Richard Armand for pulling together this event. A hand, please, for our wonderful manager."

Applause erupts in the echoing ballroom.

The man whom she motions to, a squat figure with a bald spot and a sweaty forehead—gives a mini bow. Antonia waits for the noise to die down.

"As per tradition, we would like to welcome this year's lead to grace you with a song. Her audition was certainly something to behold. Carmen Driver, if you would please come onto the stage."

Claps smatter the air. Everyone glances from left to right.

The phantom, on stage, shrinks more and more into his suit as the din simmers. Suspicions confirmed, he definitely drove her away for some reason.

"She—" A crowd parts to reveal Meg in her chair. "—quit, I believe. Just a few minutes ago."

Antonia's chin flicks to the phantom for a moment. Anger? Pity? Sorrow? Her expression betrays nothing.

Ribcage expanding in her form-fitting dress, she flares her nostrils. "Quit?"

The manager blanches. He too shrinks like a tortoise.

"Yes, Eric?" Meg blinks at the phantom. "Do you know what happened in the Japanese Garden?"

Showing his profile now, Eric refuses to look at the crowd. Whispers exchange between the partygoers. Sweat collects on my forehead and thighs. I need to get out of here. We've no business getting in the middle of family affairs.

"Never mind about Carmen. We'll—" Antonia puffs out a long breath, trilling. A musical type of warm-up. "We'll deal with her later. I suppose we shall move on to—"

Her eyes deadlock into mine.

I back into the wall until the cool stone presses against my back, and my skin can feel every divot.

"You're not supposed to be here."

I clasp my wristband. In my periphery, Raph's chest bounces up and down, fast. Nervous too. "Oh, my goodness. That explains so much. No wonder me and my friend were so confused. We'll see ourselves out now."

Gathering my skirts, I wedge my way through the crowd. Then a voice pipes up.

"She can sing, apparently." Meg says.

Prickles of heat ignite on my face. I whirl around and Meg shrugs at me, wrinkling her nose. Shaky breaths rattle my throat, and I face Antonia. "Nothing really to write home about. Again, really sorry to barge in—"

"Maybe we don't have to forgo tradition." Karim chimes in. "Maybe Tina can do the aria in Carmen's place?"

It's at this moment that I realize this entire room didn't know my name until now.

Something about me doesn't like that they just found it out. As if my name was my own little secret, my own little half-mask that I could hide behind.

Nails bite into my palms. This can't be happening. Lord knows I get nervous enough singing in front of the judges for community theater auditions, let alone—

"Are you familiar with *The Pirates of Penzance*?" Antonia blinks at me.

One of the most popular operas of all time? Of course I am...

And *of course* I can't lie.

Biting my trembling bottom lip, I nod.

"Very well." Antonia motions me to where she stands. "Grace us with a song, Miss Tina. 'Poor Wandering One' will do. I'm assuming those notes won't be too hard for you?"

I can't tell if a yes or a squeak exits my throat as an answer.

Shakiness overtakes my calves as I weave through the crowd. My heart pounds so hard that it rattles my skull.

"As she joins us up here—"

Antonia squares Eric's shoulders.

"—Eric, my son, will play Frederic." She snaps her fingers and a bubble of girls approach the stage. "And these ladies will play the sisters in the song."

Blonde hair graces most of the ladies. I'd tried, in the last few minutes, to discern the origin of the name Daaé. Swedish, most likely. Although Antonia struck me as more Italian, I guess it could go for a Nordic angle too.

I regain my balance once I'm on the platform.

A 'whoop, whoop' sounds from the crowd. Meg lifts her arms. "Don't forget to get *physical* with Frederick, Mabel."

Meg shimmies her shoulders, and a bubble around her chuckles.

Mabel, of course, being me. And Frederick being...

Facing the phantom, I notice the softness in the uncovered side of his face. He doesn't look at me, but something about him feels warm, feels safe. Something about his nose reminds me of my father.

"I—" I clasp my hands. "Do you mind if I make physical contact in the song?"

The question surprises him because his shoulders jut upward toward the painted ceiling. I realize now that they've imitated paintings of the Sistine Chapel up there.

Community theater, despite its issues, did remind us actors to ask express permission before touching anyone else on stage.

His cheeks darken. His complexion is far deeper than his pale mother's. I wonder if he gets it from his dad.

"Whatever you think is best."

Although I have no intention to make out with anyone on stage anytime soon, who knows what will happen when I get into character. I'm sure he won't mind a little hand-holding.

"Okay." I release a breath and nod at a man who has appeared at the piano. "Starting note, if you would please?"

His index finger presses down on a white key.

Wrong, I think. He starts the song half a step too high. If I drop the key, though, the crowd will notice. It doesn't help that the devilled egg I ate earlier seems permanently stuck in the back of my throat, creating a factory of phlegm.

Exhale, throat clear, here goes nothing.

"For shame, for shame, for shame…"

And then I let the music carry me away. As I sing about Frederick's character, a pirate, I flounce back and forth on the tiny stage. Many performances I've seen of Mabel show her as flighty and soaring with the notes.

I keep returning to him, in a flirtatious manner, to brush his shoulder, reach for his hand—then carry my hand away. When my dad taught me this one, he spoke of it as a cat-and-mouse number.

Electricity alights my fingertips anytime I graze them against him.

This feels different than all of the couplings I've experienced on stage before. Yes, even the number of stage kisses with guys sparked nothing prior to this. Because that felt like a stage direction...

This...this was music.

A pause from the piano.

Great, time for the high note section.

Deep breaths, girl.

I shut my eyes and trill each note. My throat feels raw, and I wait for the highest one to crack and die on my tongue. It doesn't. Instead, it vibrates, warbles—in the shaky vibrato I've been attempting to develop.

One last high note.

"Take"—this time I clasp his hands into mine. Although my abdomen hurts from how much it clenches, butterflies explode in it when his eyes pierce mine. He's untucked himself from his suit, spirits seemingly lifted—*"heart!"*

As the piano concludes with a flourish we hold that position for a few too many seconds. Antonia's throat-clear interrupts us. We spring apart. Then the applause from the crowd drowns my thoughts, and I get all wobbly again.

Stepping off stage, a buzz overtakes my ears. I only catch the final part of Antonia's speech. "—one more round of applause for our soprano."

Something taps my shoulder mid-way to returning to Raph.

I jolt and whirl around. The manager flicks up a business card with two fingers. "You got an acting resume?"

My eyebrows pinch together, and I nod.

"Great, send it over. We'll be in touch."

He disappears into the crowd.

CHAPTER 3

One hundred thousand dollars.

I almost fall out of the chair at the computer station in the library. Letting out a long, trembling breath, I peruse the email again to make sure the spots in my vision hadn't given me hallucinations.

Dear Miss Tina Whitaker,

After consulting with the casting team, we are pleased to invite you to be our prima donna in this year's traveling tour. This will take place during the summer—running through the months of June, July, and August.

Shows for the summer include Pirates of Penzance *(Mabel),* Gianni Schicchi *(Lauretta), and* Tosca *(Floria Tosca).*

We will need your response by the end of the week, confirming if you wish to accept your roles for the summer.

I have attached to this email a W-9 as well as a Cast Member agreement.

*As stated in the agreement, the Daaé Traveling Opera Troupe is willing to offer you a sum of **$100,000** for your contributions to the shows this summer—to be paid during the final Tosca performance of the season. In addition, we would also like to provide a **$10,000***

spending stipend, to be paid upfront—to cover meals, shopping,
and other endeavors with the cast, outside of what will be provid-
ed at the hotels and meal provisions backstage.

We look forward to hearing from you and do hope to be able to
work with you this season.

Sincerely,

Richard Armand

Manager of the Daaé Traveling Opera Troupe

This has to be a prank.

I slam the chair into the table and log out of the computer. Thanks to Mom's hovering whenever I jump onto social, I bought enough time in between babysitter hours to get some research done at the library. Although I'd sent in my resume to Richard two days ago, part of me wanted to get more research done about the family.

Digging my phone out of my pocket, I duck out of the library's front doors and onto the sidewalk outside. Children scrape chalk against the pavement. I think I saw something about an art-on-the-walk event.

Racing to the side of the building, I slide onto a free bench and dial Raph.

He picks up on the second ring. "Eww."

"Yes, nice to hear your lovely voice too."

"I got a two o'clock appointment with a garden trowel and some weeds. Mom thinks I'm not helping enough around the house, so you best make it snappy."

Two seconds into recounting what I found in the email, he screams. So. Loud. I have to hold the phone away from my ear. A girl on the sidewalk, two squares down, peers up at me. Then she shrugs and returns to her imitation of *Bluey*.

Once the noise dies, I place the receiver against my ear. "Okay, so before we dive into—"

"You're going to take it right?"

"—the email. Why don't you tell me what you know about the family? Google's being super enigmatic."

"Super *what*?"

"Secretive, just tell me what you know."

"That's the problem. It's all fan theories. You and I both know that they tend not to cast leads outside of their families—"

"Question on that. What happens if two characters have to, you know."

"Kiss? They do have some married folks in the family who do that. But for the single peeps...that's where auditions come in. They sometimes let people do some shows with the family for a season. They seem to cycle them out."

Except in the case of Karim. He stayed.

Maybe they liked him a lot, so they wanted to keep him.

"As for minor roles, dancers, et cetera, they hire them for a few shows, but they don't travel with the family. They do three or four shows, grab their paycheck, and leave. Which I guess isn't atypical, from what my opera friends tell me. Opera people are used to learning things fast."

"Okay." My foot taps a crack in the sidewalk. "What else do you know?"

"I know that Eric was supposed to be kept a secret."

Oxygen flees my lungs.

What?

It takes me a few moments to realize I didn't speak the question aloud. "Explain."

"He got really famous. Had an account that popped up on social media and it exploded. In later interviews, he claimed that he didn't upload them. He'd recorded them in secret, just as a hobby. Someone in the troupe must've posted them."

"Wait, why didn't he want them to go up?"

"I guess he has a...disfigurement. On half of his face. The troupe didn't want him included in operas."

So, the mask thing wasn't a gimmick?

"What you're saying is the family likes their secrets?"

"It seems like it."

"Then I *shouldn't* go for it, right?"

The thought hits me about what would happen if I didn't. Being cousins, Eric and Meg wouldn't have to kiss if Meg filled in as the understudy, right? No wonder they sought out "outsider" actors every once in a while.

"Well, I—" He sucks on his teeth. "I wouldn't say that."

A couple, holding bowls of melting ice cream, laugh as they pass in front of my bench. I curl into my gut and hiss into the phone.

"What do you mean?"

"I mean that this is the sort of family you don't want to cross. They're well-off and are known for throwing money at people they want to make alliances with."

My eyebrows arch. "Is that why they're giving me 100k? To keep me quiet about something?"

"It's possible. Did you research how much opera singers make normally?"

Indeed, and it turns out that most make $1000 or so per performance. The professionals, and I do mean *professionals*, can earn up to $200k for a year's worth of work.

But not for three months of performances.

Something didn't add up.

Sourness fills my gut. "I think I should tell them no. Blame it on the fact that Mom needs me to babysit the kids most of the summer." Never mind that the middle child had breached high-school age by now. The manager didn't need to know that.

"I'll trust your judgment. Just be careful." A buzz sounds on his end. Maybe he got a text from someone. "If you're going to burn bridges, make sure they don't know who holds the torch."

"Got it, will tread carefully."

After I hang up, I launch myself from the bench and head back to the library. AC cools the sweat that's collected on my face. Ohio summers, although less brutal than the South, aren't much more enjoyable. Pinkish residue from yesterday's sunburn still rests on my arm and face.

I nod to the workers at the front desk and head back to the computer station. Beside me, a family peruses the DVDs for a movie to watch—likely for a family movie night.

Yearning wriggles my insides. Dad and I used to love getting opera performances on DVD and viewing them together.

Sliding into a chair, I plug my library card information into the computer. Five seconds later, I've pulled up the browser for my email once again.

Fingertips hover over the keyboard.

How does one politely turn down one hundred thousand dollars?

Children shriek and giggle as they chase each other out of the picture book section. A larger-than-life bookworm hangs above the entrance to that part of the library. Dad, Mom, and I used to spend hours in that room. By the age of seven, I'd browsed most of the titles to win some summer library reading challenge. Mom took us out to pizza that day to celebrate.

Girl, focus.

I force my gaze back onto the computer.

Hold on a second...Mom.

Sliding my phone out of my bag, I shoot a text to Raph.

Tina

I think I know how I can burn a bridge without me being the one to burn it.

Three dots appear. Then his reply.

Raph

Absolutely not.

Tina

What? It's not like my mom would let me go on a tour of the country anyway. How could I sneakily even do that? She caught me one time going to the theater after-party way past my curfew, you know.

Raph

Tina, you're an adult now.

Tina

As of April. A one-month old adult. Please don't make me confront the scary opera mafia family <pleading eyes emoji>

Juvenile, I know, to tell my mom about the whole affair. But if she shut it down herself, maybe that could ease the tension building in my ribcage. Plenty of friends got out of the theater strike back in the day thanks to their parents saying, "No."

It also strikes me in that moment that I should've called instead of texted him.

Mom tends to glance through my messages online from time to time. Somehow phone companies allow her to do it. Then again, I've sent far more dangerous things Raph's way. Something tells me that she wants to give us our privacy because she operates under the assumption that we'll get married someday.

Two taps of the mouse clicks on the email. I forward it to Mom's address before I can give anything a second thought.

Much as Mom and I don't always get along, there's something beautiful and protective about a mother blockading her children from harm. I wonder if Eric feels the same way about Antonia. Does she try to protect him from others? From their derision?

Does that explain why they've hidden him away all these years? Much like my mom, sheltering me?

No, I swallow the lump in my throat.

I can't think about Eric now. Not the way electricity surged in my fingertips when we clasped hands. How, when Antonia interrupted us, it felt like someone had broken a spell.

When I click out of the sent box, I spot a bolded email at the top of my inbox. Heart racing, I recognize the sender. The manager emailed me again.

Shoot, did I forward the wrong person?

Curiosity gnaws at my skin as I tap and read.

Hey Girl,

Meg emailing from the manager's office email. Figured since most of your social media accounts aren't active that this is the best place to reach you. Planning to delete this email on our end once I send it, so please don't reply.

Popping in here to say sorry for what happened during the gathering.

Yes, part of it was to save myself. Much as I love Eric—and will personally shiv anyone who ever hurts him—I will pass out on stage if I have to consistently sing Mabel's high notes as her understudy.

But, actually, part of it was to save you.

You don't know our manager like we do. Let's just say, he would've personally had your head for barging in on a Daaé-only event.

Consider this a warning and a plea.

Accept the part they've offered you, keep your head down all summer, and you might just make it out of this alive.

Haha, jk, it's not that serious :) but for real, when you accept the roles, don't ask too many questions. Curiosity killed the cat, you know.

Soon to be your bestie on stage,

Meg

My head swims with questions from the email. Starting with, how did she get into the inbox in the first place? Does the manager really have quite the bloodthirst?

One line burns into my retinas.

"Keep your head down all summer, and you might just make it out of this alive."

Did I just write my death certificate when I forwarded the email to Mom?

CHAPTER 4

"Paper flowers?"

I hand the sheet music origami roses, a bouquet of them, to my friend, Temperance, at her graduation party. A lacy head covering is held into place in her brown hair today by some clips. Her denim skirt swishes as she places the flower stems on top of a pile of gifts in her garage.

"Sorry, that's all I have for you." I grip my elbow. "Broke, you know."

"Oh, Tina." She squeezes me in a tight hug, then releases. "They're beautiful. I know how much music means to you."

"And to you."

Temperance often played piccolo and the occasional flute in the pit for our community theater performances when we needed backups. She, Raph, and I hit it off during a grueling tech week of *Into the Woods* when I was fifteen.

The two of us, Temperance and I, pace the length of the garage.

Temperance's scrapbooks, full of photos of her friends and activities over the years, litter the tables. Photographs of her hang from strings looped into the rafters of the garage ceiling. Someone, every once in a while, taps her on the shoulder to hug her and tell her congratulations for finishing school.

I sign my name on a 3-D model T, for Temperance, in a metallic marker as Temperance's mother and mine embrace each other in a hug. They each nurse soda cups in their hands as they chat excitedly about something.

Temperance sidles beside me.

"I don't suppose," by reflex, she adjusts one of the clips in her hair, "you could make several of those paper roses for my wedding reception?"

A tiny diamond sparkles on her finger. We head toward the backyard, and grass tickles my ankles. I've opted for a long skirt today, too. Although some days I prefer shorts, I feel exposed wearing them in Temperance's more modest home.

"Oh yeah, I almost forgot that the wedding's this fall."

"I know." Temperance adjusts her thin-wire glasses up the bridge of her nose. "It's all been happening so fast."

No judgment to the girls who want to get married early.

Plenty of ladies in our church claimed they'd gotten hitched right after their high school graduations, but...I could never. I have no idea what to do with my life after this summer, let alone spend the rest of my days with some near stranger.

Two men chuck bean bags toward cornhole boards in her back-yard. I spot another gaggle of men flicking a disc golf toward netted baskets. Ladies in tea-length dresses chat excitedly at makeshift tables.

Will my life look like this?

Two Sundays back, we went to a potluck after church. A swarm of men regaled us with war stories and their time in the Navy. It fascinated me, hearing about their near-death experiences. Much like the true crime podcasts I binge under the covers on near-muted headphones so Mom won't catch me.

She doesn't know about the Spotify account. I delete the app each morning so when she checks my phone, she can't find it.

Midway through one of the stories about a submarine, a woman tapped me on the shoulder. She smiled at me, lipstick smeared on her front two teeth.

"Oh, sweetie, you don't have to listen to the men's boring stories. Come sit with us ladies for a while, mm?"

Excuses caught in my throat, like cotton, I shut my mouth and nodded. There, on an L-shaped couch, for the next two hours, I listened to them talk about their children. Many winked at me when getting to the giving-birth-to-babies portion of the discussion.

I picked at cold pulled pork and tuned out the rest of that conversation.

That was the life Temperance wanted. And good on her. She would make a wonderful mother and claimed she wanted at least six little ones running around. Temperance loved working with the babies in the church nursery and has had a steady baby fever since the age of fourteen.

But me? Could I give up the stage, *the music*, for the sake of a life planned out for me by someone else?

"So, Tina." Temperance perches on a lawn chair and crosses her legs, ladylike style. "I know my summer's going to be filled with final details on the wedding. What do you plan to do with yours?"

"Oh, likely babysitting the kids."

Temperance nibbles on a decorated cookie. Some skillful hands wove, in cursive frosting, Temperance's names on all of the treats found on tables, scattered throughout the lawn.

"That's good practice for later on."

Later on? Oh, she means when I become a mom.

Heat fills my cheeks.

"Orrrrrr." Raph's voice prickles my ears. "She's going to join an opera mafia and become super famous. Good to see you, Temp. Congrats!"

Temperance frowns. "Opera mafia?"

I shoo Raph away with a waving hand. "It's nothing. I may have had an audition for some opera company, without knowing it was an audition. Long story."

"Oh!" Temperance sets down her plate on the grass and clasps her heart. "Tina, that sounds wonderful. Although I'm so excited to marry Dustin, I do admit I'm feeling a little bit of envy right now. What I wouldn't give to be able to play in a philharmonic orchestra."

I'm losing ground fast if even Temperance is on board.

"It's likely not going to happen, Temperance. Really, it's fine if it doesn't. Gives me a chance to..." I wince but force a smile. "Focus on the more important things in life."

She nods and beams at Raph and me.

Oh, goodness. She's been on the Raph and Tina train for years. In fact, all the moms in our circle have peppered him with questions about when he planned to start "courting" me. This triggered both of our gag reflexes.

We played along with it, though. Because in a tight-knit community like this one, girls and boys didn't tend to be friends unless they planned to get hitched later on. Raph and I did try a couple secret dates together, but we decided we weren't attracted to each other. It felt more like going on a date with a brother or sister. Whenever we tried to explain the situation to our parents, though, they wouldn't believe us. Thought we were playing it coy.

Easier to just go with it than fight back. Pretend-relationships had their perks. It kept creepy theater guys away and got Mom off my back about finding "the one."

I crook my hand into Raph's arm and tug him toward the ladder toss game. For some reason, it's currently unoccupied by people playing games at the party.

"Can we please not dwell on this whole opera thing? I forwarded the email to Mom yesterday, so it's a done deal already."

"Is it, though?" He waggles his eyebrows. "Just spoke with her in the garage, and I'm pretty sure you two are *definitely* not on the same page."

A mixture of frost and warmth fills all of me.

Did I really want to do this? Something about gracing the stage with professionals felt exciting. With no scholarship, no way to pay my way through college, maybe *this* could provide an entry into the world of classical music.

Could I keep my head down, though, like Meg asked? Curiosity already niggled my gut when it came to this family.

Balling my fists, I march toward the garage.

With her free hand, the one not balancing a plate full of goodies, Mom twirls her wrist like a conductor's musical flourish. She spots me and waves.

"I was just telling Martha"—her head bobs in the direction of Temperance's mom—"about the email you forwarded to me. Sweetheart." She cups my chin. "Why didn't you tell me that you auditioned for an opera troupe?"

I scan her face for any hint of hurt because I can hear it in her voice. But she keeps her expression sunny.

Maybe she assumed that I lied about taking grad photos to go to an audition.

"It was spontaneous. I didn't realize there were auditions happening at the place we were taking photos."

"So said the woman who spoke on the phone with me. What was it? Some Italian name."

"Antonia?" I ask. "It's Swedish, actually." Indeed, one of my Google searches in the library had yielded Swedish results for Antonia's name, as well as the surname Daaé.

"Yes, well, sounds like a really sweet woman. She was going on and on about how you have one of the most beautiful voices she's ever heard."

"Of course." I bobble on my heels. Two boys bounce a basketball on the driveway. We scoot further into the garage to avoid the dribbling ricocheting off our feet. "I know I couldn't do it this summer. You work full-time and—"

Mom tosses up a hand.

"Azriel's old enough to watch Malachi. I told her on the phone that was no problem, and that you're off the hook in terms of watching the kids. That's not my main issue—"

I cock my head, bracing myself. "What is?"

"Even though you're an adult, I'm not comfortable with you going alone. I, though, can't accompany you."

There, that answers that question.

I exhale, not being able to tell whether it's a sigh of defeat or relief. Maybe a combination of both.

"That's fine, Mom. Really, I—"

"So, I told her that Raphael would be able to accompany you, and she said she would email you the details later."

Excuse me?

This same mom, who yelled at me when one of my crushes in *Into the Woods* put his arm around me, has no issue with letting a boy travel across the country with me?

"Of course, I mentioned that he'd need to stay in a separate hotel room and that you two would need a chaperone at all times. But, let's be honest, Tina, that boy needs a push when it comes to courting you. He's been using schoolwork as an excuse for far too long, and now that he's graduated, it's time. Maybe this will get him to jump-start the process."

Oh. My. Gosh. My mom has forced us into some arranged marriage.

No doubt, the one hundred thousand dollars likely sounds like a good deal to her, too. She's been against college from the start. Claims it will corrupt my mind and waste thousands of my dollars. Maybe she sees that as a down payment to a house or for our future children.

"Won't Raph need a summer job? We'll be preventing him from saving up."

"I'm sure you two will pool your resources when you finally get married. One hundred thousand dollars split between two people is nothing to blink at." She winks at me. "Besides, Raph is planning to take a gap semester, and his parents are paying his way through school after that. Something tells me the boy doesn't need the money. But you *do* need protecting. It's a scary world out there for beautiful, young, pure girls."

I excuse myself and shut myself into my car. Gripping the steering wheel, I pray the humidity trapped in my car can suffocate me so I don't have to go through with any of this nonsense.

A few seconds later, instinct kicks in, and I turn on the engine. AC blasts me all the way to the library. Although, yes, I *could* answer emails at home, I'd rather delete any choice words I have for Antonia or the troupe before Mom can glance over my shoulder to watch me type.

Relax, girl.

I force my shoulders down.

Much as I distrust this family, I can't blame them for what just went down.

Mom probably saw the forwarded email, tracked down the manager's phone number, and forced Antonia to get on the call. For all I know, it's a miracle in itself that Antonia didn't cancel the contract right then, thanks to Mom's pushiness.

I hobble over the chalk drawings on the walk. No smatterings of rain have hit us this late May, so the weather left the illustrations intact. I smile at one of a rose, etched in pink and orange chalk—the closest someone could probably get to a red.

Lemony scents greet me as I enter through the library doors. One of the summer interns must've gotten a little too happy with the cleaning wipes.

Slouching into one of the chairs, I add my information and pull up my email. True to Mom's word, a message from the manager's inbox greets me.

Dear Miss Tina,

We were happy to speak with your mother yesterday. According to Antonia, "She sounds like a wonderful person", and that you are "a very lucky girl for having such a doting mother."

Wow, these two moms really should meet for tea. They seem to be on the same page about each other.

Per your mother's request, we will allow Mr. Raphael Chene to accompany you on the tour. He shall be provided a $10,000 spending stipend, as well, and separate hotel room accommodations.

Please let us know if these terms are agreeable, and we are excited to be able to move forward.

Sincerely,

Richard Armand

Manager of the Daaé Traveling Opera Troupe

I lean back into the chair until it loses balance, and I have to grip the table to recover. Pulling myself forward, I scan through the email several more times.

No loopholes, no torches—no burning this bridge.

Glancing at my empty ring finger, I release a long sigh. Maybe this is for the best. I can put off Mom's questions about me and Raph for one more summer—and prevent her from trying to set me up with some of the youth group boys, something she threatens with great frequency.

If all goes well with these operas, maybe I can convince Antonia to get me an internship at another opera house. Or put that money toward a good program, if I get a scholarship.

I will, of course, give Raph a cut of the money. Even though he spends his summers landscaping his parents' property, earning nothing in the process, he deserves some sort of payment for the humiliation on both of our ends.

Planting my feet on the floor, I craft my reply.

Dear Richard,

Thank you so much for your generous offer. I am excited to accept it.

You will find the attached, signed documents to this email. Please let me know the best ways to get prepared for the upcoming shows, as they are a couple of weeks away.

Sincerely,

Tina

As I click send the knots in my stomach tighten. What have I done?

CHAPTER 5

"This is way too much makeup, Tina." Mom chucks a tube of red lipstick out of my suitcase onto my bedroom carpet. "Less is more when you're trying to attract the attention of a certain boy."

She's in for a rude awakening when it comes to how much stage makeup they plaster onto opera singers. Although we do wear cosmetics in theater, from what I can tell from my research, opera singers lather on far more.

As mom pilfers through my suitcase, emptying it of most of the cosmetics—which I'll sneak into my backpack right before we leave—I review the libretto one more time. Mouthing the words, instead of singing them.

Mom gave me quite the talking to after I'd spent the last few weeks reviewing the score. She claims the neighbors had called the police about disturbances of the peace.

When I suggested I could go to one of the practice rooms at the local college, she flinched. So much for that idea. But I'd really like for *her* to try and hit a high E in pianissimo.

Once I've gone over the highlighted portions of the text, I dig out a binder, into which I've slipped in all the papers they've emailed me over the past few weeks. Every day has been comprised of choreography videos to learn, vocal coaches arriving at my house to walk me through the music—and make sure I've made enough progress—and even workout regimes Meg forwarded to me. This time, she sent it from her personal address.

Seriously, though, how did she hack into the other inbox? My mind flashes back to Karim on his phone. He seems tech-savvy. Did her fiancé help her to get into that thing? Meg could've gotten the info from Karim, couldn't she?

My fingers stop on the schedule for the upcoming shows. Although I've near memorized this, my brain fills with fuzz for the dress run tonight.

Schedule for the Daaé Traveling Opera Troupe

All performances are to take place Monday, Wednesday, and Friday of each week. A dress rehearsal will take place the Sunday prior to each Monday performance. Singers will travel on Saturdays to the next destination. In the case that the drive will take longer than one day, the troupe will perform on the Thursday of that week and travel on both Friday and Saturday to the next tour stop.

June (*Pirates*)

Week One—Cleveland, OH

Week Two—New York City, NY

Week Three—Norfolk, VA

Week Four—Gatlinburg, TN

July (*Gianni Schicchi*)

Week One—Sarasota, FL

Week Two—Crowley, LA

Week Three—Dallas, TX

Week Four—St. Louis, MO

August (*Tosca*)

Week One—Colorado Springs, CO

Week Two—Las Vegas, NV

Week Three—Napa, CA

Week Four—Seattle, WA

Singers will be flown home, with a stipend for extra-fee luggage. Singers who wish to ride the tour bus back may do so.

"Tina, is this—?" She holds the shirt out in disgust. "A crop top?"

Whoops, forgot about that purchase. "Must just be a shirt that shrunk in the dryer." She chucks it onto my bed and finishes her sweep of my belongings. Lord knows why Mom even said yes to the Las Vegas portion of the trip.

Her hand touches my back and she rubs up and down. She often does this as a gesture of comfort. She's spritzed herself with a little too much peach perfume today. "Are you sure, sweetie, that you don't want me to take off work for an actual performance? I feel bad about only going to the preview."

Arching my back from her touch, I spin around in my rolling chair and smile. "You coming to the dress rehearsal is enough. I imagine there's going to be no one out there tonight, so it'll help to have someone clapping."

She echoes my expression and straightens her spine. "We should probably head over soon. They said in one of the emails that you don't need to bring luggage until they leave for New York, right?"

I murmur my assent.

Slipping on my flats, I grab my character shoes by the straps and take one last look at the suitcase. Then I lope down the stairs after Mom and into the car.

Minutes fly as we approach the opera house from the highway. Skyscrapers loom in the distance, marking the territory of Cleveland. We don't spend all that much time up here. Mom hates cities.

We park in a parking deck and walk to the theater. Heat from the sidewalk sizzles, threatening to melt the soles of my shoes.

Once inside, I gasp, taking in the vastness of the auditorium.

Community theater doesn't stand a chance against the balconied seats. I spot Antonia with a clipboard downstage and advance toward her. Although Mom came along with me, she lingers behind in the back few rows. Maybe to take in the ornate siding of the walls, which reminds me of golden vines.

Antonia glances up at me, eyes sparkling. "There's our prima donna. Ready for the preview performance?"

I nod and stop myself before I fall into the pit. Whoops, forgot that places like this don't have stairs from the audience that lead up to the stage. Antonia, catching on, bobs her chin at doors, house left.

"Why don't you go through those, and I'll meet you for a tour?"

I swerve to the left, out the doors, and into the hallway.

"It'll have to be a quick tour." Her bony silhouette is highlighted in green under the exit sign lights. "You need to get to the vocal warm-up soon. Maybe you can visit the props mezzanine? Everyone gets a kick out of that."

Mezzanine? I do recognize the word props. And I can attest from my theater experiences that when we started incorporating candlesticks and fake grapes onto the stage, the scenes did come to life.

Mom's shadow lingers behind me as we traverse a large backstage area that smells of wood shavings. Angling to the left, we spiral up a staircase and toward a large upstairs room. Dust perfumes everything.

Lights flick on with a hum.

The first shelf, right by the door, hosts a gaggle of haunted-looking dolls.

Nope, nope, nope, gonna pick up my pace and go right past that. Once we sail past shelves full of buckets, severed hand props, and various busts and statues, Antonia directs us to a helm.

She crooks her bony fingers around a spoke on the ship's wheel.

"That." My throat goes dry. "Looks like real wood."

I got so used to everything being made of Styrofoam or chicken wire.

"One of our favorite props for the show. Although it's a little unorthodox, I decided to have them keep it up here until curtain. One of the most expensive ones in the show too, I might add." She taps her finger against her nose.

Something about her—like her son—feels warm, inviting. Unlike the frost I usually get from my own mom.

Those deep brown eyes of hers look like they've embraced the beams of many spotlights in the past. This woman lives and breathes opera.

"Where is your friend?" A lacy cover-up sheaths her thin arms, as she triangles them on her hips. "The one with the beautiful photographs of you?"

This tells me two things:

1. Antonia, and maybe other people in the troupe, did their homework on us. They managed to scrounge up his social media accounts.

2. This explains why they didn't have me rehearse with them until now. They wanted to vet us first.

Guess I'm not the only one suspicious of all these circumstances. I wonder if that manager had anything to do with this. After all, he started the whole thing with sliding me that business card. Maybe Antonia didn't *want* me in the cast in the first place. If so, her body language doesn't betray anything.

Yet.

"The what?" Mom's voice pipes up behind me.

Yikes on all the trikes, I forgot that he frequently uploads pictures of me onto his Instagram page to get more business. We've reenacted Raphaelite scenes, like Ophelia, in rivers in the Metro Parks found in Ohio. Mom grew suspicious the day I returned, clothes stinking of pond.

Might I add that the dresses worn definitely didn't meet Mom's modesty standards for me?

Time for a quick subject change. "Raph? He's planning to sit in on the performance tonight. I don't *technically* need a chaperone until we travel."

"True." Now I spot the hook in her nose. It makes her even more beautiful. I can tell she sang soprano back in the day; prima donnas always carry *the look.* "However, the cast does often enjoy going out to eat afterwards. Best he joins you then, so Mom can be happy, mmm?"

"That's right, Tina, listen to your director."

Holding back an eye roll, I grimace. "Of course. If we go out, Raph will join us tonight. Speaking of the cast—"

This whole time I've listened for the faint arias of the other singers. Even in a labyrinth like this, their voices *have* to echo, right?

"—where are they?"

"Oh, doing some physical warm-ups to loosen their bodies, I suppose." Dark red polish decorates her nails. "Your body is an instrument after all."

Your body is an instrument. That phrase peppered almost every email communication they sent me.

"Although." She spun the helm once more. "I do think that Meg had to sit out her physical warm-up. Not feeling all that well. Karim may have gone with to check on her."

A moment later, I realize Mom may not recognize these names. I run her through them fast.

"Not feeling well, Mrs. Daaé?"

"'Antonia,' if you please, Tina. We're all friends here. And yes, she can get a little woozy from time to time. I think Eric may also be missing from the physical warm-ups. Probably picking out a mask for tonight."

A mask.

Rocks collide into my stomach. For some reason, I'd thought he'd wear the Phantom one. That doesn't make sense for the show, though. They'd probably put him in something a little more life-like.

What does he wear when he goes into public?

Does he go into public?

Before I can ask more questions, a phone buzzes. Antonia reaches into her bag. Glows highlight the shelves of storage bins, each labeled with the names of different shows. A bright white angel statue lingers over Antonia.

From what I can recall from the score of our third opera, an angel statue existed in that show. They made me go over all three scripts. Apparently, opera singers work on multiple pieces at one time.

But we couldn't take that honking thing on the road with us, right? They never once mentioned if we would transport the props and sets with us, or if theaters would have them at the ready. I guess that's not for the actors to worry about.

Antonia shoves the phone back into her bag, features sagging.

"I'm afraid we'll have to conclude our tour for now, ladies. Tina will be here for a week, so I imagine she'll get to explore the rest of the facilities at another time. I'll lead you to where the rest of the cast is doing warm-ups. Then"—she pats her bag—"I have a few things I need to take care of."

Silence carries us down the steps and into a room full of mirrors.

Ballet dancers stretch on barres. The emails made it clear that we would have different dancers and background characters for different locations. No use in getting to know these people here; actors and the dancers kept their distance.

Water bottles line the back corner of the room. I want to kick myself for leaving my emotional support Hydro Flask back at home.

Bubbled in a corner, a group of actors lay on their backs, letting out zzzs of air. After searching their faces for Karim, Eric, or Meg—unsuccessful—I lie beside a blonde girl and join them in the exercise.

Ballerinas whisper near me. I catch traces of conversation like "full house tonight" and "sold out of tickets." Good thing I convinced Mom to purchase her admission for tonight early, but my nerves seize in my neck.

Exhaling, I pray that we have a perfect performance tonight. Because if something goes wrong, I don't know if I can handle that *and* the fact that I have to hit high notes in front of well over one thousand people.

Why didn't they warn me we'd perform the dress rehearsal for so many people?

Did they do it on purpose? Hoping I'd fail, so they could replace me?

If so, why do I care so much? Didn't I want to get booted from the shows in the first place?

Images flicker of Temperance's graduation party. If I quit now, does that fate—her fate—await me? Several minutes pass as I replay the scenes in my mind while the woman leads us through some yoga poses. We sprawl on our backs once again.

"Hey, bestie!" A mezzo voice breaks up my thoughts. My eyelids fly open as a figure collapses next to me in my periphery. We've moved on to an exercise where we go up and down scales with lip trills.

"Hi, Meg." I insert this in a pause between the solfege.

"You ready to be smooching up my cousin tonight?"

"Umm."

"Better you than that Carmen. I did some research on her and, mmm." She clucks her tongue. "She puts the prima in donna. So anyway, you guys ready to get spicy?"

What was with this girl and me getting physical with Eric? Nerves constrict at the thought of the stage kiss. I force myself to relax. It's not even a real one.

We do a dipping move. Our choreographer, according to my video calls with her, figured it made no sense for me to try and full-on kiss him with the mask and all.

Disappointment pooled in my gut when she told me that.

Why did I want to stage-kiss him? Did the show feel less authentic without it?

Still, my chest tightens at the thought that I will go through all of tonight without having practiced with the troupe. According to several articles I perused at the library—in between learning the show and babysitting the kids—entire casts for operas didn't perform together until the dress rehearsal.

This was normal...not sabotage, right?

"Are you feeling better?" Maybe if I can get her mind off of me and Eric...

"Yeah, just had to get my legs propped up. But on my way back here, I heard two juicy pieces of news. You want in on it?"

"Umm—"

"Great, so news piece number one, our maestro is missing. Won't answer his phone and we don't have a replacement at the ready, as far as I can tell."

No conductor?

I sit up and force myself to go slack against the floor. Relax, girl, relax.

Things like this happened. They wouldn't cut the music director just so they could watch me crash and burn.

"Ready for piece number two?"

"I'm not sure if I—"

"The ship's helm is missing. It's not in the props mezzanine."

No way. Ten or fifteen minutes ago, we'd seen it with our own eyes. Without it, several of the dance numbers make no sense. The Pirate King swerves the ship from side to side, using the helm, at the top of the act.

"Who do you think—" Silence shrouds us as the solfege stops. I lower my voice to a whisper. "Took it?"

"I don't know. But I'll tell you what. They would have to know that's one of Antonia's favorite props, and"—she sucks in a breath—"they would probably be trying to get back at the Daaés by trying to ruin the show. Can bet you whoever took the helm may have a hand in getting rid of the maestro."

It *was* sabotage then.

I hate it when I get it right.

CHAPTER 6

Thirty minutes before curtain, Antonia locates a replacement maestro.

Little luck in getting another helm, though. The choreographer, during our makeup session, walks the pirates through alternatives to the scene. She and the Pirate King have to walk the stage and re-block part of the number without the ship's wheel.

Thoughts buzz as I waft away clouds of hairspray. Even though they have us in wigs, they still wanted to make sure the curls stayed in place.

Half an hour passes in a blur as cast members run through lines in the hair and makeup room. Meg claims I'll get my own dressing room once I get out of Cleveland. "Everything's better away from Ohio."

Considering I've only been out of state once to do a missions trip in Tennessee, I'll have to take her word for it.

Curtain.

Songs blare through the speakers hoisted in the makeup room. We listen as the Pirate King sings about, well, being a pirate king.

Minutes blur past, and then our number approaches.

The gaggle of women in cream dresses and I approach the stage. I adjust the heaping hat they've perched on the wig, tied under my neck with a red ribbon. Sweat forms around the mic, placed on my center part, and resting on my forehead.

The girls swarm the stage and surround "Frederick." Indeed, Eric wears no phantom mask tonight. In fact, the half-mask matches his skin tone and the contours of his cheeks. If not for the line going down his nose, it could've passed for the real thing.

"No, no, not one." The girls shriek this, as they run away from Frederick. In his song, he asks if one of the women will marry him, despite the fact that he's an ex-pirate.

Deep breath. It's almost my time to go on stage.

"Not one?" His mournful note.

"No, no—"

"Yes, one!" The note warbles in my mouth as I fly onto the stage. My dainty umbrella sailing in my gloved arm.

"Tis Mabel," the sisters croon.

Thus we begin the song, like I had back at the mansion. Perhaps my imagination, or fried nerves, have decided to play tricks on me, but I spot a genuine half-moon smile from him. He gets more into the music this time around.

The choreographer told me to ad-lib my steps and act like a flighty bird. He follows me, arms mirroring mine.

Thankfully, they've also given me permission to cadenza the heck out of this thing. I ad-lib a series of notes during a pause in the music.

When we conclude on the final high note, the audience erupts in applause.

The rest of the show passes in a mist until I find myself on center stage taking a bow for the curtain call. Two scarlet curtains shut before us, and the cast exits stage left to meet with the audience in the atrium.

I whirl around to tell Eric congrats. He handled the stage kiss well. Asking before our number—during intermission—to practice the dip, to make sure I felt comfortable enough with it.

He's disappeared.

Maybe I've lost him in the cast that surges around me like a river. We gush into the auditorium, fanning ourselves in relief from the lack of stage lights.

Patrons, most of them elderly, shake my hand and chirp about my voice. My heart soars so high in my chest that I swear it'll burst right out of my rib cage. Sabotage aside, from whoever stole away our maestro and ship's wheel, I could get used to a summer like this.

Meg squeezes my shoulder. "You were brilliant, girl."

"You too." She nailed her solo during "Go Ye Heroes" where she told the policemen to bravely die like heroes. "What's the plan after this?"

Dying conversation quells in the lobby. My ears have been buzzing from the last few minutes from the noise.

"Cast is going to Mongolian barbeque and then a bubble tea place. We know the owner of the latter, so they're keeping it open late for us."

Bubble tea. Ooh, boy, I could go for something like that.

We peel off our costumes that now stick to our bodies like a second skin. I pray that someone in the costuming department will wash these suckers before our first actual performance tomorrow.

Once reacquainted with my civilian shorts and t-shirt, I meet with Raph in the lobby. He flattens me into a hug and then presents a small bouquet of carnations.

I cradle them. "Don't encourage Mom. She's dying to get us together, you know."

Mom texted me that she had to leave a number early, thanks to a minor family emergency at home. No way could she get either of my siblings to sit through an opera.

"I know." He swings his key ring around his fingers. "Okay, Mabel, where to?"

We meet the cast at the Mongolian buffet. Karim lets Meg get first in line so she doesn't "pass out."

My stomach rumbles from a lack of dinner today, so I scoop unhealthy amounts of uncooked shrimp, baby corn, and noodles into a bowl. A chef cooks it in a wok, dousing it with the bowl full of teriyaki I ladled at the sauce station.

Once the cast gets acquainted with my "chaperone" we partake in the meal. I notice the absence of three people—

Eric, Antonia, and the manager.

Maybe they'd stuck behind to help clean up the stage. Guilt gnaws at my gut. Should we have really run off like that without asking if they had anything for us to tidy up? In most theater productions, the director needed us to help with something post-show.

Or did professional operas hire people for that?

We inhale the late dinner and scoot back to our cars before I can notice anything more.

Fifteen minutes and a drive later, we find ourselves in an adorable tangerine and teal themed restaurant. Meg perches in a wicker chair, the shape of a mango, and pats a small space beside her.

"Let's get a picture, girlie."

I scrunch myself next to her. "Do you want Raph to get one?"

She clicks her tongue. "No, my wonderful *fiancé* is the troupe's official social media guy. On your tour, did you happen to spot some of the cameras he has posted in different rooms for B-roll? Maybe not. Antonia is horrible with technology. She probably couldn't see the cameras in the room, let alone point them out to you." She snaps her fingers at Karim. "Do you mind, sweetheart?"

B-roll?

I scan through my memories.

Yes, I think I do recall spotting a camera in the scenic shop, the room that smelled of wood. Hopefully Karim didn't stick any cameras in the dressing rooms. Doesn't seem like the type.

Squeezing me closer, she smiles. I imitate her and glance at the camera. Karim is clean-shaven. I hadn't realized he *wore* a beard for the show.

He snaps the photo and allows us to take a look.

Once we finish the shoot, we bundle ourselves around a table and order desserts. Once more, no Eric.

I poke a straw into my green tea smoothie and inhale the sweet mixture. Probably shouldn't have too much dairy, with us having a performance tomorrow.

Meg digs a spoon into her mango ice cream. As she goes for a bite, I swallow.

"When are the others going to get here?"

She coughs and slaps her chest. "Sorry, wrong tube. What's that?"

"The others. You know—Antonia, the manager—"

"Not cast members. Sometimes they can come after the show but—"

"—Eric."

The table goes dead silent. Laughter from conversations at the surrounding booths prickles my skin. I've said something wrong. Time for a recovery.

"I just figure he didn't stick around for the meet and greet in the lobby. He tired or something?"

"Something like that." Meg sets her spoon back on her glass bowl. "He's a bit of a recluse. Doesn't really join us at these sorts of things."

"Oh, no worries, then."

Shoulders relax. Got it, the more I prod into Eric's life, the more trouble I can get in.

Curiosity niggles at my intestines though. Who posted those videos on his page? Why didn't the family want word to get out about their son's face?

Maybe I could get him something to go. That wouldn't count as detective-ing, right? Just a congratulations for a job well done in the show.

He did blow away the audience tonight. Goosebumps rippled on my arms during several of his numbers. How did his family keep him a secret for so long?

I ask our server for a strawberry smoothie, a safe option. Unless he has some sort of Fragaria allergy, we can present this as a peace offering.

Cold beads of sweat on the cup caress my fingertips on the way back to the theater.

Raph drops me off to swing around the block.

"Just need to grab a few things I forgot. Thanks. Will text you when I'm out."

I race into the building and to the dressing rooms. Darkness shrouds everything. I often have a sixth sense for detecting other bodies in the room. No one is nearby.

Huh.

After I dart into the auditorium, and can't find him in there, I return to the men's dressing room and find his bag and other items. I place the smoothie cup onto the table and tear off a sticky note next to one of the mirrors. Pen out of my bag, I scrawl a quick message.

Wonderful job tonight! You have the voice of an angel. Enjoy this congratulatory drink. The cast missed you at the outing.

—Mabel

Capping the pen, I feel a presence in the doorway. Sixth sense: alerted.

Twisting around, I squint to catch any silhouette from the hallway. Nothing.

The phantom has escaped once more.

CHAPTER 7

"*No emperor ever received so fair a gift. The angels wept tonight.*"

No signature.

A single red rose greeted me in my dressing room after last night's performance—the first true one for the cast.

Two thoughts plagued my mind in the moment I pinched the thorn-less stem.

One—did Eric give me this as a thank-you for the smoothie? If so, why didn't he sign it?

Two—it would take a lot of power to make an angel weep. From how our church described them, they were joyful creatures. So bright that men feared stepping into their very presence. What could make an angel cry?

What could make an angel weep?

After the cast went out for another bubble tea run, I plugged the quote into Google. It originated from the OG version of *Phantom of the Opera,* the book. I mused if Eric somehow could read my thoughts about him being the little phantom of the theater.

Something tells me that if I hid half of my face, it would drive me crazy if people compared me to the famous opera ghost. Any jokes about Tina Turner, attributed to my name, could make my stomach bubble in annoyance.

Come to think of it, maybe I should stop comparing Eric with the Erik from that tale. He probably deserves something more worthy.

Sweat stinks from the gym this morning.

Meg curls a barbell and quirks a brow at me. "You know these weights aren't going to lift themselves, right?"

I set my own weight down and slump onto a smelly yoga mat.

"I just don't get the point of lifting weights. Shouldn't we be doing more ab workouts?"

My abdomen burns in reply to my question. A few minutes ago, Meg forced us to do a workout that involved several burpees. Although I'd always done well in the homeschool co-op gym equivalent classes, Mom never exactly signed me up for any softball or track leagues.

Treadmills behind me whir to life. A girl, with headphones in, blasts rock music I can hear from my spot.

Mirrors cover the front end of the gym. Nearby, a man suckles on his emotional support water bottle. I cradle mine in the crook of my knees.

"Every bit of it's important." Meg clacks her barbell onto the rack that holds weights of various poundage. "Your body—"

"I know, I know." I pant. "Is an instrument."

"And if you only work out one part of the body, and let the other side get all wimpy." She holds up her arm and pinches the only spare bit of fat she has on her. "You'll be unbalanced. You'll fall apart."

Is this why she faints all the time?

It feels like such a personal question. Even during our initial five minutes on the elliptical today, Meg needed to sit down for a break. She dumped several Gatorade packets into her own water bottle.

On the machines next to me, what looks like a college student towels off the equipment with cleaning solution. His dark hair reminds me of Eric's. He's got the lengthy build, too.

I reach for a squirt bottle to spritz my barbell handle with the chemicals.

"Meg, if you can tell me, what happened with—" I drop the towel and gesture at half of my face.

"Eric?"

"Yeah. I know you said that curiosity killed the cat. But I think curiosity is going to kill *this* cat."

The questions kept me up last night until I popped a melatonin gummy. Granted, the buzz from the successful performance didn't help.

And, once again, Eric hadn't joined us for smoothies after. Part of me wanted to bring him another one, but that felt too forward.

"It *is* a dangerous question." Meg parked on a bench, scorched with sweat marks from previous people who sat on it. "If you ask the wrong person that is. Lucky for you, you chose right."

Don't know if I did.

Poison laces the tone of her voice. I keep my eyes wide, and unassuming. If I've learned anything from detective books, the more innocent you seem, the more information people give to you. For good reason, people withhold juicy secrets from someone obnoxious like Poirot.

"Okay, so Eric." She pats a spot on the bench next to her.

Inches between us, I sit.

"It all happened during a camping accident. He was in Scouts. Well, I guess Cub Scouts at the time. I don't know when you graduate into Boy Scouts."

Ten years old. Which means it happened to him before then.

Malachi turned nine this past March and has to make a decision to stick with it or not.

"He was in charge of tending to a campfire. Making it big, and stuff like that. I guess one of the counselors had brought a bottle full of gas, maybe for grilling or something. Campgrounds can sometimes have those."

Her fingers run up and down her knee-high socks. She sports a pair of scarlet ones today.

Maybe the girl played softball because everyone else in this gym wears no-shows. Ankle-high ones at best.

"Anyway, the fire was starting to die and so Eric grabs the bottle. It's not squirting at first, so he aims it at his face, because, you know—eight-year-olds do that sort of stuff."

I nod.

She shifts her posture, so she's bent in half.

"Nicks himself a little in the face. Tries to wipe it off, but doesn't get all of it. Then he aims the liquid at the campfire. Do you know what happens when fire hits liquid gasoline?"

Yeah, I do. But I want her explanation of it.

Once, I met a teen journalist who worked on our local paper, another homeschool gal. She told me, "You always ask the questions you know the answers to. Because you want to make sure they answer right. If they don't, you know you've got a real story."

"What happens when you do that?"

"The fire travels up the gasoline. So in this case, into the bottle."

I let out a hiss of air. She mhmms.

"Yeah, made the bottle explode, and got all over his face. Although a counselor spotted him and had him stop-drop-and-roll in the grass nearby—fires burn fast and they burn hot."

She takes a long pause. Her foot bounces up and down.

"Anyway, that's the story. You can imagine that Antonia got overprotective of him after. She's very protective of the Daaé family in general. His troop was relentless. Bullies. And that was *before* half of his face got burned. So he got homeschooled and doesn't go out much since then."

For anyone who wants to take up detective-ing in the future.

The Tell-Tale Signs Someone Is Lying

1. Not making eye contact—Although not always the case. Many of my friends with ASD don't like doing this. So don't go based on this alone.

2. Telling too much or too little—Stories that sound rehearsed.

3. Fidgeting and restless movement from the legs and feet.

4. Posture shifting.

5. Changes in speech patterns, sounding abnormal.

Although she didn't lie about the whole thing—or props to her for excellent acting—she missed something in the story. Can't find out now, though.

Get too pushy and this cat gets killed.

"Thanks for letting me know." I lift myself from the bench and return to the safety of my water bottle. "Curiosity, quenched."

"Good to hear." She pulls out her phone and wipes the moisture off the screen. Humidity clings to us in this gym. "Probably should head out anyway. We have a morning roundup meeting on the stage before today's rehearsal."

In between show days, we rehearse. We catch up on problem areas in *Pirates* and start everything else for *Gianni Schicchi*.

Once, in community theater, one of the actors participated in three plays at one time. We told him he would die, but now...I wish I could hit him up for some survival tips. Soreness covers my body.

Maybe one hundred thousand dollars did seem more reasonable, now that I take into account how much physical labor goes into the show.

"They may have some breakfast at the theater." Meg jabs a finger at me as she scoops her bag strap over her shoulder with her other hand. "What's your biggest enemy, Tina?"

The question catches me by surprise.

Does she hope to warn me about something?

"Umm." Play it off funny, girl. "Fortissimo."

"Dairy. Now that we're under the watchful eye of the manager, you can't consume any. Except maybe you can sneak some chocolate here or there on travel days."

Soon as she states this, my stomach yearns for some cheese, even at nine AM.

Yep, we've definitely earned that 100k.

Sliding into my car, I spray some coconut-scented antiperspirant onto every area that needs it and rev my engine, off in the direction of the theater. Raph offered to join me today, but I told him to soak in the last of his days of summer here. Poor guy has to accompany us everywhere. Hopefully his stipend—and what I pay him at the end of August—makes up for it. Once parked in a parking deck, I head into the grand auditorium. A bubble of actors surrounds Antonia...and a new man.

He reminds me of the manager—who didn't make an appearance at last night's performance. Everyone gossiped about whether the manager attempted to sabotage the preview performance. Someone in the dressing room even mentioned something about an email going out from the manager's office to the maestro.

The message must've told the maestro that we'd double-booked for the night. That we didn't need him.

This new guy looked like the old one.

Same squat figure. Same withering hairline.

But this guy wears a suit today with a rose stem poked through the lapel. A rose stem.

Did he have something to do with the "gift" in my dressing room after last night's performance?

I shake the thought away.

Short men don't get a monopoly on flowers, Tina.

Racing to the stage, I find a gap in between Karim and Meg. Across from me stands Eric. At least he showed up for this.

"Sorry if I'm late."

"You aren't, dear." Antonia tilts her head up toward a swoop of scarlet curtains that hang above the stage. "Singers know to get places very early. They'd learned this in school. Show up for classes five minutes early, you're on time."

Glares burn into my forehead.

Did they blame me for getting a part without spending years in a school setting? They couldn't, right? All of these guys, except for the people who played little parts, came from the Daaé family. That meant they got an automatic pass to perform in opera.

Speaking of the background characters, I don't spot the ones in the bubble.

Must be a Daaé-only meeting.

Antonia motions for everyone to sit. We do so.

"Now, before we go over some corrections from last night's performance—you all did a wonderful job, by the way—I want to introduce you to someone."

She places her hands on the shoulders of the other guy in the center of the circle.

"We, unfortunately, had to say goodbye to our old manager, Richard Armand. Although we do appreciate his years of service to the troupe, we found it was best to part ways with him."

Part ways?

So, Richard *did* sabotage the group. Must have.

Meg mentioned at the gym how much Antonia likes to protect the Daaés.

"Therefore, we had a generous friend of the theater offer to serve as our new manager. Everyone, please give a warm welcome to Mr. Roger Firmin."

Sourness fills my gut as we clap.

Something feels really off about this guy. Maybe it has to do with his lopsided grin or the greasiness of his scalp. But my intestines wriggle at the sight of him. Some detectives call it a hunch.

But I don't have any evidence about him.

Yet.

Once the applause dies, Antonia reaches for a clipboard. She'd placed it beside Eric.

"Now for everyone's *favorite* part of the day."

An amused smile plays on her lips as everyone mock groans. Musicians, from what I researched, faced a great deal of criticism. In competitions, judges would—in the most brutal and illegible handwriting—tell them every dynamic they missed in the music and every note that went flat.

I braced myself for the notes from last night. Mistakes raced through my head. Did she notice the struggles with the cadenza? That in "Here Is Love" I almost fell over during the dip, because I lost my balance?

Her eyes look like they see everything. Take in everything.

Like mine.

"Pirate King, don't forget to forgo the helm choreography. Last night you went to where the ship's steering wheel used to be. Caught yourself, but remember the changes."

She refers to all of the singers by their character role.

"Ruth, we need more projection in 'When Frederick Was a Little Lad.' Some of your notes were hard to hear. And that's a good note to everyone." She gestured at her diaphragm. "More power, more projection, and more diction, please. These songs are in English—you have no excuse when it comes to pronouncing everything correctly."

Our next show, however, contained Italian lyrics.

Meg—in the smoothie restaurant last night—got me set up on a Duolingo account to learn individual words. "You have to know what you're singing. It's not enough just to have a basic translation. Every word counts."

"And Mabel—"

My chest constricts.

"—it was beautiful, but it was not powerful. You have no confidence in your voice."

Fingers fly to my throat. True, on certain notes, my vocals tremored.

I winced. "You could tell?"

"Whatever emotion you bring to the song, it will appear in the individual notes. Although I've assigned you to soubrette parts, I don't want you to be weak."

Soubrette means a weaker voice part, got it.

"Therefore, I'm having you work with a vocal coach during our rehearsal days. We can catch you up in between sessions." Her hand flies in the direction of Eric. "He will start practicing with you today to develop more power behind your voice."

"What?" Eric and I say this at the same time.

He shrinks into his hoodie. I pinch my leggings and slap them against my calves.

"He did learn from the best." She gestures at herself. "And we worked ages on getting more confidence into his voice. He will be the one to work with you. Starting after we take a ten-minute break."

"Thank you, ten." The singers chorus this.

As the circle disbands, Eric and I don't leave our spots. We stare at each other, frozen.

What have we gotten ourselves into?

CHAPTER 8

"Ah yes, Eric, these filing cabinets really put me in the musical mood."

"All the music rooms are taken by the cast and by regular performers at this opera. This was the next best thing."

It takes me a moment to remember that we aren't the only people to put on a show here. We interrupted the regular season of this opera house. I wonder if the other places we travel to get annoyed by us moving in.

I bump into a filing cabinet and hiss as a bruise probably welts on my hip.

Eric fled to the archives during the ten-minute water break. He perches on a desk next to a bust of Mozart. Musical scores and librettos litter every surface in here. I notice how he hasn't flicked on the lights.

Doing so, I watch in my periphery as he cowers. Maybe my imagination played tricks, but he might have hissed.

"Okay, Mr. Vampire, teach me how to sing good."

"Did you bring your libretto for *Gianni Schicchi*?"

I hoist it up in the air.

"Good." He snatches it from my grip and chucks it across the room. Papers butterfly as they go sailing. "You won't be needing that for today."

I flinch. "Seriously? You *do* realize we need to go over the *music,* right? Not all of it's memorized."

Yes, I'd gotten Lauretta's song "O Mio Babbino Caro" down in terms of the notes, but the rest operated in a fuzzy limbo in my mind.

"We don't need music today."

"Ah yes. How silly of me. Thinking to bring music to a music rehearsal."

He returns to his spot on the desk and wilts. Already, I've tried his patience.

"As you may know, your body is an instrument. Before we can play any notes, we need to make sure the instrument is 'tuned.'"

Ugh, that probably means more burpees.

I salute him with two fingers and start on push-ups.

"What—" His unmasked eye blinks at me. Instead of his phantom mask, he's gone for a black one today. "What do you think you're doing?"

"Push-ups, huh," I pant, "but according to Meg, my form is, huh, terrible, so, huh—"

"Okay, please stop doing that."

Arms shaking from the earlier workout, I oblige and collapse onto the carpet. Cheeto dust coats one of the desk legs.

"Today, we're actually going to work on breath support. Did you bring your water bottle?"

With a groan, I roll myself to a sitting position and locate where I've placed my chonker of a water bottle. I hold it up for him to see.

"Eric, meet Lenny."

"Hello, Lenny." He leans forward and pats the metal. Then he swivels around and grabs something in a plastic container. Tearing open the top, he pulls out a straw and hands it to me. "Now poke this guy about two centimeters into Lenny."

"A straw?"

"A special singer straw."

"Ooo, fancy." I unscrew the top of Lenny and plunk the straw in. Pinching it, I hold it a few centimeters into the water.

"Right. Breath support today. Now, sing solfege into the straw."

I squint at him.

"What?"

"Is this a prank? Is one of Karim's cameras nearby to post this whole thing on social media?"

Eric releases a long breath. "No. Karim only puts those up on show days, and I don't think he ever films anything in the archives. Just sing into the straw."

I turn my back to him and hunch over the cup.

"What are you doing now?"

"I don't want you to see."

"You don't want me to see you singing into the straw?"

"It's weird. Let me have an alone moment with Lenny, okay?"

A long pause. "Okay, you weirdo."

Heat rises in my cheeks. Feeling self-conscious, I double over the bottle and blow the notes into the straw. Bubbles form in the plastic straw. I sing through the solfege twice and emerge for a breath.

"That exercise will help you to clear your throat and loosen up everything in that area, speaking of."

Right as I turn back to him, he has his hands inches away from my throat. My hands fly up and smack his arms away. He blinks at me, realization dawning. "Sorry, should've asked. You need to get those lymph nodes massaged out. Do you mind, if I—"

I force myself to steady.

His fingers press into my neck and knead up and down. I force my lips into a line because they keep curving upward. This feels nice.

He releases and stifles a laugh. "You're not very good at trusting people."

"You're one to talk."

The words escape me before I can take them back.

He doesn't flinch but takes in the sentence one bit at a time. Then he speaks. "What do you mean by that?"

It's not angry, or cold. Just curious.

"I mean, you run off after performances, don't spend time with the cast, hide wherever there aren't people. I can probably guarantee there are practice rooms available, but you chose the archives because you won't run the risk of having to talk to anyone."

Anyone *besides* me.

He lifts himself. At this moment, I realize he's doused himself in some sort of piney cologne. Did he have that on for the cast meeting? If so, for what purpose? I barely managed to wind my hair into a messy bun this morning so the cast wouldn't have to take in all the sweaty gloriousness of it.

Maybe Eric liked to keep clean all days. Though, I don't recall this scent ever being on him for past performances.

His voice breaks up my thoughts.

"Thanks for the smoothie. Strawberry was a good choice."

He edges himself into one of the rolling chairs at one of the desks. Rubs his fingers over a kink in his forehead.

"You're—not wrong, Tina. People are scary, untrustworthy. The minute you show yourself to them...all of yourself..." Fingertips fly to his mask. He yanks them away as if something burned him. "They run away. So sometimes, you want to beat them to the punch and hide yourself."

I draw my knees under my chin. Ghosts of his fingertips still rest on my throat. My skin tingles.

"Did that happen to you, Eric?"

His exhale shudders, like he's holding back a watery emotion. "Yeah, yeah it did."

My mind flashes back to the Japanese garden. Carmen charged up that hill, face sheet white. He must've unmasked himself to her. To get him to trust her like that, he had to have liked her. Maybe they'd spent the summer together, practicing for the upcoming shows.

Jealousy twinges my chest.

Why?

Sure, he and I acted like love interests on the stage. I'd done that plenty of times in theater. Why did this...why did *he* feel different?

I rub my thumbs up and down on my knees. "I'm sorry that happened."

Plastic wrapping on something crinkled in his fingertips. "It's fine. Learned my lesson. People don't want to see all of you, only the parts they like."

Wish I could argue, but plenty of guys ghosted me over the stupidest things.

Over the fact that my dad died, and they didn't want "that kind of red flag" for a relationship. Over the fact that I could sing semi-well, and they let that intimidate them. Over the fact that my mother, and all her sheltering, stifled me from any prospects.

They enjoyed the pretty Tina, the demure one. Not the confident one. So we buried her somewhere along in the music.

"Anyway." Eric pulls out something that looks like the end of a black stick. "We should keep loosening that jaw and that throat."

He pads over to me and kneels. With two fingers, he taps his own throat. "I'm going to move this thing up and down on your throat and neck. It's going to feel a little weird, all right?"

Tingling fills me once more by his nearness. I nod.

Right before he places the black thing on my throat, he arches a brow. "Do you trust me?"

"I think I'm starting to."

CHAPTER 9

I never would have thought that music practice would mean keeping a ball in the air using a straw, but so went the rest of our time in the archives.

We joined the cast for some choreography and cleanup.

After we finished, Meg invited us to her house.

At first, I expect Eric to decline.

He flicks a glance my way and says yes.

Heart catapulting into the edges of my ribcage, I locate my car in the parking deck. Ever warned by my mom, I keep the keys between my fingers. Eric walks me to my car before going to his to make sure I get into my vehicle safely.

A twenty-minute drive takes me to a beautiful split-level home in the suburbs of Cleveland. Vines wrap their way down a trellis outside of the house. This doesn't feel like a Meg home. Something about the stark white paint doesn't scream vibrant enough for her. As for Karim, I don't know enough about him yet.

As I kick off my shoes at the front door, it occurs to me that Mom would never approve this outing without my "chaperone." Thank goodness she works later today, so she won't question why

I come home at the time that I do. It'll be good to get on that tour bus at the end of this week and ship off to New York.

When I step inside, Meg greets me in an instant hug.

As she releases, she jabs her thumb over her shoulder. "Karim's making cucumber dip. Always the host. Come sit."

She leads me to a couch. Eric has already beaten me here because he squishes himself in the farthest corner. Part of him looks like he hopes the couch cushions will swallow him whole.

"Of course. Karim almost always *has* to be a host. Because Antonia bought this place for us, she often stops by. And if we know anything about Aunt Antonia, she's picky."

Meg sets two glasses, full of a pinkish type of liquid, before us on coasters. I notice the one next to Eric has a straw.

That could explain why he doesn't join us on outings. Thanks to that mask, it would make eating difficult, considering it shields half of his mouth. He must hide somewhere in the theater to consume anything.

I sip on the drink and savor the sweet hibiscus flavor.

"Shoot." Meg frowns. "Forgot the fig sauce and crackers."

I hold up a hand. "Don't worry about hosting us. I'll get it."

Before she can protest, I lift myself off the couch and head toward the kitchen. Through a window that leads into it, I spot Karim leaning against a wall. His thumb swipes right on his phone in rapid succession. Something about the red phone case irks me.

Call me crazy—since I've never gone on dating apps—but I know what swiping right means.

Why would he cheat on Meg? Especially after they got engaged?

Heat sizzles in my cheeks. He glances up at me and hastily slips his phone into his pocket. "Fig sauce?"

Biting my lip to prevent anything from slipping out, I nod.

He throws a dish towel over his shoulder and presents the food board with a flourish. I balance it in my hands so the cracker display won't topple over. Then I set it on the coffee table in the family room. Playbills from past performances line the room in glass frames.

"So." Meg dips a cracker into the cheese and fig block once I relocate my seat. Inches away from Eric. "What do you guys think of the new manager?"

Eric chokes on his drink.

He sets down the glass, coughs, and slaps his chest for several moments.

I open and close my mouth. "He—well, I don't know much about him yet."

It's the truth. He didn't linger long for practice. Something about that red rose in his lapel bothered me, though.

Meg crunches into the cracker. "If you ask me, that old manager had been on his last straw for forever. I swear, he's been trying to sabotage shows long before *Pirates.*"

Eric sinks into the couch.

"Really?" I ask.

"Yeah, which is unfortunate. Because Aunt Antonia really liked the guy. They did so many shows together, and I swore he was going to be with us until his heart stopped. But I *had* been noticing little things here and there."

She picks out a paper plate for herself and plunks several crackers onto it.

"Curtains not pulling at the right time. Mics failing to work. Things falling from the rafters. At first, we thought that he was accidentally hiring incompetent staff. But after he insisted we take on Carmen, we knew something was up with how eager she was to get to know Eric. Probably to get plenty of dirt on the family. Especially after that girl ran away, she must've known she was way in over her head."

Wanness creeps into Eric's skin.

Something tells me he doesn't want to revisit the scene at the Japanese garden.

Subject change time. "I'm sure the new guy will be great."

"You." Meg points at me and then at her feet. "What shoe size are you?"

Oh, she can apparently segue too. This throws me for a loop.

"Umm." My thumb rubs my palm. "Seven?"

"Great, because your character shoes look like they're a million years old. Antonia says she wants you to borrow one of my extra pairs. You'll find them in the room back there"—she gestures behind me—"on the right. Left is Karim's. Middle one is the bathroom."

They sleep in separate rooms?

My save-yourself-for-marriage mom would probably approve. But with Meg's "let's get physical" attitude, something tells me that doesn't fit this couple's vibe. Possibly, they could need their space from each other from time to time.

I click open the door, and it opens with a creak.

Stepping inside, I advance toward the closet. Something blocks my path.

My pulse spikes.

It's the helm of the ship. The one that went missing.

"You find it, Tina?" Meg's voice calls from the family room.

Shoving open the closet doors, I locate the shoe bin and pull out the most-worn pair of character shoes. They barely contain any scuffs on them.

"Got them."

Did she *want* me to find the helm? If so, did that mean the manager didn't steal the prop piece the night of dress rehearsal? Why would she frame him?

Heat prickles my neck. I grab the nape of my shirt and fan myself. I need to get out of this house.

"Hey, Meg." I shut the door to the bedroom and pad onto the hardwood floor. "I'm not feeling the greatest. Think I overdid it at rehearsal. Mind if I go?"

"Sure thing. Text us when you get home safe, okay?"

I nod and dart out the door. Soon as I make my exit, I dial Raph. He picks up on the first ring.

"Eww. Way to ruin a good weeding session."

I roll my eyes. We often answer the phone in a mock-eww. It's an inside joke from a long tech week during one of our previous performances. "Shut up and listen. I have tea."

Glancing over my shoulder back at the house, I explain what I saw in Meg's bedroom. Cicadas scream at me as I slam myself into my car and crank up the AC.

"Hold on, in *her* room? Do you think she didn't actually faint? So she could steal it right after your tour?"

"I don't know."

Meg did join me minutes later. Probably enough time to stuff it into her trunk and head back into the theater.

"But, Raph, that doesn't explain about the email to the maestro. Someone had to have hacked into the inbox—"

I stop myself short. Meg did that. With the help of Karim. The two of them must've framed the first manager. So Antonia could hire the second one.

"I just don't understand why they would do this."

Raph draws in a long breath.

"Maybe the guy knew too much."

What happens if I do that too? I already had gotten too curious about Eric's mask. The nape of my neck slaps my headrest.

"Tina, listen, I know you don't want me to be with you until the tour bus gets going. But I think I need to be with you for everything. Rehearsals, performances. Even in Cleveland, I don't think you're safe. Not without some protection."

Long sigh.

If I get too much info from the family, they may just replace me too. Like I had done to Carmen.

"I think, Raph, you're probably right."

CHAPTER 10

"I swear, Tina, if you put down a plus-four on me, I will end you." Meg fans her UNO stack of cards in front of her face.

The road rumbles, causing us to jump in our seats. Most of the bus ride to Gatlinburg, Tennessee has been smooth sailing. Except for that brief bout in West Virginia. We left at the ungodly hour of five AM and, with all of our food and gas stops on the way, plan to arrive sometime in the evening.

I tuck the plus-four card into my stack and instead toss a plus-two onto the pile. She glares at me as she scoops up cards from the pile.

"At least it wasn't a plus-four." I shrug.

This sends giggles throughout the rest of the group. Karim, some of the other sopranos, and even Eric have joined us in our mini circle to play UNO at the back of the bus.

Little by little, we've gotten Eric more involved in our tour happenings.

Back in New York, I couldn't drag him to the Broadway show, *Into the Woods.* During intermission, Meg complained the whole time about how Little Red sang with a nasal, instead of getting breath support from her diaphragm.

I noticed how the other opera singers in the audience appeared to scrutinize every note from the singer.

"It happens." Meg had told me. "Once you get classically trained, you realize when people take the lazy way out on certain notes."

Although the comment sizzled my blood, Raph sided with her. Said that after some photographer classes he sneaked into at a local college—when he was sixteen—that he could tell when someone cheated in Photoshop or got lazy in post edits.

Alas, we couldn't get Eric to that show.

His face did light up when I brought him back a New York slab of pizza. We broke the dairy rule, but we didn't care. We ate it in the large opera house underneath the glittering chandeliers.

Raph hung out in a nearby room. Not wanting to be an imposing chaperone...

But at the ready in case something happened.

After the discovering-the-helm incident, nothing has sparked my interest. True to Meg's warning, I've kept my head low. For now.

Eric and I continued our voice lessons, moving from massaging muscles to running through notes. He didn't let me pronounce the Italian words at first.

"You have to get the rhythm down. Before you can sing. Before you can add the words in."

Speak first.

Then sing the notes in one syllable, *Oooh.*

Then add the words. He would correct my Italian pronunciations and make me mark up the music in pencil for where I got tripped up.

By the time we reached Norfolk for our next tour stop, I managed to convince him to join us in the botanical gardens. We finished our show late, and they allowed us in after-hours for a tour. Meg claimed this happened during international tours. She and Karim had once gotten a front-row view of the Mona Lisa in the Louvre after they finished a performance of *Candide.*

"That thing was a postage stamp. Totally not worth the normal crowd around it."

At the botanical garden, Eric trembled as we reached a burbling fountain. Memories from the previous garden encounter at the mansion must've raced through his head. So, I had us park and take in the stars above.

Minutes passed. His shoulders relaxed.

And we drank everything in. Phone flashlights guided us through the rose gardens and butterfly statues. Body drained, I leaned on Eric's arm on the way back to the tour bus that chugged to the hotel that night.

Little by little, he unmasked.

Unlike Carmen, I liked what I saw.

"Was it just me—" Meg's voice dissolves my thoughts. She claps a red eight onto the pile. "Or did you all also spot our ex-manager in the audience last night?"

"Nooooo." One of the sopranos hissed. "Didn't someone also see him in New York?"

Chills rest on my bones.

That someone in New York was yours truly. I spotted him in one of the box seats. It reminded me of the scene in Phantom, where the opera ghost claimed a chair for himself.

When I caught Richard leering at us, his expression said everything. "You can't get rid of me that easily. I *own* this group."

Meg did mention, forever ago, that the manager had quite the micro-managerial grip on the troupe. If Antonia let him go, he wouldn't release himself just yet.

Blood drains from my cheeks. Eric meets my eye, eyebrows pinched.

"He won't do anything. Even if he's following us, we have security." The next part he says in a whisper, as if just to me. "He can't hurt us."

My body relaxes. Several policemen, with holsters, stationed themselves at our various shows. I lost count of their number in New York. The Daaé protected their own. And for these next few months, I'd become a temporary Daaé.

I clear my throat.

"You've been doing that for the whole bus ride, girlie." Meg tapped her throat with a French-tipped finger. "Do you know what your best friend is?"

"Jesus?"

"Nope, honey and lemon tea. How about, when we get to the hotel, we get you a nice cup of that good stuff?"

Despite a healthy diet, workout, and sleep schedule, my body ached.

Our new manager encouraged us to steer clear from loud venues—so we could always speak in quiet tones—and against staying up past midnight. Most of the time we complied. Sickness still caught up to us.

Everyone in the cast had an off day. Sprained ankles and coughs littered our journey across the states.

It was my turn for ailments.

"We could." I winced at the crackle in my throat. "But aren't we planning to stop somewhere first?"

"Oh yeah, that's right."

Meg's voice drops as she massages her calves. Once again, she's bedecked herself in her long socks. She turns in her seat and perched her ankles against the chair in front of her. She cranes her neck at Karim.

"You don't think we'll be at the aquarium long, do you?"

"You can sit down if you need to."

I don't know why I thought she faked fainting the first night. With whatever health condition she's dealt with, if she's made it up, she certainly plays the part well. Granted, she does act for a living.

That still doesn't explain the ship helm, though. The mystery of that has stumped me for weeks.

A figure staggers towards us.

Raph, next to me, slumps into a seat and waves me in for a secret meeting.

"You'll never guess what, Tina."

"Okay, I'll take your word for it."

A pause.

"So I need you to say 'what?'."

I gasp. "Whatever do you wish to tell me, dear friend?"

He rolls his eyes. "Yes, that works too. Anyway, Antonia was looking over the photos I took of you all in Norfolk during your dress rehearsal."

"And?"

Trees blur behind him in the background. One of the sopranos gasps and says something about spotting a black bear.

"Aaaand, she says they look amazing. May even have a job lined up for me in their marketing department after this season. Isn't that crazy?"

Raph and Antonia warmed up to each other before we even left Cleveland. Whenever Raph and I met in hotel lobbies to decompress for the day, he mentioned all the compliments she had for his photographs.

Maybe I'd pegged her wrong, thinking she vetted us to deem us worthy enough to be in her troupe. She could've scanned through Raph's social media to scout a future photographer.

"That's huge, Raph. What about school, though?"

"What about it? I'm already taking a gap year to figure out what I want to do. If you have a job lined up, why waste all that money, you know?"

Although I nod, I don't know.

Thoughts have plagued me about what happens after August. If the troupe likes me, will I end up in it full-time like Karim? Do I want that for myself?

What if I get a year into it and discover I hate it?

That will start me on square one, blackballed by one of the most famous opera groups in the nation.

Our bus slows as we approach the buildings ahead. Flanked by mountains, this feels like a far cry from our previous venues.

Once we park in front of a building, whose top story looks like all glass, I take in the sign. "Ripley's Aquarium of the Smokies."

"This where we're stopping?" I ask Eric.

"You guys are." He flashes his libretto. Colorful tabs stick out of the pages every which way. "I think I need to study up on *Schicchi* more."

He knows the score inside and out, at least from what I can tell from our voice lessons. But I don't argue. Bright sunlight blares through the bus windows. Unless we go out somewhere in the shroud of darkness, he won't come along with us.

Still a work in progress, just like me with the lessons.

"I hear Gatlinburg has quite a few things," Karim informs us, scrolling on his phone. "A SkyBridge, mini golf, whitewater rafting."

"Let's stick to one thing at a time, love." Meg grips her stomach. "I don't know how much I'm going to be able to do."

As we disembark the bus, I spot Antonia and the new manager discussing the libretto. They'll join us in a few minutes, I imagine.

We check in and gawk at a circular tube tank as we walk through the doors. Silver fish glide in circles.

"Guys, I—" Meg's voice pipes behind us. Blue light highlights her as she doubles over. "I think I need to sit this one out."

Karim goes to her and places his hand on the small of her back. "We'll sit outside until the dizziness goes away. You two go on without us."

The rest of the group has already bundled themselves around the huge skeleton of some turtle. We wave Karim and Meg out the doors and continue on our tour of the aquarium.

As we advance to the waterfall, Raph checks his phone.

"Hope she's doing okay."

"Meg? Yeah, she comes close to passing out almost every day." Water spritzes my face as it cascades the rocks. "I think she'll be alright."

"Wanna go to the SkyBridge after we get through this place?"

But I can hardly hear him over the water and the din of voices. The only downside of arriving at places on a weekend...most attractions burst with vacationers and families in need of a Saturday activity.

An involuntary shudder passes up my spine.

"No thanks. I can't really do heights."

In the Tropical Rainforest exhibit, we stare at a tank full of piranha. Conversation wilts between the two of us. Raph knows I need to preserve my voice for the preview performance tomorrow night.

When we reach a stone slab full of poison dart frogs, I glance over my shoulder.

"Feels weird to be doing it without those two, you know. Do you think we should check in on them?"

Also, Antonia and the new manager haven't caught up to us yet. Maybe they entered and went a different way. Most of the other group broke off into the various exhibits.

"Shot a text to Karim." Raph waits. Then his eyes light up. "He says they're doing fine and to go ahead and finish the tour without them. They just need to get her legs propped up."

Something niggles my gut, but I go with it.

Scorpionfish, catfish, penguins...all the rest of it passes in a blur. Anxiety pounds my temples, and I can't help but wonder that something bad has happened to Meg or someone else.

We make a final stop at the gift shop, where Raph purchases an otter stuffed animal, and head back onto the bus. Eric lifts his head and nods at us after he highlights something in yellow on his paper.

"You guys were gone for a while, see anything interesting?"

As Raph shows Eric his camera roll, I spy Meg and Karim hobbling onto the bus. They wave at me and collapse into one of the front seats, far away from us. Minutes later, Antonia and the new manager climb up the bus steps. The rest of the group trickles in like raindrops.

"—really a shame we couldn't go to that SkyBridge." Raph clicks off his phone and leans back in his seat. "I hear it's, like, literally a seven-minute walk from here."

I Google pictures of it, and my blood runs cold.

One misstep and that plummet would lead to certain death.

"And it's pretty empty." One of the girls says this from two seats down. "Me and Annika went to check it out, and there was almost no one. Maybe five o'clock is a downtime for it."

During a weekend?

Granted, some hiking trails in Ohio could be packed full of runners and cyclists on some days. And others, a complete wilderness. Guess it all fell on the timing.

"Yep." Annika nodded. "I think it was empty because one of the pedestrians said it had been shut down earlier in the afternoon. Something about being too slippery because of rain from this morning. They'd seen a sign that stated—"

Her last words get cut off by the chug of the engine.

Annika takes a selfie with her seatmate. Even from my seat, I can tell her thumb blurs part of the camera.

We rumble for a few minutes to a hotel and collapse in the lobby. Karim scavenges the hotel gift shop for some electrolytes for Meg.

Raph and I head to our rooms, and I doze off. I can't say for how long, but a knock on my door causes me to jolt in my bed. I didn't even unpeel the covers before I conked out.

I catch my balance as I stagger to my feet.

"One moment."

The knocking becomes more frantic.

I peer out the window and notice that the sun has waned to a tangerine, a near-red. Must've slept for longer than planned.

Flicking on a light, I open the door and find Meg with her fist raised.

Eyes wide, she charges into the room and parks on the base of my bed. "Did you hear the news?"

A weird taste fills my mouth. I swallow and run my fingers up and down my pant leg. "What news?"

Her hands shield her eyes and she doubles over. "Oh, Tina, it's horrible. Absolutely horrible. Our new manager just let us know downstairs in the lobby. We thought you got the group text to come downstairs."

My heart hammers in my chest until my bones threaten to crumble.

I race to the nightstand and pick up the phone. Notifications flood the screen. Mostly, "are you doing okay?" and "where are you?" Nothing hinting at any specific news.

"Meg, what happened?"

She unbends herself and stares at the bathroom. Eyes avoid mine.

"You know how one of the girls mentioned that the SkyBridge had been closed earlier in the afternoon? Due to it being slippery. I—" A shuddering breath. "—I don't know if it was an accident or on purpose but—"

Her lip quivers.

"Meg," I whisper, body going cold. "Please just tell me. You're scaring me."

"It's Richard—our old manager. He must've followed us here, and...he...fell, Tina."

I slam my body against the wall. "Holy—"

"I'm sorry, Tina. He's gone."

CHAPTER 11

Two thoughts pop into my head right away.

First, suicide. Less likely. He'd followed us across three cities for either revenge or spite or something sinister, but not enough to give up. Not yet.

Second, murder.

More likely.

Back pressed against the wall, I regard Meg with suspicion.

I could be in the room with a murderer. I could be in the room with a murderer.

I could be in the room with a murderer...

Deep breath.

"This is—" Exhale. "A lot to take in. Do you mind if I go outside? To get some fresh air or something? Maybe talk with Raph?"

"Oh, girl, of course. I'm sorry. There's no easy way to tell someone something like that."

I would know. When Dad passed, we spent the greater portion of the week informing people. Since Mom had frozen over, unable to do basic tasks for months, and being daughter number one, I handled most of the announcements.

I can still hear the sobs on the speaker from when I dialed relatives.

Moisture dots my waterline. Although I got weird vibes from Richard, no one deserves to go in that way. I check my pants pockets for the hotel key and slip into the hallway. Meg must stay in my room because she doesn't follow.

Two doors down, I locate Raph's room.

I rap my knuckles against the door. Moments later, he opens it.

"Hey." He offers one arm for a hug.

"Hey." I shove him back and shut the door behind me. "We need to talk."

He blanches. "Did you just hear about—"

"It's totally a murder," I hiss. "And we need to get ourselves the first plane ticket home."

"Hold on."

He splays his hands and then motions me further into the room. Parking in a chair, he leans against the curtains of the window. Tangerine light illuminates his features.

"Let's not jump to conclusions, Tina."

I flinch at the word *jump.*

Raph notices a second later.

"Sorry, I mean, let's not assume anything. For all we know he could've slipped and fell. Or maybe chose to—"

"Don't even say it."

I sigh and crumple onto his unmade bed. What Mom would say if she discovered I'd entered this place alone? I can't tell if she'd wag her finger at me or praise me for finally putting the moves on her hopeful future-son-in-law.

"You of all people should be suspicious, Raph." My slit eyelids peer at the popcorn ceiling above me. "You were the one to tell me to go along with this opera thing. Not to mess with this family, or there'd be consequences."

"Yeah, consequences like they'd make it hard for you to join an opera program if you turned them down. Not end your life. We have to look at the facts."

I bolt up.

"Exactly."

"What? You're actually agreeing with me for once?"

"We need to look at the facts. Give me one second."

It takes me a second to locate the mini fridge in the suite room. They'd spared no expense in our luxury stays. Bolting to it, I throw open the door and pull out all of the bottles inside. Antonia, lax as she is compared to Mom, made sure the hotel didn't stuff anything alcoholic into this thing.

Coke cans, Pringles tubes, and sparkling water bottles all go onto his dresser.

"Tina, you *do* realize that once you remove one of those things, you have to pay for it. They have sensors and everything."

"Oh, gee darn." I slam a Fiji water onto the dresser and slam the door to the minibar shut. "If only I was given a $10,000 stipend to spend on things."

Besides, Antonia seemed to hint—back in New York—that they'd foot the bill for any hotel expenses.

"Okay, smarty-pants, wanna explain to me why you raided that poor fridge?"

"Gladly—each of these represents a different suspect."

"Suspect?"

"Bear with me."

Suspects List

Coca-Cola Can—Meg

Sparkling Water—Karim

Pringles—New Manager

Fiji Water—Antonia

"You're forgetting one."

I frown. "No, I'm not. Unless you think one of the chorus members did it. We saw all of them go into the aquarium ahead of us, soooo."

He reaches around me, pops open the fridge, and tosses a bag of peanut M&Ms next to the Fiji water.

Peanut M&Ms—Eric

"Seriously?"

"What? You said we need to look at the facts, and I think I have a good enough case against that guy. He never went into the aquarium, you know."

A growl lodges in my throat. Seconds ago, he didn't believe in suspects in the first place.

"Fine, Watson. Let's begin."

I hold up each item on the counter as I illustrate each person.

Reasons Behind Why I Suspect Certain People

Meg—She really seems to be wanting to quit opera for some reason. And her fainting spells could be faked. Really didn't seem like the biggest fan of the previous manager—she talked ill of him all the time. She could've totally been fine in the aquarium and we wouldn't be the wiser.

"But." Raph cracks the pull tab on the Coke can. Bubbles fizz before he takes a sip. "It would take a ton of commitment to act sick all the time."

"She only has to do it in front of us. Besides, there is the fact that we found the helm in her room. And that she 'fainted' right around the time it went missing."

"Not fully convinced, but proceed with our next suspect."

Karim—He and Meg seem to be a Bonnie and Clyde tag team. And he appears to have quite a bit of tech-savvy. He probably got her into the email inbox the first time Meg messaged me, and then sent the email to the maestro, framing the first manager and getting him fired. But since the manager kept following us, someone had to take action. Karim was seen leaving the aquarium with Meg.

"What you're saying, then, is that he doesn't have enough motive on his own. He and Meg would have to be in on it together."

"Unless he knows something about that first manager we don't. If he hacked into the inbox, maybe he spotted something the manager wanted to hide."

"Ehhh."

"Plus, he's a big guy. It takes a lot to throw a guy off of a bridge."

"Better, Sherlock."

New Manager, Roger Firmin—We don't know much about this guy. He slinks away during rehearsals and sends most notes to the cast—and members of production staff—over email, but he did swoop in to take Richard's spot at the last moment. It's almost like he'd been waiting years for that moment. But when his rival, Richard, kept appearing at performances, he needed to do away with him for good.

A pause.

"Nothing to argue about, Watson?"

"Nah, the guy gives me the creeps. But I thought of something.

"Mmm?" I peel the lid off the Pringles can and poke my fingers through the top.

Shame on me for eating at a time like this. But I need to give my hands and stomach something to do, other than puking.

Saltiness coats my tongue. My stomach concaves. When did I last eat?

Raph digs a handful of chips out of the tube. "Don't you think it's weird how the girls talked about there being a sign at the bridge? What if someone made a sign ahead of time for this purpose? Or got it out of the props loft?"

True, the props loft in Virginia was a labyrinth. We found all sorts of weird things in there, from rubber mice to fake pig roasts. Very possibly someone could've found a sign up there or created one from the materials at the theater.

"It *is* weird, but anyone could've done something like that. We all travel together, you know."

And likely, if someone brought a fake sign, they got rid of the evidence by now.

"Proceed."

Antonia—Fiercely protective of the Daaé family. If anyone crossed them, AKA a nosy manager, then she may be just bold enough to get rid of such a person. Not to mention, someone brought up that Richard really wanted Carmen to be cast. If Antonia suspected foul play on his part, she may have wanted to cut ties...in more than just firing him.

"Hold up."

"Great, here comes another objection."

"How could that tiny lady throw that heavy man off a bridge?"

"I don't know, Raph. Maybe she got the second manager to do it. Maybe she hired a guy. She probably has the budget to hire a guy."

He slumps, frowning at the bedsheets. Why did this argument from him sound more forceful than the others?

"I don't know, Tina, she just doesn't seem like the type to put her family's reputation on the line, simply to kill off a guy."

"Wait a second." I jab a finger at him. "You're just defending her because she said she liked your pictures. We're supposed to be unbiased, Raph."

"I *am* unbiased. And I just so happen to like the fact that she appreciates my art."

"Whatever."

"Speaking of biases, let's go to the next suspect, mmm?"

What could he possibly mean—

He shakes the peanut M&Ms. Oh boy.

Eric—No one knows who posted his videos. The family clearly wanted him to be kept a secret. Maybe he posted them to thrust himself into the spotlight so the family would be forced to allow him to perform with them. Well, when Eric saw the manager sabotaging the shows, he decided to take matters into his own hands. He did stay on the bus, after all, when we went into the aquarium. Maybe the manager knows something about Eric that we all don't. Something sinister, something ugly.

I stare at my feet in silence for a few moments.

Then speak. "You've been thinking about this for a while, haven't you?"

"What do you mean?"

"I'm saying that story was quite the stretch. Just because he's a recluse, doesn't mean he's a murderer."

"Something tells me you need to check your feelings for this guy."

"And something tells me you need to stop reading fan theories online."

Scrolled through plenty of them at the library. People made constant comparisons between Eric and the Phantom from both the book and the play. Rumors buzzed about people going missing, family deaths—all pointing back to an ugly creature hiding in his mask.

One of the theater kids told me they didn't like to watch horror movies for that reason.

"They purposely hire people with facial deformities. Because something about that scares people. Something about ugliness justifies that we can kill them off in brutal ways."

"Yeesh, Sherlock, maybe we should revisit this stuff later." Raph side eyes me.

My voice came out harsh. I'm not sure if I meant it to or not.

"Yeah." I steady the timber of my tone until it comes out even, cool. "Maybe we should. On our plane ride home. Murder or not, something's off. And we shouldn't stick around to find out why."

I push myself off of the bed, head to the hallway, and slam the door behind me.

When I reach my room, I notice that the door has been left open by the key latch. Heart quickening, I step inside and spot something scarlet on my dresser.

A red rose, with a black ribbon tied in a bow on the stem.

Tremors overtake my legs as I approach the flower. Six words, in scarlet ink.

"Past the point of <u>no return</u>."

They've underlined "no return." And by it, drew a small illustration of a house.

I can't go home. The murderer won't let me.

"Okay." I set the rose down and take in a sharp breath. "If you won't let me leave, then I'm going to sniff you out."

CHAPTER 12

T ricky business, trying to casually ask a person if they've murdered someone.

Antonia gave us the day off yesterday. Canceled the preview performance to give us "time to grieve," and had the box office assistant refund those with tickets. After we ordered room service, Raph and I spent the day planning how we would tackle the mystery.

He would interview Karim and the new manager.

Me? Meg and Antonia.

As far as Eric went, he tended to disappear during most warm-ups. Neither of us would get a chance to corner him—except me during voice lessons on Tuesday. If Raph trusted me enough to "check my biases."

Meg and I get ready in her room this morning.

I spatter my face with warm water from her sink. "So, Meg—I wanted to talk with you about something."

Her shoulders seize up toward her ears. *Gotta approach this carefully.* She rubs some sort of moisturizer up and down her cheeks.

"You, umm, kept my door open by accident when you left my room the other day." A towel wicks off the excess moisture from my skin.

In our list of questions to ask, this came up first.

Why would she leave it open? To allow someone to put down the rose and the vague threat? Or did she make it seem that way, and left the flower herself?

Raph and I *did* draw the conclusion that whoever put the rose down probably committed the murder.

"Oh, sorry about that." She rubs her fingertips on the other small white towel. "I was just so out of it that I wasn't even thinking."

A lie.

Her eyes flicked to the side, and her voice went up.

I decide to drop it for now. Tension fills the air like a strong whiff of hairspray in a dressing room.

We return to the room and loop our bags for the day over our shoulders. My fingers pinch my emotional support water bottle Lenny. Uncapping it, I take a long swig.

She flicks off the lights, and we step into the hallway.

Silence carries us on the elevator ride down to the breakfast hall.

Oatmeal.

Used to love it during my school days. I would get *fancy* by sprinkling some brown sugar or blueberries on it. But considering most of the breakfast options at the hotel restaurant contain dairy, we have to go with the oatmeal bowls once again this morning.

A waiter takes our order and sets down iced goblets of water at our table.

Water streaks down the sides of the glass.

Picking up the glass by the bowl, I drink in a long, frosty sip, and set it down on the table. "Everything's so much to take in, you know? I'm surprised we have a performance today."

The straps to her tank top scrunch when she shrugs. "Although he was a big part of the theater, the people of Gatlinburg don't know that. We can't keep canceling."

Or people will ask questions.

I finish her sentence in my mind.

Art Deco decor covers every inch of this restaurant. In a booth beside us, two women saw knives into Belgian waffles and French toast. Although not-dairy adjacent, Antonia also warned us against sugar the day of the performances.

Meg's fingertips prattle against the tablecloth. "Wanna go over lines while we wait for our food?" The tapping stops. "I just feel unprepared without a dress rehearsal, you know?"

I find this odd because we've spent the past four weeks performing this show. Two days off, Saturday and Sunday, wouldn't make her forget everything. Plenty of theater productions I did in the past had a whole week between performances. Sure, we'd do a line-through—where opera singers run through the lines together—right beforehand, but for a professional opera singer like Meg?

Probably a subject change.

"Sure. Take it from wherever you need."

"Let's do from my solo. I definitely tripped up at the last performance."

"Go ahead."

She taps out the rhythm by drumming her fingers against her palm. *"Go, ye heroes. Go to glory. Go and die in combat gory."* She winces. "You know what? I think I know it."

Ah, didn't like the *die* portion of that solo, did we?

The server returns with our steaming bowls of oatmeal. He sets the tray down and I grab a spoonful of blackberries.

Purple blotches stain the mixture.

"I'm sure you do, Meg. Although a question I've often wondered, does passing out ever affect your memory on stage?"

This throws her for a loop. I can tell by how she leans back in her chair and how her eyebrows pinch the bridge of her nose. She's trying to figure out my angle. "Actually, no. It does take a few minutes to come to, but usually, concussions are what can make a memory faulty. And I have plenty of concussion stories I can tell you from when someone wasn't able to catch me when I passed out."

She recounts one as the server plops more ice in my glass.

"—and that's how I couldn't remember the first half of my junior year in college."

Junior year?

Girl must be in her mid-twenties by this point then, right? I hadn't asked the ages of most of the cast. Online searches at the library yielded little results. Everyone seemed to know Eric's age, though. Twenty. Because so many people clamored for a video of his first time at a bar.

"That sounds scary. It's so good that Karim was there at the aquarium. With how many kids were running around, that would've been a horrible place to pass out. You could've gotten trampled."

"Yeah, for sure. It was definitely awful the one time I fainted in a high school hallway. It's like soda trying to escape from a bottle's neck, it's so crowded."

"I imagine. Does it take forever to come to once you've fainted?"

"Mm, no. I think the longest I was out was maybe ten minutes. That was the concussion one. It can take me a few more minutes to be able to sit up or even stand. You're pretty dizzy after."

Gotcha.

Raph and I spent well over an hour at the aquarium.

"Really? At the aquarium, you guys were out for a while. That whole time, were you coming to?"

"I—"

She pauses, frowns, and stirs her oatmeal. She's probably caught on.

"—umm, no. Probably took me a bit to get un-dizzy, but Karim and I started to talk about wedding things, and well, I guess we spent a lot longer doing that than we planned." She moves her engagement ring up and down her finger. "I don't think most people realize just how stressful figuring out where people sit at the reception can be. Anyway."

She throws her cloth napkin on the table. Classic piano trills in the background.

"We really should get going. Antonia wants to do her director's meeting first thing, before warm-ups."

Before every show, Antonia meets with each of the main characters to discuss what to focus on during the performance. During that, I plan to interrogate her.

Itching fills my chest. I didn't get through half of the questions I wanted.

In a family like this, though, maybe I asked too many already.

"Sounds like a plan, Meg. Ooh, I think I see Raph at another table. Might just go check in with him."

He sits under a geometric fan-shaped light. Karim exits the booth, across from Raph, at the same time I flounce over.

Raph waves at me before stabbing his Belgian waffle with a fork.

"Anything, Raph?"

"Well, I did figure out in my meeting that Karim is a huge *Star Wars* nerd. We both agree that *Rogue One* is one of the most underappreciated films—"

"About the murder, Raph." A growl lodges in my throat.

"Oh. Well, no."

He shares what Karim did. Which, is, basically nothing. Karim and Meg's stories do match up. Granted, they share a room in the hotel, so maybe they had time to corroborate.

"Did you ask him if he got any pictures at that time frame? So he could show us time stamps and if he has an alibi?"

"Well, no. But you don't exactly take pictures when your fiancée passes out. It is weird how they couldn't do, 'wedding planning'"—he tosses up air quotes—"inside the aquarium, though. Feels like a flimsy excuse."

"Not enough to convict them, though."

"No."

He stirs a waffle square in a glob of syrup. Butter, in the shape of a rose, perches on a small plate.

"What I'm wondering—" my stomach gurgles at the scent of the syrup. I miss normal-people food. "—is how they found the body so fast if someone wasn't looking for it."

Because I missed out on the group huddle in the lobby, the day of the murder, people filled me in on little details here and there. The group chat offered no help. Just smatterings of "I can't believe he's gone <crying emoji>" and "Does anyone have an extra hair straightener? I think I left mine behind in Virginia."

"It *is* a popular area." He says this through a mouthful of waffle, so it comes out as "isth."

True.

Guess we gotta keep the interviews going and hope for the best.

Humidity prickles my cheeks as we head onto the bus and toward the theater. A glass building cocoons us as we enter the auditorium. A circular ceiling, lit up, illuminates the auditorium.

Antonia circles us up and says she wants to convene with the actors one by one. She's worn no makeup today. Wrinkles show themselves, as do the dark circles underneath her eyes. Poor woman hasn't gotten much sleep these days.

She motions me up first and dismisses the rest of the cast.

Two chairs face each other on the stage. A stage manager sweeps the area behind it with a broom. Antonia asks her if she can wait until she's finished with the one-on-ones.

Footsteps pad away.

Alone, with a potential murderer.

I slide into the left chair, and my leg bobs up and down. I force it to still.

"How are you feeling, Tina?"

Her eyes form the shape of teardrops, crinkled, concerned.

Caution; I have to exercise exactly that as I answer. The questions might try to bait me, force me to give up the fact that I've decided to play the detective.

"It's all a lot." Not a lie. I make direct eye contact as I say it. *Time for a softer voice, Tina.* That came out harsh. "I know I didn't know him like you all did. I can only imagine what you're feeling."

She blinks, fast.

Moisture fills her waterline.

"Yes, well." Her voice crackles. A tear escapes down her cheek, and her hand flies to her face, to wipe it away. "I'm sorry, I—"

"No, please, Antonia. You've had to be the strongest one out of us all. I'm okay if you need to let it out."

Her lip quivers, and she nods.

"Yes, I suppose it could be good to talk about it." Shuddering breath. "Although Richard and I had our creative differences, we've worked with each other for years. After Eric's father passed—"

She doubles over and sobs. It takes her several moments to unbend herself and continue. Blotchiness covers her features. She apologizes again for her tears.

"—he really was like another father figure to the boy. I knew he was not all with it, cognitively, when things were starting to go wrong with the shows. I let him go to start his retirement. I just—"

Her lip quivers again.

I can't tell if she's lying. She makes eye contact, doesn't fidget. In past shows in theater, I've learned how to fake cry, and this snot dribbling out of her nose feels like the real deal. This woman—so full of grace and elegance—doesn't show emotion often. It would take a lot to get her to sob like this.

She sucks in a deep breath through her teeth and lets it out in a hiss.

"—can't imagine that somewhere between me and Roger looking at the jellyfish and the sharks that he would...that he would—"

Words don't come.

So I supply them for her. "We can change the subject. How about the jellyfish? Did you happen to get any photos of those?"

A watery chuckle escapes her throat.

"Absolutely, those moon jellies were stunning. Here, let me see if I can find it on my camera roll." She squints at her phone, finger taps becoming more frantic. "Oh, I'm terrible at technology. Mind looking through for me?"

Antonia hands me the device. I click on the photos app and locate the jellyfish photos. I check the timestamps. Sure enough,

Antonia found the jellyfish display ten minutes after Raph and I did. Enough time to have a meeting on the bus with Roger.

Definitely not enough time to go to the SkyBridge and back. The walk alone would take fifteen minutes. And who knew how long it took to toss a man overboard?

I return the phone to her.

For now, we could cross Antonia off the list, unless something else came up.

She still could've hired someone to do it.

I'd have to look into her hiring practices later.

For the rest of our meeting, Antonia and I go over the performance tonight. She tells me that she's proud of my progress in my voice lessons with Eric. Now, she hears the confidence in my vocals and the power behind certain notes.

"You must keep in mind, dear, that he's had years of lessons. First with his father, and then with me. It can take a while to develop that voice. I hope you don't mind continuing your lessons with him for the remainder of the summer."

"Of course not."

Free voice lessons from a professional? Yes, please. In fact, when I think about it, they were paying *me* to take these.

Once we finish the meeting, I locate Raph in the wig shop. He's placed a wig, with wire braid pigtails, on his head.

"You *do* realize that the wig ladies are going to kill you if they catch you."

They must've gone on break. Because in all hours they brushed, hair sprayed, curled, and teased the heck out of these things.

"What a way to go. Murdered by a wig lady."

"Anyway." I fiddle with a pin that sticks a green-and-blue wig to a Styrofoam head. "You get anything on the manager?"

"Haven't had a chance to meet with him yet. Guy's more slippery than Eric. But I'll try to get to him before the show, I promise."

Speaking of Eric, I explain my meeting with Antonia to Raph as he places the wig back onto the severed head. He pins the hairs in place and ruffles his own, which has gone all wild with static.

"That's what you get for not wearing a wig cap, dude." I observed how some of the other actors also wore a plastic cap of sorts, instead of a cloth one. At first, I thought they'd wrapped their heads in saran wrap.

"Yes, yes, I get bad hat hair...or wig hair in this case. But you said Antonia seems to have a good alibi. Ha, told you."

"Pictures, for now, with time stamps. And some pretty believable crying. But remember in a mystery, everyone is guilty until proven innocent."

I glance over my shoulder at the door. None of the stage crew has returned to tend to the wigs. Tension releases in my gut. Crazy that he and I can talk about these things with such normalcy. Numbness fills my chest. I don't think the murder has hit me yet, at least, not in full.

"Anyway, she mentioned that I'm going to continue voice lessons with Eric, so I guess I could prod him tomorrow."

"Or tonight. Someone mentioned him setting up his ring light in the basement. To film more videos for social media. But—"

He picks up a yellow tack off the linoleum floor and tosses it onto one of the workstations.

"—can I trust you not to get all biased?"

I sigh. "Again, when I say *everyone* is guilty until proven innocent, that includes everybody. In fact, you could be guilty. You could've hired someone, you know."

"But I didn't, and I seriously didn't even know the guy." He throws up his hands. "I'm fine with you interviewing Eric. But is it really safe for you to be alone with him tonight?"

Eye roll.

"Seriously? I just had a one-on-one *alone* with Antonia. You had no problems then."

"Yes, on a stage where guys were running lights up in the tech booth, and where a whole cast can come to your rescue if they hear you screaming bloody murder."

I squint at him. "Fine. I can grab one of Karim's cameras he has stationed around for B-roll and bring it down with me. You can be in another room if you don't want to hang with the cast afterward, but you can't be in the *same* room." He opens his mouth to protest. I continue. "Everyone in this family is dodgy. If they think something's up, we're not going to get a good interview, okay? He trusts me. More than he trusts you."

He stares at the tile for several moments.

Lights buzz above us, filling the room with a hum.

"Actually." His head snaps up. "I think Karim already has a camera down in the basement. He tends to set up one in every room—besides where people get changed."

"Really? I guess that settles that then."

Fearing we could get interrupted by the wig ladies anytime soon, I head for the door.

"Tina."

I stop, whirl around, and catch the plea in his expression.

"Please be careful."

With two fingers, I salute him. "You got it, captain."

Then I make my exit, not sure if I lied just then.

CHAPTER 13

I feel like such an adorable little stalker.

In the shroud of darkness, I hang by the door frame as he sings. A simple ring light illuminates his features as he carries on in the song.

"—one day out there."

Goosebumps ripple up my arms at the last note. He reaches forward to the camera displayed in front of him and clicks the red button, finishing the recording. Once he does, I clap. This causes him to jolt in his stool, and almost fall off.

"So this is where the magic happens, eh?"

"Shouldn't you be with the rest of the cast?" He hisses this.

As he turns to me in the waning light, I take in the mask he's worn for the video. It's green, like the shirt that Quasimodo wears in *Hunchback*.

"The cast is going to a bar. Guess everyone could use a drink after everything that's happened. Considering I have a few years until I get to twenty-one—"

"Don't they have bar food or something that you can eat?"

My nose wrinkles. I think about the gasp my mother would utter at the mere thought of me brushing my lips against alcohol. "Have you ever been to a bar?"

He cocoons himself into his hoodie. We'll take that as a no.

"That was from *Hunchback*, right? It was beautiful."

He softens. "Thanks."

"Mind if I turn on a light?"

A pause. "Sure."

My fingertip probes the wall until I locate the switch. Buzzing fills the basement, washing everything in a pale glow. He flinches and straightens. In my periphery, I spot Karim's camera. Part of me wonders why he didn't take it once the cast left for drinks. Maybe Raph got to him and gave him some reason to keep it there.

"I love *Hunchback*." I shove my hands into my shorts' pockets. "I think my favorite is 'God Help the Outcasts'."

He leans against a large lamppost. Huge set pieces that wouldn't fit in the props mezzanine are stored down here. "Why's that?"

"I think it really goes to show that we're supposed to love and care for the overlooked, the downtrodden, the poor."

Half a smile cuts across his cheek. "It's a nice thought, for sure."

"Mind showing me around?"

He hesitates. "It's pretty boring."

"My whole evening's free."

He lingers in place for a moment, then motions for me to follow. "I have the editing suite up in the archives. You can watch me pull back the curtain of Oz."

We galumph up concrete steps to the ground floor. I notice how he sails everywhere he goes. If you placed a cape on him, he'd be right at home. He'd gotten so used to playing hide-in-seek over the years that he glides like a fish avoiding a net.

This time, as we step into a dark room, he turns on the lights.

We step behind a Mac computer and he pulls up an editing software. My editing experience is limited to a couple video projects in iMovie. This looks far more complicated.

Several bars on the screen indicate different film cuts and voice clips. He plays each one individually for me and shows me how he tampers with the levels.

"This is so complicated." I peer at the tiny video screen in the editing suite. "I had no idea this much work went into one video."

"It didn't use to be like this. It was just me, in my bedroom, with an iPhone. But once the videos got posted, we needed more professional equipment. I taught myself how to do all of this. YouTube is your best friend."

I chuckle as he toggles some of the voice clips, truncating them.

"Eric, you—you really have no idea who posted the videos?"

He leans back in a rolling chair. It collides with the wall. A cork board above has various programs of past shows pinned to it, as well as several sticky notes with illegible scrawling.

"I mean, probably someone in the family. Since those were the only people I showed the videos. All I know is that one day I found a note with a username and password. I downloaded the app, and realized some of the videos had millions of views."

He pinches the "nose" part of the mask. It hits me that he probably has to clean his masks regularly to remove any sweat or grime.

"It honestly surprised me that people were even into the opera videos," he says. "I figured, since most of our audience members are sixty or seventy, most wouldn't be on social media looking for opera content. But after 'Queen of the Night' videos blew up, I guess there was an audience."

Which family member could've posted? "Meg, maybe?"

"She has always been like a sister, but it would take someone who had the ability to hack my phone. I don't think I ever gave her the password to get in."

"Karim, then?"

"Nah, have only known the guy for about a year. Not enough for him to unveil the hidden Daaé child to the world. He's pretty quiet. Keeps to himself."

Much like another guy I know.

"Honestly, Tina, we could keep playing this guessing game forever. For all we know, it could've been Richard. He saw a lot of the videos too."

I park on the edge of the desk, shoving glass paperweights to the side.

"I'm sorry about him, by the way. Antonia mentioned he was like a father to you."

He's turned his face, making all features indescribable. In his hand, he grips one of the glass paperweights—a jellyfish caught in a bubble.

"Yeah, not completely a father, but definitely was there for me for a lot. It's crazy to think that he's gone."

Guilt gnaws at my insides for even prodding him. He lost his father at a young age, and just said goodbye to another one.

Still, I promised Raph I would ask the questions we prepared.

So I craft a story. "Do you remember what you were doing around the time he passed? I think Raph and I were looking at the jellyfish. The paperweight reminded me…"

He drinks in the words.

Like Meg, can he sniff out my ulterior motive? Speaking of smells, everything in this office carries the hint of orange. Someone must've cleaned up shop before we got up here.

"Yes, actually. I'd been stuck on the part where Gianni Schicchi is pretending to be the dead man, so the family can change the will and get all of the money."

"So, *all* of the opera, then."

"Well, most of it. But it is ironic that I was reading a libretto about death around the time—"

He cuts himself off. Chokes on something. Swallows.

"Was anyone with you on the bus?" *Please, tell me you had an eyewitness.*

"No, by then, everyone had left."

Darn.

This doesn't look good for him. But why would he kill off the only father figure in his life?

"I know you said that he was a lot like your dad. What was your dad like?"

He doesn't answer me.

"I—I can go first, if you'd like. Since mine is gone too."

His eyes bore into mine. Lines form on his forehead. Did he not know this about me? Antonia did her homework on me and Raph, but did she not pass along the info to the rest of the cast? Most of them were on social.

Granted, I didn't post all that much.

A long breath trails my lips. I don't maintain eye contact. If I do, I'll dissolve into tears.

"He taught me everything there was to know about music. Mom did have me do lessons with a few music teachers after that, but they didn't teach like him. He could make music come to life. He had the voice of an angel. Even more than that. He had a voice that could make angels weep, and—"

Nails bite into my skin. No crying, not now.

"—and he was an absolute monster when it came to movie popcorn. We'd go together during the weekdays when I'd finished my schoolwork for the day. He liked going at those times because we'd get an empty theater to ourselves, except for the seniors. And he'd claim he didn't want much popcorn, and that he only wanted 'a few bites.' So I'd go to the bathroom, come back, and he'd have eaten the whole bag, and—"

Hot tears build in my eyes. I shut my eyelids.

"—and, when he'd—"

Water trails down my cheek.

I finish that part in my head. And when he'd gotten the diagnosis, he sighed and told Mom, "I guess I'm just another statistic." Cancer be darned, it felt like more than numbers. It felt personal.

Like they'd ripped me from music and stuck me in an anechoic chamber. Forever echoing the silence.

"—and—"

I dissolve.

All the emotion of being gone from home this long, of sleeping in unknown beds each night, of the sudden murder. They've brought back some version of eight-year-old me. The one told not to cry at the funeral because, "Your dad is happy now. He's in a happy place. Heaven just got an angel. You shouldn't be sad about it."

Something brushes my hand.

I open my eyes. Through the blur of tears, I spot Eric's fingers on mine. I dare not move. Something about his touch grounds me.

"He sounds like a wonderful person."

"He was." I sniff, wincing at the moisture in my nostrils. A trail has probably started streaming from that too. "I'm sorry."

"No, it's fine." He wraps his arm around me and presses me into him. Warmth tingles on my skin. "We've all had a lot to deal with these past couple of days. Why don't we do something fun to get our minds off of it? All I had planned for the evening was editing, so I'm down for anything."

I *would* invite him to whitewater rafting with us tomorrow afternoon—after we do our voice lesson—but he would never venture out in broad daylight.

My mind flashes back to my basement when I was seven. Dad and I used to pretend to paddle in a cardboard box boat down the "river." He would sing *Phantom of the Opera* and drape himself in a blanket to symbolize a cape.

Could we replicate something like that?

"Do you know if there's a box or large set piece we could sit in? Maybe in the basement?"

I can recall the lampposts, but little else.

He releases me and frowns.

"I think there's an upside-down set piece that is shaped like a box, why?"

"That's perfect. Follow me."

We fly down the steps into the basement once more. Sure enough, a box, large enough to hold three people, rests next to the lampposts. I climb inside and motion him in.

"What are you—"

"Since you'll likely not be touring Gatlinburg with us, I figure I'll bring Gatlinburg to you. It's a step up from bringing you back pizza and smoothies all the time. Now you can *experience* it." I toss up jazz hands at the word 'experience'.

He stares at me. "What?"

"Get into the raft, Eric."

"The raft?"

"Get in, or the black bears will eat you."

I motion to the blank wall behind him. He stares at the bricks for several moments before shrugging and hopping into the box, right behind me. I can feel his shadow over me.

"Welcome riders to the wild whitewater rapids in the Smokies. I'm your tour guide, Tina. We'll be going down class four rapids today. Keep in mind that class five rapids is a waterfall, so it's going to be a bumpy ride."

I mime strapping on a helmet.

"Be sure to have those helmets strapped on tightly and have your paddles at the ready. Don't ever let go of that T-shape on your paddle. You want to hold on to it at all times."

"How do you know so much about whitewater rafting?"

Memories blur back to the mission trip I did in Tennessee, several years ago, not too far away from here. Our group had done a bit of rafting in the rapids then.

"Why, dear rider. For I am a brilliant tour guide."

"Okay, weirdo."

"Now, get ready for our first rapid, it's a class three, so a nice starter-offer."

I grip the sides of the box and swivel my body back and forth. Based on the movement I feel behind me, Eric has decided to follow suit.

"Okayyy, riders, we just got past that rapid. Good work. Did you know we have cameramen stationed in different parts of the surrounding forests? Make sure you smile when we go down the bigger rapids, so you can take the photo home to Grandma, okay?"

"Okay." He snickers.

"Oh, crikey. Look, everyone, to your left. You'll see some cute otters. Wave hello to the otters."

"Are there even otters in Tennessee?"

"Otters who escaped from the aquarium. Tsk, tsk. Oh, everyone hang on, we have a class four rapid ahead. Please stay in the boat. And if you fall out, let your body go slack. I'd hate to have you be pulled under. Here we, goooooooo!"

I jerk left and right, up and down.

"Oh no, riders, it looks like your tour guide may be falling out of the boat. Do not panic. I repeat, do not—"

Arms band around my midsection and pull me back. My back presses against his chest.

I...do not mind this.

"What—what are you doing, rider?"

"Uh...protecting you from the rapid?"

"Much obliged." I giggle.

Footsteps echo in the basement. I glance toward the direction of the door and spy Raph advancing toward us. Shimmying out of Eric's grip, I lean toward the front of the "raft."

"What's up, Raph?"

He's paled. "Erm. Bus is leaving for the hotel. The group is back from the bar. It's stopped by here to pick us all up."

Already?

"Right, okay, thanks, Raph. We'll be there in just a moment."

He regards me with narrowed brows, but nods and heads out of the room. I pull myself out of the box and offer my hands to help Eric up. He accepts them.

"That was fun." He steps out of the "raft." "So much fun that I...I might actually be up for going with you all tomorrow?"

I cock my head. "Really? It's going to be in the afternoon." In broad daylight. "Are you sure?"

"Yeah. As long as we can ride together, I think I can handle it."

Squeezing his shoulder, I grin. He lopes off toward the door. Two seconds after he vanishes, Raph appears. I grip my neck and rub.

"Sorry, umm. I have very eclectic interviewing methods?"

"Never mind that right now. But don't think we're not going to revisit"—he gestures at the box—"whatever that was."

"What's up?"

"I didn't get a chance to interview the manager. But I did see something super sketch."

"Tell me. I live for the sketch."

The glow of his phone screen stings my eyes. I spot someone snipping red rose stems in an office.

Although fuzzy, I make out the figure with the scissors.

Roger Firmin, the new manager.

CHAPTER 14

"A waterproof mask, eh?" I grip the handle on the raft as our group travels down a rocky hill. Our tour guide directs us toward the shore of the river. "Why do you have that, Eric?"

Across from me, gripping his handle, Eric shrugs. A spandex mask, the color of blue, shields half of his face.

"When you live from theater to theater, you learn a thing or two about sewing."

During our voice lessons, he hinted at several things he taught himself. Other languages, how to cook in the opera kitchens, and now, apparently, sewing.

"Glad you could make it out with us today, cuz." Meg's voice sounds behind my ear. She, Karim, and Raph have all joined us to raft.

Sunlight beats down on our necks, despite the tree cover flanking us on all sides. My coconut-scented sunscreen bleeds into my eyes. Blinking away the sweat, I peer up at the cerulean sky. Even on summer days, Ohio doesn't come this bright and this blue.

"Eric." With my hand holding a paddle, I knuckle the sunscreen out of my eyelids. "Now that you're joining us for this, think you could come with the cast on our next outing, after tomorrow's show?"

Meg hisses.

"Umm, girl, it may be best if you and Eric stay inside for the rest of the Gatlinburg trip. Apart from outings like this, of course."

I frown. "Why?"

"Trust us on this, okay?"

Water burbles on the shore. Rocks dot the dirty sand as we set our raft down. Our tour guide rehashes the rules to us. His slight accent hints somewhere in Eastern Europe. Glasses shield his eyes.

Like us, today he wears a life preserver vest, a blue helmet, and shorts. All of us sport *Pirates of Penzance* t-shirts, covered by the vests.

"Remember, if you fall out of the raft, do not panic. Grab the raft's side—"

He twangs a cord that runs the length of the inflatable blue boat.

"—and allow the rest of the group to pull you up. Can I have a volunteer?"

Meg must raise her hand because he waves her forward. He has her "pretend" to fall into the water—the sand—and she grips the cord on the boat. Our tour guide grips her life preserver and yanks her into the raft.

"Just like that. Any questions?"

We have none. Our raft, along with us, surges into the river. Cool water splashes my calves and bare feet until we've made it out to knee-high depth. We climb into the raft, one at a time. Eric settles in beside me in the back.

Raph, up front, tosses me a withering glare.

On the bus ride over here, he had insisted he park beside me in the raft.

"Again, any one of these people could be a murderer." He whispered this. The driver at this moment decided to blast classical music on the bus speakers. "You didn't exactly get a solid alibi from him yesterday."

Nor from Meg and Karim.

"Okay, but we're all going to be rafting together. It's a little hard to drown someone when everyone else is looking."

"Yeah, unless everyone else is in on it."

That thought hadn't occurred to me until then. What if they'd decided to go all *Murder on the Orient Express* on this? If everyone played a role, no wonder we couldn't patch together all the details.

Tsk, tsk, Tina. Stuff like that only happens in books.

Our paddles beat a steady rhythm against the water. Eric nudges me with his elbow and points at his yellow-tipped paddle.

"It's like a metronome."

"Ohhhh." I give him a playful shove. One not hard enough to eject him from the raft. "Don't even get me started on that thing."

During our voice lessons, he employed an electric metronome to keep me steady on the beat. Within several measures, I would get off and we'd have to start over.

Foamy water greets us at the first level three rapid.

As our boat dips down, water splashes us. My shorts stick to my thighs like a second skin. Maybe should've asked Eric to sew me an extra pair with the same fabric as his mask.

After several more rapids, our tour guide tells us we could take a break. We've entered stiller waters so I perch on the end of the boat, soaking in the sun. The inflatable fabric of the raft singes my fingertips as I lean back. Don't care.

We've gotten so little free time that I will take it all in at once.

Everything smells wet and green, like water cascading over a mossy rock. Insects flitter to-and-fro in the shafts of sunlight that poke through the trees. One would think, in a peaceful place like this, that a murder didn't take place earlier this week.

Someone behind us swears. I crane my neck and spot another boat gliding alongside ours. I don't recognize the passengers.

Two girls in the back gawk at us. Helmets obscure most of their features. I can tell one of them is taller than the other, even from their sitting positions.

One of them, the taller girl, curses again. "It's totally them."

Passersby on the streets of New York and Virginia did recognize some members of the troupe from time to time. As if by instinct, I catch Eric sheltering behind me. No wonder. He doesn't get out much, let alone to be spied by a fan, and he doesn't go to the meet and greets after shows.

Taking the lead, I wave and offer a warm smile. "Hi."

"You're the one who stole Carmen's part from her, aren't you?" The shorter girl growls.

Ice taints my blood. Did I hear that right? "Stole her *what*—?"

They scramble to one side of the boat and slap water at me with their paddles. I scream and lose vision, as they've aimed most of the splashes at my eyes. Wobbliness overtakes my body, and I lose balance.

I don't remember falling, but seconds later, I feel the water hit my back.

Coming to, I realize I've plunked right into the river. Derisive laughter sounds from nearby. Sputtering, I grip the side of the boat. Hands clutch the end of my life preserver and hoist me back into the raft.

Knuckles fly to my eyes to wick away the water. Someone hands me a towel and I wipe my face.

Meg, meanwhile, issues a string of curses at the other boat as something prickles my foot. No wait, stabs. *Hard*. Like, a million times. I crumple the towel and hold up my foot.

A black and slimy creature suctions to it.

I shriek and kick my legs up and down. It must dislodge at some point and thunk back into the river because moments later, I find a pink spot left behind by the leech.

For several moments, I pant and grip Eric's hand to find grounding. By then, the other boat has sailed past us, towards more rapids.

"What—*pant*—just—*pant*—happened?" I release him once I've realized how blue his hand has turned.

Meg glances back at me, eyes squinting. "We'll explain when we get back. Sorry, girl. Didn't realize they'd be here."

We take the rest of the rapids in silence. I imagine the picture they snap at the level-four rapids captured morose expressions. Definitely not one to "take home to Grandma."

Shivers run up and down my body when we disembark. Someone runs back to the bus to grab more towels as I curl into a ball on the sand for warmth. Arms band around me.

Once Karim shows up with several more towel bundles, Meg digs her phone out of her bag—also left on the bus, also brought by Karim.

"Okay, so I was hoping not to show you this until we were out of Tennessee, but let's just say that Carmen has a posse. And Carmen has been spewing all sorts of lies, and... We'll let you see for yourself."

She holds up her phone for me.

Illuminated by a ring light, Carmen roosts in a beanbag chair, legs crossed. She sips on some concoction from Starbucks and leans back on her arm.

"Okay, y'all, story time."

It's now that I realize she has a distinct Southern twang to her voice. Wonder why I didn't spot that back at the mansion.

"So I was scheduled to be on a summer tour with the Daaé family, right? Sign the contract and everything. Trust me, I have a trail of emails, right?"

Pop music from a Broadway show plays in the background.

"And so I've been waiting a solid month to hear back from them. We *were* supposed to start shows in June, but I didn't know if they postponed, or what. Put my whole summer on hold for this when I could be applying for grad school, you know?"

She siphons a splotch of whipped cream off of her crop top.

"So I find out, through a friend, that they've been apparently performing? Not only that, but they've replaced me with some girl named Tina or something? Yeah, never been to music school. Probably never had a proper audition. I don't know if a family member got the part for her or what, but definitely seems sketchy."

Her fingertips move to a ring-shaped necklace pendant. She moves it from side to side.

"Anyway, as y'all know I live in Nashville, and Gatlinburg is just a four-hour drive away so—"

She leans in close to the camera, winks.

"—may just have to pay them a visit. Feel free to say hello to them for me, okay?"

The video loops.

Meg clicks pause and sighs.

"There were...protestors outside of the theater yesterday when we left for the bar. We ended up just hanging in the hair and makeup room. Waited to look for you guys until the crowd cleared out."

That could explain why they'd gotten back from the bar so fast.

"They're mad at the family, yes. But, girl, they're mostly mad at you."

Anger prickles my skin.

"But I didn't do anything—"

"Wrong? I know. Hopefully, this'll all be over when we ship out on Saturday. Until then, hang tight. We'll get lots of takeout."

They huddle around me as we head to the bus. Eric and Raph flank my sides. Something about this wall of people fills my gut with warmth. As the oldest sister, I always played protector, played mom. I didn't often get to receive the same safeguarding.

Karim places several towels on a chair before I sink into it.

Eric hands me Lenny, and Raph, my phone. The group chat has texted me several memes to cheer me up.

"Oh, and girl, one more thing." Meg stands in the center aisle and leans her arm against the headrest. "You may not want to go to the meet and greet for the rest of our Tennessee trip. Although security has been able to prevent people with signs from coming in, I did hear some boos last night. Best to stay on the safe side."

As the bus chugs to life, I press my knees against my chest. I replay some of the conversations with the people whose hands I shook last night. Some of the younger crowd did seem to say passive-aggressive comments like "wow I could understand *most* of the words you sang last night" or "man, you look so young for being an opera singer. What school did you go to again?"

Yup, should've read more into that.

So much for worrying about a murderer.

A mob of fangirls may take me out before he or she gets the chance to.

CHAPTER 15

True to Meg's word, the audience does boo on Wednesday night.

Not the whole crowd. Most clap. But during "Think of Me" in still moments, I catch snippets of hisses and jeers.

Eric pulls me into the basement after the show. He's shut off all the lights, except for the ring light stationed in the corner.

"What are you—"

"Just sit on this stool, okay?"

"Okay." I park on a wobbly stool, gripping the base to steady myself.

"It was ridiculous tonight. What some people in the audience pulled. So we're going to fix it, okay?"

"Okay?"

"Be yourself. You'll do great."

He leans forward and clicks the record button. I realize he's only set up an iPhone tonight, not his usual camera. LIVE in white letters shows at the corner of the screen. *Oh shoot, I'm going to be featured in his account.*

I pull back a few loose strands of hair as hearts appear on screen.

"Hey, guys. We just got done with a performance." He nudges me with his elbow, and I force a smile at the camera. "Tina did amazing tonight—"

Butterflies explode in my stomach.

"—and I know I don't usually go live, but I wanted to clear up some things."

He lifts a finger.

"First, Tina didn't steal anything, except maybe the show each night of our performances. She didn't intentionally sabotage Carmen. She had no idea she was up for the parts that Carmen was intending to perform this summer when she sang for us."

Another finger.

"Second, our former manager reached out to Tina after hearing her audition. Tina had no prior connections to our family and presented an aria, just like every other auditioner we will hear. Like the auditions being held tomorrow—"

Ah yes, someone mentioned in our group chat that we had a dark night tomorrow. Once a season, the group would hear from new auditioners. Gatlinburg's, and the nation's best, would appear in the auditorium to serenade the group.

One more finger.

"Third, Carmen had a very clear verbal agreement with me that she had no intentions in doing the summer shows. Carmen, if you're watching, I think you'll recall exactly what you said to me in the Japanese garden. Our manager saw you were unwilling to commit to the shows and sought an understudy. It's nothing personal."

There's a bite to his words.

All of it…very personal.

"Anyway, now that we've cleared that up, I hope you all come out to support Tina as we continue on our tour. She's going to kill it in our final *Pirates* performance, and she's going to do amazing as Lauretta in *Gianni Schicchi.*"

He holds me with a smile. Then breaks off to hit the LIVE recording.

Once he finishes, part of him shrinks into himself again. He'd been a giant moments before.

"Two things, Eric—one, you come alive when you're on camera."

"Thanks. It's one of the only places I can be fully me."

Yes, I understood.

Often in the photoshoots I did with Raph, I could dress how I wanted. Hang off trees in the woods or dip into an algae-crusted pond without my mother clucking her tongue at me. In theater, in photos, in opera, I too sprung to life.

"Two—you really didn't have to do that."

I cringe at the thought of the flack we will surely get.

"Yes, I did. We protect our own here, and I'll personally *take out* anyone who tries to hurt you."

That sends chills up my legs—not the good ones. "Take them out on a date?"

Hope the joke lightens the mood.

"Haha, no. Now, we should probably find out what everyone's ordering for takeout. I could kill for some Chinese right now."

Spicy General Tsos still lingers in my mouth the next day, Thursday.

The day of auditions.

Meg warned me to stay out of sight of the actors, but I can't help it. Arias serenade me in every corner of the building. They've taken up every free space possible to practice their audition pieces.

A sweet alto with kind eyes verbal processes with me before her auditions in the hair and makeup room.

"I'm a huge fan of yours, by the way." She clutches her arm. Nails make white imprints into it. "Your voice is absolutely beautiful. I've seen videos, and you seem to be getting better with each performance."

"Thanks." I split open a packet of Oreos, the cast gift yesterday. "Most people seem to be pretty upset about me getting these parts in the first place. Said I should've gone to school first."

Most of our chorus members and supernumeraries receive a snack of sorts before performances. Those in the larger roles may get a pastry from the on-site chefs.

She suckles on her water bottle straw. Lets out an *aaah*. "That's to be expected. Because school is often awful."

"Yeah?"

"Yeah. You always get that soprano who thinks the world loves her—very Carmen type if you ask me."

Comradery buzzes in my chest. There's something very warm about the bond of two friends who hate one enemy.

"And then there's the tenors who literally never practice and manage to land roles all the time because there's always a lack of men in opera. Or the fact that every school is now classically training singers, so there's more competition. Or when you go to competitions, and those judges—"

She cuts herself off.

"Sorry. All to say, school, for me, sucked. If anything, I'm glad you can dodge it. At least for a while. I hear that if you do well with this family, you can probably book gigs at most places."

No wonder I got the hate I did at the river.

If I went through all of that, I would also feel a twinge of envy at anyone who landed a role without paying their dues.

"Well." She blows out a long breath. "I think I'm up soon."

"Want me to watch? I can cheer you on from the tech booth."

She grins. "I don't think you're allowed to cheer, but the support would be nice."

"You got it."

As she enters the hallway, I sail down several corridors and up the steps toward the tech booth. Not a soul exists inside the large area full of electronic controls—except for one.

"One of your hiding spots, Eric?"

Perched in a rolling chair, he cuts me a smile. His finger caresses the button on one of the controls, labeled "Go". From my stage manager days, I remember smaller versions of this. I got good at operating spotlights and pressing the cues when the assistant stage manager told me to do so.

"I try to find several at every theater."

With an *oomph*, I shove myself into a chair and trundle beside him. "Any good auditioners?"

A tenor finishes the note of his final aria. He bows, picks up his binder from the pianist, and trots off stage.

"Yes, and no. Not good enough to get a main role, I imagine. And Antonia and the manager tend to pick from a trusted free-lance pool for the others. We tend to tour in the same places."

Every other year, they'd go international. Their troupe would hit up places such as Milan and France.

And years like this one, they'd keep it national.

"Freelance pool?"

"Yeah. Not super uncommon in most artsy areas."

"True."

In theater, a girl who acted with us also did modeling. Said that because her agency tended to work with the same designers, the designers would pick girls they'd worked with before.

Something felt very safe about collaborating with trusted peo-ple.

Judges in the audience below huddle to discuss the most recent singer.

"So, tell me, Eric, what exactly makes someone a winning can-didate for the next season?"

"Someone who can learn on their own." Check.

"Someone who can sing well, obviously."

Again, check.

"Someone who is good at keeping secrets."

I stare at him to make sure I heard the last part well. His expression melts.

"Kidding. Someone who can sight read. Sometimes our maestros like to mix it up and give us their own interpretations of pieces."

Unease spikes in my gut.

The girl from the hallway ambles onto the stage. Bright lights wash out her face. No wonder they smeared so much makeup on us for shows. She didn't even come without any cosmetics. Several contoured lines carved up her face in the makeup room when we spoke.

"Hello, my name is Kimi Davis, and I am auditioning for the fall season." She holds up a slick, black binder. "I have four to six pieces prepared, starting with "Smanie Implacabili" from *Cosi fan Tutte*.

Kimi sucks in a deep breath.

Then begins.

Several measures in, I gasp. "She's amazing."

Eric's finger moves to the Coke can on the tech booth counter, dangerously close to a stack of papers and the electrical equipment. "She won't get it."

"Why not?"

"There are so few parts for altos. She's lucky she's not a contralto because there are even less opportunities for people like them. Even if we did have an alto part available, it would go to the family or the—"

"Freelance pool." I finish for him. "What's the point of auditions, then, if you guys only let in the same few people?"

"That question." His pointer finger goes to the air and draws a circle. "Is *the* question singers have been asking for decades, probably centuries. Nothing about the theater is fair."

A murmur in my throat hints at assent.

Kimi finishes her pieces and squeaks a "thank you" before marching off the stage. Deliberation lasts mere moments with the judges before they call in the next singer. I can feel my heart sag against my ribcage.

No wonder so many people wanted me off the stage.

If directors and managers picked favorites, everyone would scrutinize every note I sang, every expression. My mind flashes back to Meg's sneer as we watched *Into the Woods* in New York.

Opera pitted everyone against everyone.

Cowgirl boots pound the stage as a familiar figure steps out into the spotlight. A sharp gasp fills my throat. Eric blanches when he stares out the tinted glass of the tech booth.

"No," he hisses.

"Hello, my name is Carmen Driver, and I am auditioning for the roles I was *originally* contracted for." She opens her binder and pulls out a stack of stapled paper. Holding them up, she releases and lets them butterfly to the floor. "I'll let you take a look at those later as a reminder."

Heels from the boots thump as she sashays to the piano. Unlike Kimi—who sported a silk dress—she wears a bohemian-styled number. Not opera-ready, for sure, but maybe appropriate for a rodeo.

"How did she get into auditions?" Eric slams his palms against the counter. The Coke can rattles.

I realize I have my hand pressed against my mouth and I remove it. "Don't know. Maybe she barged in during someone else's time?"

If so, no angry singer trampes onto the stage to dispose her.

Carmen passes the binder to the pianist and returns, center stage, with her hands clasped.

"All of my audition pieces will come from the upcoming show, *Gianni Schicchi*. I am extremely familiar with the choreography and blocking of the show, as I was sent videos in May. Prior to the family gathering at the mansion."

Coldness pierces my veins.

Antonia or the manager can't boot her out, right? She deserves a fair audition like everyone else.

"My first piece will be 'O Mio Babbino Caro.'"

A throat clear.

I swallow and find my esophagus has dried out. Something stabs my gut. Betrayal? Anger? No sense in identifying the emotion, because when she opens her mouth, shivers run up and down my arms.

Gooseflesh raises on every part of me.

This girl isn't just good.

A voice like that could make angels weep.

With Antonia's, the manager's, and the rest of the judging panel's backs facing us, I can't make out their reactions. They exchange whispers over clipboards in between measures.

I turn to Eric and take in his expression.

Stony, hardening. He catches my stare.

"You're better."

I snort. "You're delusional."

"Yeah, well. It's like Antonia said back in Cleveland, you can hear emotions in each note. Your music sounds kind, gracious, sweet—like you." His cheeks darken.

I can feel mine do the same.

He clears his throat. "Hers are arrogant, loud, demanding for attention."

"And yet, she has more followers than I ever will." One of our troupe members called her a prodigy back at the mansion. Carmen even had fangirls willing to sic leeches and water on me.

"People like her always seem to."

She finishes and gives a mock curtsy. Doesn't even sing the rest of her audition pieces. Can't blame her. That alone probably blew away anyone else who showed up to perform today.

Air sucks in between my teeth. "So, Eric, what does this mean now?"

His fingers massage his unmasked temple. "Nothing good."

CHAPTER 16

Payday, the Friday before we leave, always sends the background characters into a tizzy.

I wait in a queue outside of the payment office. My eyes trail the line to the door, and I spot a paper sign with, "Collect Checks Here" on the glass window.

Fingers tap my shoulder.

Whirling around, I spot Meg's pinched brows. She cradles a bundle of flowers in purple cellphone wrapping. Strangers sometimes gave us gifts after the show. "What are you—?"

"Roger told me to meet him in the office. Waiting for everyone else to collect their checks. How did the meet and greet go?"

"Great." Sparkles shimmer in her eyes. "There was a little girl who told me I was who she wanted to be when she grew up. Said I reminded her of princess Tiana, 'with bigger hair.'"

"That's adorable."

"Yeah."

Her shoulders slump.

"What's up, Meg?"

"Don't get me wrong, I *love* opera. But my body doesn't love it." She hobbles between both feet, neither standing on the ground for a long amount of time.

During our dinner last night, Karim informed me that Meg couldn't stand for long periods of time without the blood pooling in her feet. Guilt gnawed me then. Maybe Meg hadn't been making up her fainting spells.

Or maybe, like a good actress, she pulled off the role of the season.

Guilty until proven innocent.

"I just—" She rubbed a spot on her forehead with her thumb. "I honestly don't know what *I* want to be when I grow up, or if I'm allowed to be anything else. This family is such an opera family, you know?"

My chin bobs.

Everyone in my extended family plays sports and runs marathons for fun. You can imagine how much they wilted when Dad pursued opera for as long as he could.

"It's fine." She hugs the flowers closer to her chest, smooshing the top irises. "Most opera singers tend to feel like this at one point. Although places do hire older singers, mezzo and soprano parts go to younger people. So I'll have to face this at one point. Anyway."

She cocks her head at me. A loose leaf catches in one of her curls.

"What do you want to be when you grow up? An opera singer?"

So I thought.

But hearing the horrors of school, seeing the hopefuls lose a little fire in their eyes at auditions, the aches in my body, the sabotage from Carmen yesterday...

"I don't know, actually. Might take a gap year to figure it out."

She thumbs her nose. "Love it. That sounds like such a beautiful thing. Don't ever let anyone tell you any different."

As the line wanes, we discuss the highs and lows of our final *Pirates of Penzance* performance. Carmen must've called off her goonies in a post because we didn't hear a single boo tonight.

The last tenor, with an envelope in hand, exits the office. I twist the knob and enter. Antonia and Roger loom behind a desk. With solemn expressions, they wave me in.

The door clicks shut, and I park into a black chair.

Anticipation throttles my throat, and I clear it to make sure I have access to my airways again.

This isn't going to be good.

"Hi." I keep my voice high, pleasant. In church circles, when I did this and cocked my head, the ladies would coo about how "precious I was." It tended to lessen any blows someone might dole on me.

"Tina." Antonia smoothed a wrinkle on her pencil skirt. "As you may have heard, Carmen Driver made an appearance at auditions yesterday."

I clock the bookshelf behind her and read the titles, trying to keep my mind off the buzzing in my brain.

To ground myself, I take in the scents of the dark office. Something minty, maybe a cleaning solution, or the gum Roger chews right now.

Gripping the chair arms, I force a smile and nod.

"Yes, I was informed that she had auditioned."

Roger steeples his hands and places them down on top of a full-sized desk calendar. "Carmen met with us earlier today to discuss the agreement she signed. Although she made a disappearance during the family gathering, she is still contracted to play the roles of Tosca and Lauretta in our upcoming shows."

Rocks lodge in my throat.

I choke on them. "Does this mean...you're letting me go?"

"Oh, darling, no." Antonia weaves around the desk and places a hand on my shoulder. "You signed a contract as well, and we intend to uphold it. All payments will still be issued to you, and we intend for you to continue on our tour through the end of summer."

She bends down, eyes crinkling.

"I believe you have extraordinary talent and potential. We'd still like to tease that out more before we part ways."

Relief pools in my intestines.

So why does it feel like a little insect is chewing holes through them?

"Why did you call me into—"

Roger cuts me off. "Unfortunately, because we signed the contract with Carmen first—and because she does know the choreography and blocking—we must let her play the parts you were originally signed on for."

No Lauretta.

No Tosca.

My insides wilt.

"What parts will I play then?"

"We"—Antonia returns to her spot behind the desk and triangles her hands on her hips—"don't know. We figured out whom you will play in *Schicchi.* Since actors have already signed W-9s for the speaking roles, or our own Daaé troupe has already been assigned to them, we're giving you the part of Buoso."

Cracks form up and down my stomach and rib cage.

Buoso, the guy who dies in the beginning.

The dead body the family stuffs into closets and under the bed throughout the show.

That guy.

"A supernumerary part, then." My voice cracks in my throat.

That means that I won't sing or act with the cast. I will play a literal body for the next month.

And Tosca? Would they even let me carry a single note for that?

"Oh, Tina." Antonia clucks her tongue and wrings her hands. "I'm so sorry that you got caught in the middle of this. This is certainly less than ideal. But we hope your experience is helpful nonetheless. Our intention is to introduce you to the world of opera and help craft your skills."

I unfurrow my brow.

What on earth is wrong with me? Pouting in this office? They still plan to pay me. I can hang out with Eric and Meg and Karim. If anything, this gives me more time to sleuth about what happened with Richard on the bridge.

My fingernails clack against the armrests. "I'll make the most of this opportunity, I promise."

"Good girl." Roger winks at me.

That sends my gut wriggling.

He shoos me out of the office. Soon as he does, my pocket buzzes to life. I pull out the phone and answer the FaceTime call from Mom.

"Hi, sweetie!" She pulls the camera back from a view of her nostrils. "I'm with Temperance and her mom, doing some wedding planning, and we just wanted to check in with you."

Mom could've used anything as an excuse to call me.

Off to take the car to a wash? Time to check in on Tina.

Taking Malachi to summer soccer camp. How's Tina doing?

She calls at least once a day and insists I send her pictures anytime we head to a new venue or do something new.

Mom flips the camera to face a kitchen table. Temperance and her mom hover over several index cards. Maybe they've gotten started on the seating chart for the reception.

"Hi, Tina." Temperance waves. She picks at a roll on a small plate. "Sorry to bother you on the night of the show."

"No worries." I rub my smudgy blush to make it more even. "Honestly, I'm glad you did. Bus is leaving tonight instead of tomorrow. We have a longer stretch ahead of us, so we're going to pull an all-nighter drive."

"That sounds great. Now, a question that I've been wondering about. Does the pit ever travel with you? Or do you work with a different orchestra every time?"

"Different one every time."

I chuckle at Temperance, ever curious about the instruments. A flautist through and through.

"Although, now that I think about it." The image of a small woman, cradling a violin under her chin, surfaces. "There is a woman I see in the strings section that I swear has been at every show. Maybe she travels with us."

If so, I never spotted her on the bus.

Sometimes our manager drove in a separate vehicle, though, when he and Antonia didn't need to coordinate stage plans. So it wasn't outside of the realm of possibility.

"Another question I wanted to ask you." Temperance bites her lips, cheeks pinking underneath her glasses. "Would you be one of my bridesmaids?"

I gasp, sliding down the wall in the hallway. Various members of the crew step over me.

"Oh, Temperance! That sounds amazing."

"I know it's last-minute, but so has everything else been about this wedding. Dustin and I are very eager to start our life together, you know—"

No, I didn't.

The thought of even kissing any guy, besides maybe Eric, blared alarm bells in my head. People went at different paces, though, when it came to relationships.

"—and I would normally ask you to be my maid of honor. But I really should ask my older sister to be the matron. Since I'd been maid of honor at her wedding, and—"

"Temperance, I'm glad to be part of the wedding party. Thanks for asking me."

"You're welcome."

Mom must've set the phone down because she and Temperance's mom hold an animated discussion in the kitchen.

"Anyway, Tina, have you and Raph had any chance to spend more alone time together?"

Ah, I knew we couldn't have any sort of conversation without escaping the question of arranged marriages.

My fingers run up and down my yoga pants. I've made sure to keep them out of view, otherwise I'd earn quite the gasp from Temperance.

"Haha, not yet. Maybe soon."

She nods, expression turning earnest. "There is still time. I admire you for your patience with him, and for the fact that you have not given in to temptation. I am sure that with you two staying in the same hotel that it could be very hard not to give into desires of lust."

Oh. My. Goodness.

It burns my insides to think of what Temperance, or Mom, would do if I came home with someone like Eric. Would they approve of the match? Because I got with a man, any man?

Several guys in my youth group didn't seem to care about personality when it came to girls. As long as they were, in fact, a girl and wanted to give birth to at least four kids, they put a ring on it.

"Of course. Gotta love abstinence. Now, I'm sorry, Mom, but I really should go. We took our suitcases with us to the theater today, so we're loading up on the bus soon."

"Oh, well, I hope you have a safe journey. Definitely keep us updated on the Raph situation."

She hangs up before I can even formulate a response.

A shadow looms over me. Carmen, suitcase in hand, simpers and heads toward the door. I bolt to my feet and advance toward her.

Not sure why, but I feel the need to talk. Make amends—even though I technically have no apologies to make.

Mom called me "ever the diplomat" back in the day. Trying to stay in everyone's good graces.

"Hey, Carmen."

She spins around, eyebrows raised in an oh-this-should-be-good fashion.

"Hey, I know we really haven't met." Outside of the Japanese garden. "But I just wanted to say sorry if there were any hard feelings. I really didn't know about—"

Her suitcase plunks against the carpet, and she throws a hand up. "Yeah, yeah, I saw the video Eric posted. Also, that's super spineless to get him to stand up for you like that. I'm a firm believer in fighting your own battles."

Excuse me?

He pulled *me* into the recording room and filmed the video on the spot.

"No, wait, he didn't—"

"Yeah, I'm sure you've rehearsed the story a million times in your head. Just know that it's a very good thing that Roger is letting me do the rest of the season with the cast. And planning to pay me what they agreed to. Otherwise, let's just say, it would've been quite the show in court."

Hold on.

"Pay me what they agreed to."

Did they also offer her $100k to take on the part?

Is that why she returned?

Auditioners yesterday told me that most opera singers work a side job on top of doing opera. That gigs once in a while could pay the rent, but not always. That being the case, no wonder she fought so hard to get her parts back.

Her lips twitch. She eyes me up and down, surveying my reaction. I make everything go slack. She will not win this from me.

"Happy to help mentor you, Tina. Since I'm certain you won't be needing any more voice lessons from Eric for the remainder of the season. I'm sure you'll make a fabulous Buoso. Seems like a part that's more your speed."

She smirks, grabs the handle of her suitcase, and pads down the rest of the hallway.

My fists roll into balls. Nails dig into my palms until everything goes numb.

It's a good thing that I'm not the murderer.

Because two seconds ago, if you'd given me a knife, I can guarantee I would've spilt a lot of blood.

CHAPTER 17

"You're very bad at being dead, girlie."

Meg holds me up by the armpits until they ache. She insisted, the second we arrived at the hotel, that she would help me get ready for the part of Buoso. Since we wouldn't rehearse today, and we'd do the preview tomorrow…"Tina can use all the help she can get."

I stagger to my legs and wobble forward until the sores under my arms cry out in relief.

"What was I doing wrong?"

"You didn't go all slack. You have to keep in mind that we're shoving you into closets on stage. It has to look believable."

I crash onto the bed, shielding my eyes with fists.

"I can't even play a dead guy. Carmen was totally right, I'm in way over my head in the world of opera."

"Stop that."

Meg slumps beside me. We collapse and stare up at the white ceiling. In my periphery, blue Florida skies pierce my vision out the large glass window. When we arrived in the morning, humidity soaked every article of clothing we owned. We would spend most of this week indoors, I imagined.

"Carmen's been getting on everybody's bad side, not just yours, girlie."

Images of the bus ride flicker. She'd parked right across from Eric and shoved her legs against the seats. That way no one would take up that row. When Meg sneered at her, Carmen jabbed a finger at her nose.

"Don't think I don't know about your and Karim's secret. If you're going to judge, look at yourself."

Meg muttered on the way back to her seat, across from me, about how she had no idea how Carmen could've even figured that out.

Normally, the word secret would've tingled my insides.

But drained from weeks of performances, and the confrontation with Carmen in the hallway, I conked out for eight hours of the journey to Florida.

I angle to the right and stare at the beach view. Bright blue ocean waves lap over white sand. Too bad the heat registers in the nineties. Otherwise, I may take the opportunity—as a dead guy with no voice lessons—to go splash in the cool waters.

"How do people—" I draw in a breath and phrase every word by choice. "How do people like her get away with acting like that?"

In community theater, divas like Matilda would utter passive-aggressive things from time to time like "Oh, you're such a good *chorus member*, Tina" or "Oh, well, I just love it when people give it their best effort in auditions. It goes to show that anyone is able to try out for community theater, even if they aren't very good."

But never.

Ever, *ever* would Matilda say what Carmen did to me.

"Cutthroat jobs do that to you." Meg taps my leg with a socked foot. "I've seen so many people exit school either burnt out and never wanting to do music ever again, or they see everyone as competition. So they will cut you down. No matter the cost."

No matter the cost.

"She has to know she's making enemies, though, right?"

Enemies with me means I may kill them off as a character version of themselves, if I ever get to writing detective novels in the future. But making an enemy of someone like Meg or Karim, or any of the other people in the Daaé troupe? That's the death of my future in opera.

"Well, chica, we have to think of things from her perspective. In her mind, she *did* audition. She *did* get the roles. She never *did* say she was dropping out. And suddenly, some bright-eyed girl who's never gone to school gets the role."

"Ugh, trust me." I rub my hands up and down the cool sheets. These beds don't have comforters on them. They rest in the closet, probably unused even in the winter months. "I get it. But it's still ridiculous she's acting this way."

"It's a reason. Not an excuse."

She slaps my leg and lifts herself from the bed.

"Speaking of the prima donna, she and the others are planning on having lunch at the pier. You joining us?"

Burning fills my stomach.

When had I last eaten? No dinner last night, because show nights meant eating after. And if the bus made a pit stop for food, no one woke me up to inform me.

"Yeah, that sounds good. Let me get some sandals on."

As we leave the hotel room, Meg vows to paint "those sad little jagged toenails" when we get back. As we meet up with the group on the bus, Meg and I station ourselves toward the back as Carmen once again bars us off. This time, Eric hasn't joined us. Probably to avoid Carmen.

Thanks a lot. She's undone weeks of work, where we finally got him to join us for whitewater rafting.

Karim and Raph, behind us, get into a heated debate about *Clone Wars* versus *Star Wars Rebels*.

We reach the destination, and sand kicks into every crevice of my shoes as we pad up and down the hot boardwalk.

Sunlight scorches us, and we stop by a food stand that sells gator bites and other fried goodies.

I overhear Carmen as she orders.

"Just to be extra clear, there are no peanuts whatsoever in the catfish. You're not even cooking with peanut oil? Like, are you absolutely positive there are no peanuts?"

"All canola. No peanuts." The worker taps a sheet that must list the allergens included in any of the foods. A wheat symbol indicates gluten.

He drains a fish filet from its oil and slides it into a boat that he hands her. Once she returns to an umbrella table, I order a boat full of gator bites with dynamite mayo sauce.

True to the internet theories, they taste like crispy, rubbery chicken.

I slide into a seat next to Raph, and he sneaks away a few gator nuggets. I slap his hand and tell him to get his own.

"Hey, guys." Meg shimmies her shoulder as she places her boat of gator pieces next to mine, the free seat left available. "Can you believe it? The guy said there are *no* peanuts whatsoever in this. I made extra sure there were *no* peanuts, not even peanut oil. I just can't stand the Peanuts. Stupid Charlie Brown and that stupid football."

I pipe up. "Hey, Meg, love you, but that probably isn't something to make fun of."

Much as Carmen has been a diva about everything else, I sympathize with her for her peanut allergy. We had a girl with a terrible latex allergy in one of our plays. The director made a big deal about how we couldn't have balloons at the cast party, to the point where she had a nervous breakdown, "worried she'd let the cast down by her allergy."

Something tells me someone exaggerated how picky Carmen was about the restaurant choice. Everyone had villainized her from the start. Girls who got leads in plays tended to get the worst criticism from castmates.

I can only imagine how frustrating it must be for Carmen that she can't eat at certain places. For the slightest moment, Carmen passes me a grateful glance. Then her face hardens.

"Not all peanut allergies are the same." She lifts her chin, embracing the teaching moment. "Sometimes people can get hives.

But other people get stomach cramps. Their throat can close, skin turns blue. Definitely not something to be making fun of."

Meg buckles her chin into her chest and mutters something I can't hear.

Palm trees flicker in a brief, merciful breeze. Clusters of people amble past, several lobster-red from the sun. I can feel the sun singe my skin. Carmen insisted we eat outdoors. Her skin tans like a Grecian goddess.

I shrink underneath the remaining shade of our umbrella.

"So." Karim crackles the fried fish skin with a plastic fork. "What is everyone planning to do for the rest of the day off?"

Meg's hand shoots up.

Karim frowns. "Umm, yes, Meg."

"I'm planning to paint Tina's toenails."

"Umm, that's great, Meg."

"You don't understand, Karim. The girl needs some desperate help. This is a *big* deal." She blows away a curl that fell onto her nose. "And then, who knows? Beach looks pretty nice. Maybe you can finally teach me how to body surf."

Carmen fluffs out her napkin that almost sailed off her lap from the wind.

"I don't know about you guys, but *I'm* going to study the libretto. We're all getting paid to do this, so we probably shouldn't slack off, even on non-rehearsal days. The only person here who doesn't need to work on the music is Tina." She gestures at me. "So if she wants to take a day at the beach, that's fine I guess."

Everyone prickles.

You can tell by how their shoulders go up, their cheeks darken.

"Forgot about me." Raph raises his hand, and tension ebbs. "And after your pedicure, Tina, I think you and I need to," he drops his voice, "hang out."

Desperation laces his tone.

Did he find out something new?

Eyes press into me from all sides, so I force a sunny expression. "Of course. Sounds like a plan."

An hour later, Raph knocks on my door. I swing it open, race back to the bed, and display my now scarlet toesies.

"Yes, Tina, those look very nice."

"Meg said we *had* to do the red. Since red is a very romantic color, she says it's going to attract all the boys." I hobble on my ankles toward him, still uncertain if the paint has dried yet. "Raph, are you falling head over heels?"

He snickers. "Oh. Absolutely."

It's sarcasm, an offense that must be avenged.

I chase him around the room, saying my toes are going to "get him" and "make him fall in love with me." He wheezes and throws an arm up to indicate we need to stop the chase.

I return to my place on the bed and brush my fingertips against the nails. By now, the paint has smoothed to a hardened shine. She went with the gel today, so these bad boys won't get stripped any time soon, no matter how long I hold them under scalding water in the shower.

"Two things, Tina. One—you know that you and I are not going to ever be a thing, right? We already tried dating each other and figured we just weren't all that attracted to each other." He gives me a pointed look.

Duh. "We'll always be like a brother and sister, and are only keeping up a ruse for our parents so they stop pressuring us to find other spouses and get married." I wink and flash my toesies again. "And will keep up the ruse until one of us finds a significant other."

"Two—if a man seriously falls in love with you, because of your *feet,* you should probably run."

"Eww. Noted."

I dangle my legs off of the bed and swing them like two pendulums.

"Anyway, you wanted to meet with me?"

His features slacken. "Yeah, I did. Now, I know you're not on social media."

Raph parks next to me and pulls up Instagram. He taps the search bar for a handle.

"But I'm sure you've known from the numerous selfies and photos that Annika takes, that she's not the world's greatest photographer."

Her profile appears on the screen. In every picture, the blur of a thumbprint rests in each corner. Huh, I *hadn't* noticed this, but Annika and I don't pay much attention to each other. She hasn't looped me into many photos.

I giggle at a picture of her and a golden retriever, a selfie.

It hits me that several of these singers must leave pets at home. None accompanied us on the road. Besides their three-month break period between March and May, did they ever get to see them?

Perhaps she'd posed with someone else's puppy.

Raph steers me back on track. "Okay, what mistakes are you seeing?"

"Her thumb is in all the pictures. And yeesh, the girl really likes her filters."

"Yes, the second one is terrible, but not the focus of today. You remember how you asked Antonia to show you the pictures of the jellyfish when you interrogated her?"

Memories blur back to that day.

"Yeah, the time stamp said she and Roger weren't far behind us."

"*She* wasn't. I'm not too sure about Roger."

"What do you mean?"

He clicks out of the Instagram app and onto his camera roll. Several photos of our mini group—Karim, me, Meg, even Eric—flit through his fingertips. He stops on pictures of moon jellies.

"I asked Roger if he could send me some pictures of the jellyfish. Said I was working on a project and was asking the cast if they could all get me the photos they took of them."

Even before he zooms into the individual ones, I catch the thumb blur at the top corner of several of them.

"Were these the ones he sent you?"

"Yeah, but Annika clearly took them."

My stomach drops. "Maybe he's really bad at technology? And he asked one of the younger people to take some?"

"Had that thought too, until—"

We once again flick into Instagram. He taps on Roger's profile and shows me the feed. Photographs of city backdrops and the picture of a woman holding a violin flood the screen. Although taken on an iPhone, lacking the quality of most professional cameras, Roger tags himself for the photo credits in his descriptions.

"You're not supposed to tag yourself, right?"

"Yeah, it's very cringe. But we know he can snap photos. At least, on a phone."

The weight of his words press down on me like concrete.

"Did you—get a chance to check the time stamps on his photos? Just in case? Maybe he took some pictures, but it didn't work out, and so he asked Annika to do that."

"Thought of that too, and yes, I did. The time stamps are when Annika stopped by the tank. And before you ask, I did ask her to show me *her* photos. And I checked *her* timestamps. Roger handed her his phone and asked her to take some pictures."

"Why?"

"So it looked less suspicious, that's why."

"Why would Antonia say they were walking together?"

He grabs a pillow from my bedspread and tosses it in the air. He catches it.

"Thought about that, but I had to go to the bathroom. *Then*, it hit me."

"What?"

"He probably said he had to go to the bathroom. See it hit me, because I *was* going to the bathroom. All the best ideas happen in there. Probably even hinted that it was going to be a long one. You know, like when Temperance gets 'surprised' in public."

Temperance never liked to say the word "poop." It felt improper for the refined girl, so if she took a long time in public restrooms—thanks to that fibrous diet of hers—she would tell me, "Sorry, got surprised."

"If we gave him fifteen to twenty minutes in the bathroom, maybe it wouldn't have alerted Antonia to how long he'd been out. Enough time to go to the bridge, chuck a guy over it, and come back."

Thoughts race through counter-possibilities.

This doesn't look good for Roger.

"Plus, Tina, I did see him with the roses. You haven't gotten any more of those lately, have you?"

I bite my lip and shake my head. Eyes dart to the door. Gotta make sure to do the double-locks tonight. Just in case.

"What do we do, Raph?" Shivers run up and down my arms.

"Wait for more evidence, I guess."

"More?"

Even as the question passes my lips, I know it's not enough. Maybe Roger'll claim he went to the restroom and asked Annika to take photos during that time. We didn't have any witnesses near the bridge.

"Hey." He wraps me in a one-armed hug. It doesn't provide the same warmth and fuzzies as Eric's did, but I'll take it. "I know, I'm sorry. Hopefully, we'll get more soon."

"Not from that murder." Tears itch my waterline. "No witnesses, very little evidence. It's going to take another murder, and a sloppier one at that, to nail this guy."

I can't tell if the silence from Raph, or my last-spoken statement, scares me more.

CHAPTER 18

"A masquerade ball? Eep!"

Meg tears a poster off the wall in the back hallway. She turns and displays it for me to see. A purple mask, smothered in sparkles, glitters next to the curly font that spells out "Masquerade" in golden letters.

"Tina, we *have* to go."

My fingertips brush my upper lip, the ghost of a stage mustache still leaving behind an imprint. After the preview performance tonight, my heart goes out to all the men and women in trouser roles who sport fake beards and goatees.

I will say though, the darkness in the closet on stage provided comfort.

Except for the fact that my thoughts buzzed back to Roger. I dodged him these past twenty-four hours, after what Raph showed me in my hotel room. The more I think about it, the more it makes sense.

A theater manager takes charge of everyone in a production:

- Technical Directors

- Master Carpenters

- Box Office Assistants

- Main Directors, like Antonia

- Etc.

Even if Roger *had* gone to use the restroom, he could've hired someone out to take care of the old manager. Maybe could've placed the blame on someone else, a scapegoat.

And if he paid off whoever well enough, he'd earned their silence.

After all, they gave me $100k for the summer. What else did they dole out?

Good thing he slinks away for most performances. Don't have to deal with him much, for now.

I almost caught some zzzs' in that onstage closet, before they pulled my limp body out and stuffed it underneath the huge bed on stage.

Tried as I might, I couldn't stop the twisting of my stomach during Carmen's songs. Nor the roaring applause that followed them. Or the standing O she received at the curtain.

Maybe she'd been right. I didn't deserve to perform with this group.

"Tina." Meg squeezes my arm. "You listening?"

"Wha—yeah. Of course I'll go with you tomorrow."

I snatch the paper out of her hands and scan over the details.

"We'll need dresses, though."

"Oh gee, Tina, if only we had a costume shop that we could borrow some outfits from."

"We can do that?"

From what I could tell from the seamstresses, who chased Raph out of a shop when he stole one of the hats for a camera shot, they didn't like any fingers touching the clothes. But maybe the ones in Florida worked very differently than the ones from Virginia.

"I think your measurements are posted somewhere in there." Meg meanders down the hall toward the shop. "I'll go looking for a dress for you. And—"

She waves her finger like a maestro with a baton.

"—make sure to ask Eric if he wants to come. I'm sure you're going to be the only one to get him to go."

"Eric?"

Dryness fills my mouth. He and I haven't spoken these last few days. Carmen claimed she needed to play "catch up" and work with him on the music rehearsals she missed in her absence.

"Yeah, you know, my cousin. Real emo and broody type. Hides in basements, especially when his new stage girlfriend is monopolizing where we can go out to eat after."

"She is?"

Meg flicks a glance over her shoulder and rushes to me. Voice a-whisper.

"Tonight she's turned down pretty much all of our food suggestions because there's nuts in some items on the menu. Never mind the fact that she can order something else. She says that she used to work in restaurants and 'cross-contamination' happens and blah, blah, blah."

Much as I love Meg, I really hate her sometimes. If anything, she's acted more like a diva than Carmen at times. Especially when it comes to this peanut allergy thing.

You'd think that the opera, of all places, would be accepting of all people with all conditions. The theater in my hometown had been.

Maybe I'd gotten all my ideas about the opera wrong.

"I mean, maybe her allergy is really serious, Meg." Once again, I think back to the girl from community theater with the latex allergy. Of all the frustration Carmen had to have experienced when explaining to people that they couldn't stop at certain restaurants due to an allergy. "You think the chefs here know?"

"Of course they know. We all fill out the medical emergency contact sheets at every new theater we go to. What I'm saying is, it's excessive. She's excessive. Either way." She backs away from me once more. "Get Eric to go to the masquerade. He keeps hiding and is all mopey. And it's affecting his singing."

She presses a nail talon against her earlobe.

"I can hear it in his notes. They're like little musical cues telling me how someone is feeling."

If only everyone in the world had Meg's talent. Then we wouldn't wonder. All we could do is ask someone to sing, and they'd bleed out for us.

What would Eric sound like if he sang while thinking of me?

Meg slips into the costume shop and disappears. Although Eric didn't tell me where he'd gone after curtain call, part of me knows. I find a staircase and sail into the basement.

Candles, dozens of them, flicker around a blanket. He parks in the middle with a basket hoisted on his crisscrossed knees.

"Are you...expecting someone?"

I ask this as my blood chills. What if he planned to do something with Carmen since they spend so many hours together now?

All of him relaxes as he squints, making me out in the flames. "Yeah, *you*."

"*Me*? You knew I would come down here and meet you at this really weird picnic?"

As I move toward him, he flinches. "Careful." He gestures at one of the candles near my foot. "Dangerous."

"It's not like one of these could burn the whole place down."

"You'd be surprised."

His voice goes cold, vicious. I've plucked some unknown nerve. "Sorry."

"And yes, I knew you'd come down here. I figured that you'd want to escape a certain prima donna."

Tension ebbs in my gut.

We still share the same animosity toward her.

With ginger steps, I weave around the candles. Flames flicker along with the movement. He's left little space between him and the rest of the blanket, so I park inches away.

"I've felt so bad for you. She's been dragging you away for line run-throughs all the time."

Groans, playful ones, pass through his lips. He rubs half his face up and down. Candlelight illuminates the string that holds on the veil. No idea how the Phantom in *Phantom of the Opera* manages to keep his on without anything holding it in place.

Christine tore off the mask at one point in the show.

My fingers itch to do the same. I refrain. Secrets belong to someone, and you can't simply snatch them away because you want in on one.

"Don't even get me started on her." He flips open the lid on the basket. Out pop several treats in plastic wrappings. "I have no idea what her end game is."

"What do you mean?"

"I mean." He tears off the wrapper on one of the treats. In the glow, I recognize its shape. A brownie of some sort. I reach for one as well. "She runs away from me in the Japanese garden the moment she sees my face, and from that, made it clear that she didn't want any roles in which we'd have to have stage chemistry."

A corner of the treat slides into my mouth.

I frown at the cranberry and chocolate chip combo as they crunch on my molars. Can't tell if I hate or love these.

He continues. "But now she's wanting to spend every waking moment together and go over the libretto."

"She does love her libretto."

I recount for him what happened on the boardwalk docks.

"Also." I hold up the brownie. "Where did you get this and what's in it?"

"Chef is experimenting for tomorrow. You know how they like to leave treats backstage with the cast."

A nod from me.

"Well, I guess this is for Wednesday's performance. I think for Monday's performance, he's planning on doing cookies or something. He calls it a trail mix brownie. Got cranberries, M&Ms, peanuts, chocolate chips—"

"Hold up, peanuts? Carmen has a nut allergy, right?"

"Oh, trust me. He knows it. She made sure to walk him through her medical sheet a million times. Says he's going to make a different batch separate for her and put it in that dressing room, so no one else takes from it."

That eases my shoulders. Still, Carmen hasn't described how severe her allergy is. Wouldn't the chef be playing with fire by having any peanuts at all in his kitchen?

Much as I can't stand the girl, after the Richard incident, I wouldn't want anyone else to get in harm's way.

"Speaking of Carmen and why she wants to spend so much time with me. I think I know why, after that docks story."

Heat from the firelight warms my arms. "You do?"

"Tina, I think she's trying to get to you in some way. She's taken the parts from you, and now she's trying to isolate you from friends. Until you either leave the tour, or break, or both."

Revenge.

For me "stealing" her part.

A scoff fills my throat and I roll my eyes.

"She's ridiculous."

"She's not going to get away with it."

I wince. Last time he stood up for me, it backfired in the hallway with Carmen.

"Please don't feel the need to fight my battles for me. I'm a quiet fighter, but a fighter nonetheless. Never underestimate an introvert."

As I lean back, he snaps forward. "Careful."

My fingertips bump a candelabra. I clasp my hands and double forward.

"Sorry, forgot."

"Fire's dangerous."

"Yeah, Meg told me about the campfire incident."

Odd choice to bring candles down in a room, when they clearly caused so much physical and mental pain and suffering for him.

"I." He sucks in a deep breath. "Lost someone to it."

Silence. I blink several times, weighing the words.

"Eric, I—I had no idea." I clasp his arm with my hand, and he doesn't flinch away from the contact.

We hold ourselves there for a while. Then he speaks.

"Yeah, my dad, he..." He shuts his eyes, turns his head to the left. "Was notorious for leaving the gas from the stovetop on. Mom would always yell at him for it. And he was a big fan of lighting candles. Usually never both at the same time."

I already know where the story is heading.

Dread forms puddles in my intestines, but he continues.

"One evening, when Mom and I were out, he was making us dinner. Even though the ingredients were done on the stovetop, he'd forgotten to shut everything off. Lit a few candles beforehand too. Did it for Mom because he was a romantic kind of guy."

Gotcha, Eric associates romance with candles.

Definitely not relevant in this room full of candles right now.

Focus, girl, on his story.

"I don't know what caught on fire first, but he'd gone upstairs to nap. By the time we and the fire department got there—"

He breaks off.

"You don't need to finish. I'm sorry. I'm *so* sorry."

My arms band around him in a hug, and he compresses into me. We suspend in warmth and in sorrow together. His shoulder budges against me, indicating he wants to let go. We release, and I steady myself on the blanket to avoid the candles.

"You *do* realize we are in a room full of fire right now, though, Eric."

"Yeah, something about facing your fears, yada yada yada. There's something about you, Tina. Something that brings out the brave in me. The same way the videos do."

Everything ignites in me at these words.

I struggle to hold myself together. So I beam and fight the urge to cup his chin.

"You know what, Eric? I think you do the same thing to me."

He leans toward me, and I let him press his hand into the small of my back. *Holy crap, we're going for it.*

We don't need background music. I can hear it in the candlelight.

Faces two inches away...

I hear someone clear their throat at the door. We break apart, and I squint to make out the silhouette.

Her voice reaches me before my vision clears. "You guys coming onto the bus with us or what?"

Carmen.

Eric shrinks behind me. No matter how brave I've made him, it could take him extra courage to face the girl who unmasked him in the garden. I block him like a shield.

"Thanks for the offer, Carmen, but I don't think we're going with the group to dinner tonight."

"Not dinner." Carmen leans her hip against the door frame. "Back to the hotel. We couldn't agree on a place to go, so we're getting room service back there." Her long fingertips cover a yawn. "Probably a good thing too if we're going to do a matinee tomorrow, and then a masquerade right after. Not a great idea to stay out super late."

"Masquerade?" Eric whispers this.

"So." Carmen flicks on the lights. We wince under their harsh beams. "Bus is leaving in two minutes whether you two are on it or not." She vanishes into the hallway.

My hands press into my cheeks and pull them down until they form taffy under my fingertips.

"Great, she's going too."

"Are you"—Eric cocks his hand—"planning on going tomorrow?"

"I mean, Meg's roping me into it. And I was planning on asking you. But after I just found out that Carmen is—"

"I'd love to go." His face illuminates. A grin cuts up his cheek. "With you. Not Carmen."

"That's pretty brave of you." I tap his shoulder, feeling put out by Carmen spoiling the moment. "Proud."

"Well."He lifts himself to his feet and offers a hand to help me rise. We start to blow out the candles.

"It's much easier to be brave when you're brave together."

CHAPTER 19

*"O*ur *lives are one masked ball."*

Once again, the rose on my hotel dresser contains no signature. Guess Roger wants to have a happening time at the ball tonight too.

Right after the first performance, we made a pit stop at the hotel to get ready for the ball. Meg vows that as soon as she finishes her hair, she'll bring the dresses into my room, so we can finish "hopping into our getup" together.

Fire burns my fingertips. I hiss and yank my hand back from the curling wand.

Might as well give up on the effort. No use in corralling my crazy hair into beach-like waves. I reach for a bobby pin and secure a section of hair in place to make it look like I put more than a few minutes of effort into the whole ordeal.

A knock from the door breaks up my thoughts.

Unplugging the curling wand, I head to the door and open it.

Swaths of fabric consume me. I stagger back as Meg stumbles into the room with ten different dresses raised above her head.

"Okay, chica, I have options."

Images of the costume designer flash before my eyes as the oceans of tulle brush my legs and venture to the closet. The short woman, with a wart on her forehead, holds a permanent frown on her lips.

I can't imagine how much grayer her skin could get if she realized how many costumes Meg nabbed. "Edna is going to kill you."

"Edna, humph." She grunts as she shoves the hangers onto the bar in the closet. "Can handle one night away from these. We're not using any of these outfits in *Gianni Schicchi* anyway. Now."

She steps back from the closet and smooths her silk robe. "I already picked out mine in the shop, so it's back in my room. Since Miss Prima Donna forced us to go onto the bus before you could try these on, you get to take your pick now."

I move to the closet and check the sizes. Yup, close to my measurements.

"Ooo." She claps her hands and moves to the rose on the dresser. "Secret admirer?"

Eww, Roger?

"I guess you could call him something like that." Hangers shove to the right. Yellow, although beautiful, would look terrible with my skin tone. The white lacy one? Too wedding gown. "Any chance you know what Eric is wearing tonight? He really wants to go with me."

Wince.

"I mean, not *with me*, with me. Just, probably someone he knows he can dance with. Someone who isn't his cousin. And isn't Carmen."

Just stop, girl, stop. I bury my face into the plume of tulle from one of the gowns.

All of these dresses stink of musk and deodorant. Worn before. According to Meg, actors tend to share costumes across shows. Costumers only make new outfits if the new actress had a major height or weight difference from the previous ones.

"Actually, I stopped by his room to borrow some full-face masks. Since he has a plethora of those, along with the half-face ones. I believe he's wearing a red tie."

Red.

Scarlet snags my attention in the closet. I grip the hook of the hanger and pull out the ball gown.

Sparkly beads make their way up the midsection into the bodice. It reminds me of crimson snow.

"It's strapless."

"It's perfect, Tina. Get in."

I shimmy into the gown, and Meg laces me in. A corset tightens around my midsection. Guess someone named Tina won't get a chance to eat much food tonight. Images from homeschool dances flit across my vision. Even at homeschool dances where the dresses weren't super tight, you couldn't stuff down so much as a granola bar. In a corset like this? Impossible to keep down anything.

"Makes you really miss the dresses on stage, doesn't it?" Meg snickers.

"Yeah, well, at least I don't have to sing tonight." Breath support and corsets didn't get along all that well.

Once she fastens me into the dress, Meg pulls out a bag she must've brought in with the other dresses.

"A red mask for you."

When she hands it to me, my fingers run up and down the sequins. Scarlet glitter flakes onto my thumbs.

"I love the gold stitching in this thing."

"Thought you might. Also, Eric has a gift for you. Says it'll go with any dress."

Meg holds up a plastic Ziploc bag. Inside it, something gold glitters.

"What is it?" I clock the white, circular pendant. Gold veins form jagged, lightning bolt patterns on the pottery.

"So he was trying to explain it to me. Used some word. Basically, ordered some Japanese pottery necklace. They break apart the pottery, and then stitch it together with gold."

"Kintsugi."

Although not always with necklaces—the same principle applied to all pottery. Japanese craftsmen would take broken shards and twine them together with a precious metal. Illustrating how brokenness and beauty could join hands together.

I clasp the necklace around my neck. Cool to the touch, the pendant chills my heated chest.

When we slip on the masks, I wriggle my nostrils.

"Seriously, how does Eric breathe in these things? It's clamping down hard on the bridge of my nose."

"People get used to things if you give them a long enough time." Her voice drops to a morose note. Then lifts into a high one when she claps her hands. "Gotta go get my dress on. Meet you downstairs?"

"Be right with you."

After I finish my makeup, and shove several bobby pins into my curls to hold up the hair, I float toward the elevator. My dress bubbles into half of the shaft, so I thank my lucky stars that no one else has come to join me.

When the doors part, I spy Eric in the middle of the hallway, near the pool.

Empty, the corridor doesn't boast of any guests or trundling suitcases. Granted, we got back from our matinee in the evening. Most people checked into their rooms earlier in the day.

Chlorine from the pool room punches me in the nose. Despite the efforts of my mask to cut off all sense of smell.

Speaking of masks, Eric holds his up to his face. He's worn a full-face one today that covers all of him. Through the eye slits, I catch his wince.

"You look beautiful."

"You look like you need help."

"Thanks. It's the strings. I'm used to an elastic band. Not having to tie a bow in the back."

"I got you."

Padding to his backside, I hear an elevator ding. Carmen's dress showers silver glitter onto the linoleum tile. She spies me, rounds in my direction, face purpling. Her finger jab almost pokes me in the eye.

I stagger back and let go of the strings. Eric keeps the mask pressed to his face. My heels click against the tile as I regain my balance.

"Carmen, what the—?"

"*You*. It wasn't enough for you to take the parts away from me, but now you're leaving me threatening notes?"

Excuse me? Threatening notes?

"What are you talking about?"

Did she mean the roses? Had someone left flowers in her room, too? And did this happen to other members of the troupe?

If so, Meg would've commented such when she spotted the rose in my room. Maybe Roger felt like plaguing both of the newest members to the troupe—the non-Daaés.

But why wouldn't Raph get any notes? Then again, he isn't a member of the troupe. Maybe they've targeted people in the opera.

"Don't play dumb with me. I don't care that the note is typed, I know you did it. You've been jealous of me since the moment I stepped on stage, and so you're trying to stop me from going to tomorrow's performance."

My mouth sinks into a gape.

"Carmen, seriously, I didn't leave any—"

"And what's with you trying to hang out with Eric all the time? Think that buddying up with Antonia's son is going to get you in good with the Daaés? That you can convince them to replace me again? Well, let me tell you what *isn't* going to happen."

"Carmen." Eric growls this. He can't push her away from looming over me, though. Not with his hands on his face.

Also, buddying up?

Hold on. Is *that* why Carmen spends so much time with him? Because if she can get into his good graces, he'll pass the word along to the others?

Fire prickles my skin.

"I don't really see how any time I spend with Eric is any of your business, Carmen."

"Oh, it's plenty of my business. If you're going to act all smitten with the director's son, you might as well know what you're in for."

She takes two steps back and shoves an elbow into Eric's gut. As a reflex, his arms snap down to protect his abdomen. Carmen takes advantage, grabs the mask from him, and whips it away. In a lightning-fast movement, she seizes his wrists and holds them down, twisting him to the side so that he has to face me.

Now I can see all of him.

And honestly?

On a scale from Freddy Krueger to Two-Face from the *Dark Knight* series?

At first, I can understand why she screamed in the garden. It looks like someone took a knife to his face and carved up several inches of skin. And what was left behind droops over permanent, red scars.

I take it in for a moment.

Relax.

Like Meg said upstairs, you can adjust to anything if you give yourself enough time. Then I make out his eyes, the beautiful eye untouched by burn marks. His pinched brow on the unburned side of his face.

His pupils bore into me. Daring me to flee, to hide.

No wonder he does it first, to beat people to the punch.

Every word I speak next, I weigh. Because something tells me we will both remember this moment forever.

I pad up to him. By now, Carmen has released his wrists, but he doesn't shield his face. No use at this point.

My fingertips reach up to cup his chin. "Oh. Is that all? You hyped this up way too much, I must say, Eric."

He brightens. Soaks in the words. Ones he's needed to hear for years. His lips twitch, and a scoff sounds from my left. Carmen's.

"Here." I unclasp the kintsugi necklace and place it in his palm. "For you to wear tonight, as a reminder. You can return it to me once you remember who you are."

We hold a stare for several seconds.

Then I twist my head to the left, toward Carmen, smirking.

"Whatever. You're still in way over your head." She jabs a thumb into the elevator button. "And after the note you left me, I'm not going anywhere with you tonight." The elevator dings, and she slips inside.

Glancing over my shoulder, I spot the group huddled a few meters away in the lobby. Did they...catch all of that? Roger stands amongst them, half-smile cutting up his cheek. I don't like how he looks in a black mask.

"Come." Antonia motions to us with a wave, positively glowing. Maybe she'd yearned for someone to see her son the same way she had. "Our carriage awaits."

Eric slips on his mask once more, and I help him to tie a bow in the back with the strings.

Five minutes later, we disembark the bus and head inside a large building. Bass throbs the bricks outside.

A larger heat wave, than that from the outdoors, hits us the moment we step inside the large dance floor. Masked men and women in gowns and tuxes bump up and down to some song called "The Wobble."

"You know," Meg shouts this and finds an open chair to park in. "When I thought of a masquerade, I'd pictured dancing to music from *Bridgerton* or something."

Eric leads me to the outskirts of the dance floor by hand. I'm grateful, because the closer you get to the center, the more *into it* the couples appear to get. We sway to the music as Karim escorts a stranger a few feet away from us into the movement.

I flick a glance back at Meg, and she shrugs.

"He knows I'm not going to be able to dance, so, might as well let him have his fun."

My mind flashes back to him swiping left and right on his phone in the kitchen at his house. Did Meg know about the fact he's on dating apps? Did Meg just not care?

Eric's hand laces into mine, and I forget. About...whatever it was I'd just thought about. He guides his hand to the small of my back as the music fades into a slower number. Gripping his shoulder, I glimpse Raph parking next to Meg as they chat.

We, Eric and I, spin in lazy circles.

String lights, woven onto the ceiling and columns of the ballroom, wink at us. Sweat glistens on our skin after the number finishes, and Eric motions, with a jerk of his head, toward double doors.

Skin prickling with overheating, I nod, and he seizes my hand.

We race outside. Scents of tangerine sunshine fill my nostrils when we pass through the double doors onto a balcony outside. To my surprise, no couples linger out here. Probably because, despite the change in temperature, we still swim in the humidity.

Sea salt peppers the air.

Twenty degrees cooler, and I could spend a forever here.

I lean my wrists against the stone balcony and take in the palm trees and flower gardens sprawled out in front of the building. Ibises soar in the skies above.

"Tina."

His voice tickles my ear. I turn and find him inches away, unmasked once more. He gauges my reaction. I can tell by how his eyes flick back and forth, like a sensor awaiting movement.

"Listen, I know you were trying to protect my feelings, and I appreciate it. But you didn't have to lie to Carmen back—"

"I didn't lie." It doesn't come out as sharp as the words sound in my head. My tone is soft, like the blurring of a sunset. "Really, Eric, I didn't. It's unfortunate that you can't see how beautiful you are."

"Beautiful." It comes out in a whisper. Pianissimo.

He fingers the necklace pendant. Per my instructions, he wore it.

"Yes." My palm flies under his chin, rests there. "So beautiful."

He surges forward and plants a kiss on my lips. A long one. We suspend on the balcony for a moment as warmth fills every vein, until I swear my blood vessels will pop one by one.

We pull apart. His cheeks darken.

"Sorry, I wasn't thinking. I—"

Grabbing fistfuls of his suit, I pull him in and kiss him again.

CHAPTER 20

"**A**re you *just* eating the chocolate chips off of that brownie?"

An apparently very judgy ballerina squints at me as she stretches at her mini barre. Each of the dancers practices their flexibility at one of these stations.

I glance down at my trail mix brownie I snagged from the wicker snack basket.

"Maybe."

"What's in that thing anyway?"

I swallow a nutty taste. "Umm, berries, peanuts, chocolate chips—do you want me to get you one?"

Gianni Schicchi required no dancers. But the group for the upcoming opera, the one that would take place after we left Florida, booked the dance room for today. The ballet mistress allowed me to huddle in here. Everywhere I stood, I felt like I'd gotten in the way of the cast or crew.

"No thanks. We're on a pretty strict diet regimen for the next show."

"Suit yourself." I nibble the corner of the brownie.

The bright side of playing a dead guy? You can eat whatever you want before the show. May even sneak into the kitchens and down a whole glass of milk, just for the principle of the thing.

"Shouldn't you be with the others warming up?"

She clasps her ankle as she says this and points her foot toward the ceiling. *Show off.*

I shake my head. "Don't have a singing part in the show." Thanks to a certain prima donna.

Speaking of, true to her word, she's avoided me at all costs. I caught a glimpse of her at breakfast. Soon as she spotted me in the restaurant, sawing a Belgian waffle with Meg, she flounced off.

I wonder why Roger left threatening notes in her room.

It strikes me that Roger would have to get doubles of each key to access our rooms like that. Since Meg only left my door open the one time...

Maybe, when he booked the hotels for the groups, he told them we'd need two key cards per room. He did only hand me one on the bus. Perhaps he kept a slew of them in his bag in case he had to drop roses onto dressers from time to time.

The ballerina twirls. I clap.

"You're incredible."

She simpers. "Thanks. I will say, dancers aren't afraid of anything. Except turning left. We hate it when they make us do that." Once again, she squints at me. Her face brightens, recognition dawning. "You're that Tina girl, right?"

My pulse spikes.

Will she slap me with a whitewater raft paddle?

"Yeah?"

"You wanna learn some dance moves? We have a little more time before the mistress is getting back here. I could walk you through the basic positions."

I don't have the heart to tell her that I did participate in dance for a few years, and could second position in my sleep.

Well, anyone could. You just stood there with your feet slightly apart.

Still, best to oblige her and keep things amicable.

I pitch the rest of the brownie into a trash bin next to the door and join her at the barre.

"Okay, so." She claps her ankles together and forms "pretty fingers" with her hands. One of the principal dancers in musicals at the community theater taught me that term. "This is the first position."

My feet imitate hers.

"Great. Now, make sure to make your middle finger go slightly up. Perfect. Now you look like a dancer."

A snort. "Thanks. Pretty sure if you give me anything more complicated, I'll fall flat on my face."

True story. During one of my dance recitals, back in the day, the teacher instructed me to Chaîné. I spun twice, and when I lifted my leg, I lost balance, wobbled, and smacked into the stage floor during the final performance.

"Okay, so before we go into position two, you're pretty close with Eric, right?" She buckles into her neck, cheeks pinking.

Was she...a fangirl of his?

I slide my feet into second position before she can show me.

"Umm, yeah I am."

She clasps the barre and leans on her hip, more casual than before. "Girl, I'm *obsessed* with his videos. Do you know if he's going to do an unmasking soon? We've been begging him to do that for months."

"Uhhhh."

Gasp. "Have you seen what's under the mask? People have so many theories about what he looks like under there. Can you see the skeleton poking through?"

"Tina?"

Relief floods my gut as I whirl around to see who called my name. At the door, clad in all black, the stage manager drops a headset onto the resting position on her neck.

The stage manager?

Although I didn't interact much with her, I know she imitated several of the songs backstage. She'd pretend to lip-sync them, and would swivel her hips back and forth in an exaggerated fashion to mimic the dance moves.

"Yes?"

With two fingers, she waves me toward her. I bolt toward the door frame and we hold a mini huddle in the hallway.

"What's up?"

"Carmen is not feeling the best. Something about cramping and vomiting. Asked us to take her back to the hotel so she can rest in her room."

Blood drains from my cheeks.

"Oh gosh, is she okay?" Although, if I could wish anyone ill will, it would be Carmen. But I wouldn't sic puking onto someone, not even a worst enemy.

"Yeah, probably just that time of the month. When I get mine, I'm in a fetal position for the first two days." She shakes a fist at the sky. "Curse the girls who don't ever experience cramps."

Heat floods my cheeks. In my community back home, we would never talk so out in the open about...the time of womanly shame. Most of the time, Temperance referred to hers as "red dragon week" or "strawberry week."

"You think you're up for the part?"

My fingers fly to my throat, and I knead the skin. "Oh gosh. I haven't warmed up with the group for ages."

Thank God I avoided chugging that milk in the kitchen.

The audience will totally tell that I haven't had days of practice. During vocal warm-ups, Antonia would send me out to help various crews with securing props or setting up the stage. To give me something to do, to "earn my keep" for the summer.

"No worries. Eric's in a practice room. He's agreed to run you through lines and get you ready. But." She glimpses her watch. "You don't have much time. We need you in hair and makeup in twenty."

"Thank you, got it, in twenty." I breathe. Anxiety drums in my ears until all I can hear is buzzing.

She leads me to the practice room, and I find Eric stationed at the piano. The stage manager vanishes, likely to tend to more of her preshow tasks.

"Ready?"

I shake my head. "Don't have a choice, though."

He runs me through scales. I cringe at how much I strain at the top notes. Halfway through one of the higher solfege, I break down and crumple on the floor.

"Tina? Hey." His legs spin around the piano bench, and I feel fingerprints on my back.

Eric and I didn't have much time for conversation after our kiss last night. We'd pulled ourselves back onto the dance floor, avoided the eyebrow raises from our friends, and went back to our rooms at the hotel.

Uncurling myself, I toss him a pitiful look. "Hey."

"What's up?"

"Eric, they're going to know I'm out of practice and boo me off that stage again. They're here for Carmen tonight, not me."

"No."

He grits his teeth and he slides onto the floor beside me. Arms band around me, drawing me into him.

"They're here for Lauretta. The Lauretta who is sweet, compassionate, and kind. Not the Lauretta who is arrogant, mean, and apparently sick. If you ask me, karma knows exactly what it's doing."

I don't like his tone on that last sentence. It sounds sinister, dark. His voice softens.

"You're going to do great because you have it within you to be great. Let's run through 'O Mio Babbino Caro,' okay?"

A feeble nod.

He returns to his place at the piano and plunks the starting chord.

"O mio babbino caro."

Voice strains against my esophagus. I remember our jaw and throat exercises and relax.

"Mi piace, è bello, bello."

The notes flow out smoother, stronger. I shut my eyes and embrace the music. Measures carry me to some faraway place, where I float, fly. Sailing through the high notes like Peter Pan in the cumulonimbus.

"Babbo, pietà, pietà."

My eyelids fly open. I clock his expression. He glows.

"How did that sound?"

"Like an angel."

Rushed to hair and makeup, they wind my hair into tight braids, slap the wig cap onto me, and bobby pin the heck out of the wig into my scalp. Meg eyes me from her station and spritzes her natural curls with hairspray.

"So, Tina, you want to tell me what happened between you and Eric on the balcony last night?"

Heat rises to my cheeks. I hold myself very still and bite back a yelp when the hairdresser digs a bobby pin into my skull.

"Oh, not much. We were just talking."

"Right, so was that before or after you two were eating each other's faces off?"

Pain bites my forehead. I grip the chair arms and grimace. "Oh my gosh, Meg, you saw it? I thought you were sitting down."

She giggles into her hands. Then she sets the hairspray down onto the counter and smooths out the highlighter in the corner of her eyes.

"I mean, it's not like I don't have working legs that can transport me to the punch table or anything."

Snack tables for the night held up foamy punch bowls, guaranteed non-alcoholic, due to the fact minors could attend the ball as well. Eric and I did snag cake pops between numbers of songs we didn't know.

"Are you two an item, or—?"

"Oh, I don't know. We haven't had a chance to talk about it."

"Oh." She silences. "Probably something to discuss after the show tonight. If I know anything about the Daaés, we take care of our own and take relationships very seriously. So you better tell me you're serious about this, or I will personally take you out."

Although she laughs at this comment, my gut wriggles.

I chuckle along to save face.

"Don't get me wrong, I wouldn't *mind* if we did get together. If he feels the same way—"

"He does. And after everything that happened with Carmen, it's nice to see him get with someone much better for him."

"Carmen?"

She unmasked him in the Japanese garden. This I do know. But had they gotten together?

"Yeah."

She sighs and rubs blush up and down her cheeks with her thumbs.

"There's a reason why those fangirls were ridiculous back in Tennessee. They'd wanted Carmen and Eric to get together. Both were young prodigies in opera. It made sense to the social media world to pair them together. And it made sense to our old manager, who insisted Antonia cast her."

Meg dabs her tainted fingertips on a makeup cloth.

"And at first, it really seemed like the two were into each other. At least, from what Eric told me on the bus rides to various tour stops. She'd played with his feelings. Probably to get the family to like her."

She uncaps a lipstick tube.

"Eric finally felt safe enough around her to unmask himself. And probably to ask her out right after. Carmen could only act up to a certain degree, and fled Dodge."

Until the money drew her back to the group.

One hundred thousand dollars could make a girl do a lot of crazy things.

"All to say." She smacks her lips and smudges the pink lipstick. "You've seen all of Eric, and you like him. If I know anything about my cousin, he's serious about this. I hope you are too."

A headache pounds in my temples throughout the show from the stress.

I don't even pay attention to the notes when I get on stage, because all I think about is Meg's warning in the makeup room.

Yes, I'd love to date a guy. But in a community like mine, dating meant courting. And courting meant marriage. And I didn't know if I was really ready for that.

At curtain call, I force myself to relax.

Dating works differently out here. Most people are not like Temperance. You do not have to get married to someone after knowing them for a few months.

Courage surges through me once more.

The meet and greet provides plenty of laughs. Some of the younger patrons express their gratitude for the supertitles on a display screen above the stage.

"Without those," one in a gray suit tells me, "I would have no idea what the heck you guys were singing about up there."

Some of the older patrons ask Meg when she's going to get a real job or start thinking about a family. She laughs and gives clever answers. Telling me, after they leave, that opera singers tend to get typical fare like this.

After the meet and greet, I trundle the circular staircase that leads to the basement. Sure enough, Eric sprawls on the floor, staring up at the rafters.

"See something interesting up there?"

"A heck of a lot of spider webs."

"Okay, you weirdo. You may want to check this out." I hold up a plastic bag with the theater logo on it. "I decided to check out what kind of merch they have. Since apparently, we're on merch now."

Even the merchants dressed to the nines for the opera. One of them ran me through her daily schedule, where she did this for a living. Eat oatmeal, workout, sell t-shirts at opera houses, repeat.

I plop on the floor beside him, and he digs into a bag.

Out pops a half-mask, white, like the *Phantom of the Opera*.

"During the notary scene, I saw a couple people in the audience wearing them, so I wondered if someone was selling them in the lobby. Turns out, I was correct."

His thumbs run up and down the paper mache, expression indiscernible.

So I continue. "They love you. Seriously. There was a ballerina earlier who was going on and on about how she's a huge fan and can't wait for an unmasking video."

His shoulders hike, so I stop myself short.

"Sorry, I didn't mean to scare you."

"You're fine, it's just." His fingertips trace the sawdust on the floor. He draws a frowny face. "It's frightening, showing them *all* of you. I think people are always willing to accept some parts of you. But finding a person who sees you as you are, sees *all* of you, and wants you nonetheless..."

Knees draw under my chin as I wrap my arms around them.

"Trust me, Eric, I do get it. Not all of it. I haven't been through nearly what you have. But it's hard to find someone who likes to see *me* unmasked."

He cocks his head. "Explain."

And I do. I run him through how my mom expects a perfect, homesteading daughter, who can give birth to her several grandbabies.

"If she saw the photos I do for fun with Raph, or if I auditioned for regional theaters—the ones that don't do family-friendly shows like *Cinderella*—I don't think she'd like that version of me."

"What about Raph?" A bite rests in his voice. "Doesn't he like all of you?"

A chuckle bobbles in my throat. "Trust me, we'd tried the dating thing. Turns out, we're both just not attracted to each other. We're pretty much brother and sister at this point. Just making our parents think we're into each other, so they won't arrange marriages for us with other people."

Thumbs chase each other around in circles. I still my hands on his.

"You think I'm jealous, huh?" He leans closer. "Does that," he whispers, "make us something then? If I'm being protective of you?"

I take in his minty breath and hold myself back from kissing him right here.

True to Meg's word, he was serious about this. As long as we didn't have to slip a ring on our left finger in the coming months, maybe we could explore this...

"Would you like it to?"

In reply, he presses his forehead against mine.

"Can't imagine anything better."

CHAPTER 21

M y alarm doesn't go off the next morning. And when I
check my phone, I see why.

Forgot to plug it into the charger last night.

Every part of me buzzed after Eric and I made ourselves official, and shared several more kisses in the basement of the theater. No wonder I didn't have half a mind to revive my phone last night.

Mom blitzed my device with a million messages and calls. At least, I imagine she did so. Unless I send her updates every few hours, she'll leave several voicemails.

"Welp." I set the phone down on the nightstand and plug it into the charger. At zero percent, it won't show me any notifications any time soon. "That's probably for the best."

Sores run up and down my body. Maybe Meg would relent and let us skip the morning workout we tended to do on practice days. Often, she knocks on my door to tell me to go to the hotel gym downstairs. We'd take showers after, in our own rooms, to wash off the sweat before heading to the ground floor restaurant.

Maybe if I beat her to the punch and get a table, she won't make me do burpees.

Carmen's thoughts on librettos be darned, every opera singer needed days off.

I crumple the sheets as I roll out of bed and head to the bathroom. Splash warm water on my face and run my fingers up and down it with moisturizer.

As I towel off my cheeks, I stare into the mirror.

"Good Lord, I have a boyfriend, don't I?"

Sparks ignite like firecrackers in my stomach once more. I don't know if I can down any breakfast. Why did this both feel exciting and scary?

Taking a long swig from Lenny, I set him down on the dresser and finish getting ready. I pull on a crop top and athletic shorts. Even if they didn't need me at rehearsal today—depending on how fast Carmen recovered—they'd likely have me help out in other areas. Clamping in spotlights into the rafters or climbing up ladders to hang pieces required athletic wear.

I rush into the hallway, before Meg could exit her door and knock on mine, and into the elevator.

Chlorine punches me in the nostrils as I pass by the pool and dart toward the hotel restaurant. The waitress stationed at the front eyes my stomach, and lines on her forehead furrow.

Don't care.

We've officially entered the rebellious Tina phase. Next, I might get a cartilage piercing or, gasp, dye my hair. Could never go as far as to get a tattoo, though. Mom may boot me out of the family in that case.

She leads me to a table and sets down a menu in front of me.

"What will we be having this morning?"

"Can you tell me which product has the *most* dairy?"

"Most?"

Her pen taps against her notepad. She's probably gotten strange questions before, but never like this. A fountain behind her burbles. A koi pond river snakes around the tables at the restaurant, protected by a glass pathway.

"I suppose the omelets tend to have the most milk used in them."

"One of those, please. With mushrooms, and cheese. Oh, goodness, give me all the cheese."

"Extra cheese. Got it. Anything to drink?"

Milk would be overkill. "Coffee, please?"

Antonia insisted we stay on a water-only drinking diet, allowing the occasional Gatorade for Meg and her fainting spells. Coffee would give us acid reflux.

But they likely wouldn't make me sing today. Carmen seems like the type to hold onto her parts with a death grip.

Much like Matilda.

Once, our theater put on a production of *Peter Pan*. I got the understudy of Wendy and didn't get the chance to test out the flight equipment. Screamed the first time they hoisted me in the air. No surprise that the director's daughter, Matilda, played the lead.

One night, Matilda came in with a cough that sounded like she'd garbled glass. Sore throat, drippy nose, the whole shebang. Although the entire cast and crew encouraged her to go home and let Tina play Wendy *for one night* while she recovered, she refused. Red-nosed, she marched onto stage and belted the songs.

By the end of the first two numbers, she lost her voice. So she spoke the rest of the lyrics. That night, being closing night, she still never let me have a shot at the role.

Come to think of it...why did *Carmen* go back to the hotel yesterday?

Vomit must've surged nonstop. The only explanation for her to rescind her role to a hated enemy.

Minutes later, the waitress returns with a steaming omelet. I stab my fork into it and saw off a piece with a knife. Eyeing the entrance to the restaurant, I shove the wad into my mouth. Cheesy goodness explodes on my tongue.

Oh, dairy, I missed you.

As I make my way through the breakfast, I scan the restaurant. No familiar faces from the cast or crew emerge. Huh. Meg was always a be-on-time type of person. Maybe she slept in?

I didn't go with the cast to their outing last night. They headed to some river state park.

Body sore and not in the mood for hiking, I let them go do their thing.

Crumpling my cloth napkin onto the table, I shove my chair back and return to the elevator. Antonia could've texted everyone and bumped the practice time. Hope explodes in me. What if she canceled practice altogether?

Nah, can't get them up that high.

When I get to my door, the green light beeps when I slide my keycard in and out. I click the door handle down and step into the room. My chest seizes.

Another rose on my dresser.

Ginger steps approach the closet, first. If someone has access to another keycard, they could be lurking. I shove the door open and skid back. No one, except for the dress from the ball I have yet to return. Let's pray Edna didn't notice its absence.

After a sweep through the bathroom, I determine the room empty. Time to read the note.

"'Does he love you so much? He would commit murder for me.'"

Murder stirs up sourness in my stomach. Cheese threatens to launch up my throat and expel into the toilet.

Carmen mentioned threatening notes. Did someone have it out for me too? Would they kill us both?

Breaths become ragged, shallow.

I don't know how I get back to the bed, but seconds later, I find myself perched on the edge of it. A knock at the door stifles a scream in my throat. I have enough sense to shut my lips in time to trap it.

I shouldn't open it, right?

The knuckles rap again, more persistent this time.

Not here, not here, not here. I take in my open suitcase and scavenge the items, with my eyes, for some kind of weapon.

"Tina?"

Raph's voice expels all air from my lungs. *Oh, thank God.*

Shoving myself from the bed, I twist down the handle and open the door.

Paleness covers his skin. "You haven't been answering your texts."

I wave him in and slam the door shut. For good measure, I click the second lock. Once I jerk the door, to make sure that sucker won't open before I say so, I return to Raph and gesture at the wall charger.

"Battery died. Forgot to plug it in last night."

"Then you don't know?"

A fist clenches around my stomach. Eyes dart to the rose. "Know what?"

"Carmen, she..." He rubs the back of his neck with his palm. "You know how she went home sick last night? Wasn't feeling good."

Bile rises into my throat. "Mhmm?"

"I think she had an allergic reaction or something. Maybe to those brownies, but just didn't tell anyone. Must not have thought it was serious enough for a hospital. Or was too sick to get away from the toilet but—"

His neck stoops to the floor.

"—she passed away this morning. She wasn't responding to knocks on the door so Antonia got a spare key from downstairs and...found her."

Passed away. Died.

Holy crap, someone else died.

"Tina, they're canceling *Gianni Schicchi*, and possibly the rest of the season."

I don't hear what else he says after that. Because my ears fill with ringing.

CHAPTER 22

They encourage us to stay in our rooms for the next few days and just order service.

I pick at smoked salmon as Raph texts me updates. Put the group chat on mute because I don't think I can take one more "wow, this is so heartbreaking <crying emoji>" text.

Raph: Autopsy did find trace amounts of nuts in her system. Maybe it triggered the reaction.

I, however, suspected poison. It acts the same way that an allergic reaction can. Antonia says that when she found Carmen this morning, the girl's skin had turned blue. Upside to autopsies is, they can trace poison. But they won't look for it unless told to.

Raph: Doesn't look like we're going to be called in by the police.

Can only imagine the ire from online communities. All the Carmen supporters must demand blood. Raph tells me not to check any social media. Not that I'm on social media apps a lot, anyway. Just have accounts on some to like the occasional posts Raph puts up.

The police part surprises me. But as far as they can tell, the chef made a mistake. He must not have paid careful attention to her allergy sheet. Or got hers mixed up with others.

I'm sure he swears he double-checked.

I'm sure he blames it on some assistant who deposited the brownies into the basket in Carmen's dressing room.

I'm sure some annoyed worker told her, "Yes, it doesn't have nuts, now stop asking," since she liked to hound them. It's the same reason why people died on roller coasters when ride operators did the same boring tasks, dealing with the same entitled people.

Raph never informs me what happens to the chef. Part of me doesn't want to know.

Raph: Emergency cast meeting, happening in the lobby.

Although Raph isn't technically in "the cast," Antonia knows to keep him updated. That I don't use my phone all that much and might miss updates. She considers Raph "one of the family" at this point.

My fork dings against the plate as I drop it. Here, on a Friday, a day away from our departure, Roger pulls us into a meeting. Probably to tell us to go home, that they may cut part of our funds for the season.

I'll take it.

Long as Eric and I can stay in touch after, I want to get as far away from this family as possible.

A twinge of guilt bites my stomach. I've not spoken to him in the past few days. Most of the time I drifted between sleep and binging shows on the TV, to get my mind off of Carmen.

Stumbling to my closet, I slip on a pair of flip-flops and rub the circles underneath my eyes. They'd take me without makeup today whether they liked it or not. Armpit sniff. *Yeesh, could use deodorant.*

Coconut clear antiperspirant slicked on, I exit into the hallway and almost bump into someone. I stagger back, take him in. Eric.

"Sorry."

"Hey." He spread-eagles his arms. I collapse into his chest in a long hug. We do an awkward sway back and forth. "Doing okay, Tina?"

"No." Itchiness covers my eyes. "I know we weren't the biggest fans of her, but—"

Lumps form in my throat.

Back in middle school, one of my theater camp counselors caught a rare form of leukemia. We attended her funeral in a large megachurch. As the pastor spoke from Psalm 27, I reached for the tissue box stationed at the end of the pew.

Tears cascaded for several minutes.

I hardly knew her.

Death does that to people. Turns them into martyrs, loved ones—even if they were total strangers or enemies when alive.

"I know, darling." He kisses the crown of my head, lopes an arm on my shoulder, and guides me to the elevator. "I know."

It bothers me that his voice doesn't sound like broken glass, like mine.

People grieve differently, I remind myself.

Karim and Meg spot us when we step off. They've huddled onto one of the couches. The cast bubbles around the furniture and fake fireplace in the lobby.

Meg pats the seat beside her. Only enough room for about one and a half backsides. Eric sits first and taps his thighs with his fingers. Understanding, I position myself on top of him and prop my legs up on Meg's knees.

Warmth from behind grounds me. I enjoy the feeling of his breath on my neck. It reminds me, too, to breathe.

Roger waits for a few stragglers to join the crowd. I spy Raph bunched near the fake fireplace, not operational during the summer months. It strikes me as odd that a Florida hotel would even have one of these. Then again, maybe it's the type where the embers glow, but no heat emanates from it.

By instinct, I shrink any time Roger lurks near.

Bloodshot veins must still cover my eyes, like they had when I last checked the mirror. I want him to look at me. To feel my hatred. To know that I know what he did.

At long last, Annika squishes herself in an open gap between two sopranos sitting on the carpet.

"Thank you all for joining us. As you may know, our group chat has been flooded with messages, so I didn't want the information in this meeting to get buried underneath the texts."

Wonder if anyone else muted that conversation.

Roger presses himself against a brick column. Visitors to the hotel whizz by, rolling suitcases behind them.

Antonia rises from her place on a chair, a lacy top billowing in nonexistent wind. I imagine that sort of white clothing piece would work well over a bathing suit. "Before we dive into any of that, I was wondering if we could do something in memory of Carmen."

Everyone recoils.

Antonia must not have warned Roger about this detour in the meeting, because his lips form a thin line.

Not wanting to offend, nods pass around the circle.

"I'll begin. And there is no expectation to contribute. We are all still processing." Antonia fiddles with tassels on the lacy cover-up. "Carmen was extremely talented. She had a beautiful singing voice and enchanted audiences everywhere. One of my favorite memories with her was when I watched her sign the program of a little girl. The girl said Carmen looked like a princess, and Carmen returned the compliment. Saying that the little girl, too, could one day grace the stage. And that, 'I can't wait to see you shine up there.'"

Antonia presses a hand to her chest, voice crackling in her throat.

"It reminded me of when I went to my first opera. And the soprano told me something similar. I think we all had a moment like that. Where someone, a hero, told us we could sing, and we believed them."

Nods pass around the circle.

When Dad took me to my first opera, I swear the lead soprano probably spotted stars in my eyes when I shook her hand after. She, too, told me she couldn't wait to watch my debut on stage.

I wonder if she held true to that and would watch me in one of my performances with this troupe.

Fuzziness fills my stomach at the memory Antonia spoke of. I wish I knew this version of Carmen. The one who inspired little girls. The one who got fangirls so invested in her career, that they would defend her to the death in Tennessee rapids.

"Who is next?"

Silence cloaks us for the next few moments. Then Annika raised her hand. Antonia gestures at her to speak.

"Well, I appreciated how she was really gung-ho about us being serious about opera. She was always willing to run lines with me backstage. There are a few in Schicchi that the notary says that I just can't get down and—"

The last few words come out watery.

"—and I can't believe it's over. And I can't believe she's gone."

Annika buries her face into her knees. One of the girls beside her runs a hand up and down her back.

Some of the other cast members share vague memories with Carmen. Having spent a mere handful of days with us, we struggle to dredge up something. I don't speak. Every part of her death feels like my fault.

Once an uncomfortable amount of quiet shrouds us after the last story, Roger takes advantage and pushes himself from the wall.

"Thank you, Antonia, for letting us share those wonderful memories. And I'm afraid I'm to be the bad guy with our segue from here."

Automatic doors slide open at the front. Warm air plumes inside.

Roger continues.

"As you all may know, we have canceled all performances of *Schicchi*. For respect of our fellow cast mate, and to give you all time to grieve."

Anger bubbles under my skin. Good thing Eric's belted me to his chest with his arm, or I may launch myself at this guy and go down swinging.

"I believe a funeral will be held for Carmen back at her hometown. You are welcome to make travel arrangements to go see her during that time. We are more than happy to book a flight out to Nashville."

Annika raises her hand. Blotchiness covers her cheeks.

"Wouldn't we just drive back to Nashville? Isn't that cheaper?"

"Good question, Annika. The funeral will be held next week, and we will not be here next week, which leads me to my next point of the meeting."

The heels of his shoes click against the tile. For such a short man, it makes sense why he'd wear footwear that gave him an extra boost of height.

"In memory of Carmen, we have decided to put on her favorite opera. She mentioned, in her initial audition video, that she enjoyed the music from this. And we'd like to dedicate all future performances to her. Instead of putting on *Tosca*, we will be performing *Phantom of the Opera*."

Gasps and wide eyes exchange around the circle.

"I know most of this group performed it this past winter. So it will be a matter of refreshing everyone on the choreography and music. We will have three weeks to do so."

My brows furrow.

What's this guy's end game?

Why did he *really* want to put on Phantom?

Memories skitter back to a conversation I had with Temperance during one of our late-night rehearsals. She complained about the score from *Sound of Music.*

"It's really the *Sound of Money* if you ask me." She hmphed and hugged her piccolo close to her hip. "Directors always do shows like those when they need more audience members or good PR."

Bingo, good PR.

Even if they didn't look super in-depth into Carmen's autopsy, fans of Carmen would claim we tried to kill her. Poison her. Slip her food allergens.

And they'd be right.

Putting on a show like *Phantom* could distract people long enough that they could forget about the mysterious death.

In my periphery, Meg's hand shoots up.

"What about the people who haven't performed? Karim and I were Phantom and Christine last time. Same parts?"

"We were actually thinking"—Roger jerks his head in Antonia's direction—"that Tina and Eric could fill in for those parts."

Eric and I both flinch at the same time.

Boom, there it is. People online have clamored for ages for Eric to play the Phantom. Bred for the part, or, well, burned for the part.

"And you and Karim will play Madame Giry and Raul. Since we had other actors fill in for those roles last time."

Surprising, because the family tends to cast its own. But maybe they'd decided to play it dangerous last winter.

"Those unfamiliar with the show will spend the weeks rehearsing together. As for the rest, you will help us to construct set pieces that we will transport to our first theater in which we'll perform. Are there any questions?"

Flurries of arms fly into the air.

The next several minutes pass into a blur as I run through the scores in my head. Christine, although a dream role, would be difficult to tackle in a few weeks.

Tension pounds my temples.

I excuse myself to my room before the meeting ends. Don't hear the elevator ding nor the click to get into my room. Just the smoosh of the pillows as I let them engulf my face.

Several minutes later, someone knocks.

A sharp gasp from me. I still can't get over the fact that the same person who left roses on my dresser could pay me a visit. Carmen did, after all, receive threats. Then met her end.

Perched on my tiptoes, I peek through the peephole.

Raph bobbles on his ankles in the hallway. I swing open the door.

"Mom's going to kill you when she finds out how often you keep going into my room."

He glides inside and closes it.

"How did the rest of the meeting go, Raph?"

"Don't know. Roger was going on and on about the importance of minding your surroundings in new theaters. And about how someone last year got a concussion from banging their head into a pole. I tuned the rest of it out."

"Speaking of Roger."

I spot the rose on the dresser.

Room service didn't get to my room yet. Two fingers pinch the stem, and I hold it up for him to see.

"Roger left me another one. Read the note. That's a literal murder confession, right?"

"It looks bad. Except for the fact that it probably comes from *Phantom of the Opera*."

"What? Really?"

"Yeah, I've been looking up all the quotes. Most are from the book. I think one was from the opera itself. It doesn't exactly say, 'I just killed Carmen, and my name is Roger Firmin,' though."

Shoulders slump, I set the rose stem back onto the counter. Dew drops from the plant rest on my fingers.

"Also, Tina, I'm not totally sure that Roger is our guy."

Too stunned to speak, I slacken. Then I take a breath. "What?"

"C'mere. I spotted something on his Instagram page that I think you want to see."

He pulls up the app and taps on the photo, one with the woman and the violin.

"I met her at the ball. Turns out that she's Roger's wife, and plays in the pit with us at all the shows."

Huh. I take the phone from him and gaze at her picture. She did seem familiar to me. We don't interact with the pit much. They spend intermission in their lounge, playing poker on a green felt table

"Swipe the photo, though, there's a second one."

Following his instructions, I do. In the second picture, she cradles a bundle of red roses.

"When I saw him clipping the stems in his office, I guess it was for his wife."

Dizziness overtakes me. I perch at the head of the bed and hug a pillow against my stomach.

That can't be right. As manager, Roger has hiring power, the ability to replicate hotel keys without us knowing, motive for getting rid of the last guy...

What about Carmen? The thought niggles my skull.

She felt like a wild card no one in the cast or crew prepared for. Did Roger get rid of her to tie up some sort of loose end?

And if not him, who?

"Listen, Raph, even if he cuts roses for his wife, that doesn't mean he can't *also* put them in people's rooms. He could multitask, you know."

"And look super guilty in the process?"

"I don't know. It's one thing against a mountain of evidence and motive. We should probably still suspect him."

"Dunno, Tina." He meanders to the curtains and runs his fingers up and down the translucent fabric. "After I talked with his wife, he seems like a down-to-earth guy. Has massive social anxiety, which is why we don't see him most of the time."

So what if his wife gave him the stamp of approval? "Most serial killer's spouses don't suspect them, you know. They've been known to think of their husbands, or wives, as upstanding, hardworking people. The murders tend to catch them by surprise, too."

"This isn't a true crime podcast, Tina." His voice rises. Veins bulge in his neck. It takes a lot to get someone like Raph angry. "This is real life."

"I'm *sorry,* but do you not know what the *true* part of *true* crime means?"

Redness creeps up my throat. I can feel the intense heat of it. I ball my fist and rise from the bed, stalking toward him.

"And if you don't think it's Roger, then pray tell, who do you think it is?"

"Easy. Eric."

This stops me short.

I blink, several times, to make sure I heard him right.

"Are *you* crazy?"

"Listen." Curtains ripple underneath his brush of them as he turns to me, hands splayed. "When it comes to Carmen, he has significantly more motive. He couldn't stand her, she unmasked him in front of you, *and* she threatened you. You can't be dumb enough to not realize how possessive he is of you."

"Possessive? He's my fricken boyfriend. Of course, he's going to be *protective.*"

My shrieks die in my throat. Many of the opera singers border our rooms, and I don't want them picking up any of our fight. My voice drops to a hiss.

"You've been weird about him from the start. Is it because he has a facial deformity? So that makes him easy to scapegoat?"

Raph swears and rubs a hand across his eyes. Putting space between us, he roves over to the closet.

"Of course, not, Tina. But you have to realize you've let certain things blind you to the fact that he still could've done it."

"What? And you've been *so* unbiased with Antonia? With Karim and the fact that you and he both like Boba Fett or something?"

He mumbles something.

"What?"

"*Jango* Fett."

"Whatever, Raph. Point is that you're not blameless here either. And I still think Roger makes the most sense in this situation. If not him, Meg and Karim next for sure. The person with the *least* amount of evidence or motive is Eric."

"I'm not having this conversation when you're like this."

He turns on his heel and advances to the door.

"Like what? Like a reasonable detective?"

"Like a pining girlfriend."

With that, he swings open the door and bangs it shut.

CHAPTER 23

"Tina, c'mere." Meg waves me over to the seat beside her on the bus. Sparse trees blur past as we make our way into Tallahassee, en route to Louisiana. "Can you keep a secret?"

My heart catapults into my throat.

I choke on the pulse and nod. As I do, she pulls up a Pinterest app and clicks on a wedding board labeled, "Something Borrowed...from Every Other Pinterest User."

Cute.

In the seat across from me, Karim crunches on a bag of Bugles. Right before we left this morning, we made a pit stop at the theater to drop off our costumes we borrowed from Edna. Karim snatched several chip bags from the kitchen. They litter the carpeted floor beneath him.

"Karim and I weren't originally supposed to get married until winter, but—"

Her breath hitches, tone sounding nervous.

"—as it would seem, we may be pulling off a wedding in Las Vegas."

Week two of *Phantom*.

"Is it going to be in one of those Elvis churches?"

She snorts. "No. But it will be eloping, technically. So Antonia is seeing what all she can gather for us at the next theater. May help us with some pergola pieces, in between building the sets for *Phantom*."

Ah yes, *Phantom*. So many questions plagued my mind about that opera.

Tina's 2 A.M. Ponderings about *Phantom of the Opera*.

1. **How did they get the rights to the show so quickly?** Yes, they'd performed it the previous winter. But according to our community theater director, you have to schedule these things in advance and make sure theaters nearby aren't putting on the same show. Granted, a prestigious group like the Daaés could probably get an exception. Still...

2. **How could the cast pull everything together in three weeks?** Even if ninety-five percent of the cast knows the choreography, and needs just a refresher, musicals take a minimum of eight weeks to learn in the community theater setting. We put in at least one hundred hours into each one. Of course, we do forty-plus-hour weeks as a troupe. Math maybe factored out to be the same in this case.

3. **How did Eric feel about putting on this type of show?** No doubt people made comparisons between him and the lead all the time. Even I did at first. But does he

hate the Phantom? Wish that people wouldn't compare him to a psychopath and murderer?

Many more plagued me, but those three resurfaced the most.

The glow from Meg's phone brings me back to reality. She taps on a photo of a dress with long sleeves and lace needlework.

"Since I won't have time to do a fitting, I pinned a few dresses from stores in Vegas. I tend to fit sample sizes, so thankfully there won't need to be alterations."

I think back to Temperance.

Would she wear her mother's gown, like she'd vowed to do during our freshman year? Would she fit it? Didn't most dress places need six-plus months to make any alterations?

"Help me pick out a favorite?"

The question dies in Meg's throat. Her voice comes out downtrodden, instead of giddy.

"You doing okay?"

"Just nervous, I guess." She pastes on a smile. "I hear some brides can get post-nuptial depression and all that. Not everyone is super excited for the big day. And that's normal."

I flick a glance at the seat adjacent to me. Eric reads through the libretto for *Phantom* that they handed us last night. Guess they kept copies of that script lying around. Although it seems like a hassle to transport. Another question that kept me awake at night.

He eyes me over the top of the book and smiles.

Returning his expression, I turn back to Meg and muse about how I would feel if I got married to Eric. Maybe I'd feel as nervous as Meg did. She and Karim didn't even know each other for a year before their upcoming marriage.

But also, Temperance beamed with giddy glee when talking about Dustin.

Everyone's different.

And sadly, Meg could've caught on to Karim's cheating. Maybe she's upset about marrying him after that.

"I'm trying to decide between this A-line and this mermaid."

She swipes back and forth between two saved pins.

"Hmm, from what I can remember from every wedding dress show Mom and I watched,"—and believe me, she made me partake in quite a few. Probably to remind her daughter about "what's really important in life." —"Mermaids can be hard to walk in, and you need to be pretty tall to pull them off."

"Yeah."

Meg's hands run up and down her thighs.

"Don't think I have enough hip for that type of dress anyway. Thanks, Tina. Let's move on to the color scheme and flowers, okay?"

For a good five hours, we debated on the final elements for the elopement.

Then, over dinner, Meg picked my brain about what I'd want at my own wedding.

We arrive in Louisiana, and somehow the heat was even worse than in Florida. Crickets chirp as we head into the hotel. Don't even get a chance to flick on the room light before I crash into the bed.

Bright and early on Monday, Antonia calls me and Eric into rehearsal an hour early. So would be the schedule, six days a week, for the next three weeks. Roger emailed us the plan last night. Thank goodness my alarm blared this morning. Otherwise, I may have missed the first bus ride to the theater.

Schedule

8 A.M. Breakfast and a brief workout

9 A.M. Eric and Tina called in to do warm-ups and begin scene work

10 A.M. The rest of the cast arrives and starts to work on the sets

11 A.M. Eric and Tina work on songs together

12 P.M. Lunch break

1 P.M.-3 P.M. Eric and Tina continue to do scene work or whatever is needed that afternoon

3 P.M.-4 P.M. Break where the cast can go outside for fresh air, and also catch up for anything else needed to be learned.

4 P.M. Eric and Tina help the others with the set

5 P.M. Final notes

6 P.M. Leave for dinner

Meg and Karim, new to their parts, join us this morning. Karim complains about how he doesn't know if he can hit Raul's notes well.

"Yes, I can hit tenor range." He holds open the glass doors to the theater for us. "But I'm really a baritone."

On the other hand, Meg called her drop from high soprano to mezzo a "blessing."

"Seriously, I think I was the worst Christine ever. There were probably so many judgy people in the audience wondering if I'd pass out from that high E."

Antonia sends Meg and Karim into a practice room with a piano.

She pulls us into another large windowless classroom and has us begin on the scene where Christine rips off the phantom's mask. Odd place to start. But I know that in both theater and film, people tend to do scene work out of order.

Fingertips shake as I reach for the half mask he wears today, scarlet instead of phantom white. My arms balk.

"Don't be shy about it, Tina." Antonia sips from a Styrofoam cup. String from a tea bag pokes out of the hole in the cup's lid. A faint mint scent wisped from the vessel before she capped it earlier. *What I wouldn't give for a little honey tea right now.* "Christine has to be forceful about this. Deliberate."

Hands clasp together.

"Quick question before we run this. Will the audience see Eric's real face for this?"

In my periphery, I catch his stare. No sense, from this angle, in determining if his expression went soft from gratitude or something else.

"I suppose so, yes."

Eric recoils. I spot him shrinking into his hoodie.

"Antonia, if I may." I step forward in front of him, as if shielding him. "Although Eric unmasked himself for me." Not by choice, but by force. "I don't know if he feels comfortable doing so in front of thousands of strangers. Isn't it his decision to reveal himself or not?"

"The boy can speak. Eric?"

His chin buckles into his neck. When his stare meets mine, his face hardens, in resolve, I believe.

"Yeah, Mom, to be honest, I'm not the most comfortable with it. Maybe hair and makeup can do prosthetics or something?"

Antonia pinches her brows as she sips again.

She sets the cup down on a lidded piano and sweeps her arm toward the door.

"I believe someone from the hair and makeup department is here. Ask her what is possible."

Even if that particular person—the hair and makeup staff member—won't be with us for the rest of tour, they can give us some pointers.

We both mutter a thanks and bolt into the hallway. Eric squeezes my shoulder from behind.

"Thanks."

"It's your secret to reveal. No one should force you to before you're ready."

No Carmen should ever snatch that opportunity away from us.

My stomach twists as I think of both Carmen and Raph as we meander down the red-carpeted hallways.

Raph and I didn't leave our conversation on good terms.

He slumped in the back of the bus and scrolled on his phone for hours. Once that died, he feigned sleep. How do I know he faked it? Because Raph snores like nobody's business. Discovered this on a long tech weeknight in our community theater back in the day.

And on the bus, he didn't even so much as labor heavy breaths.

As for Carmen...

No, nausea climbs into my throat every time her face flashes before my eyes. Guilt knots my insides because I won't attend her funeral. Seems like a disservice to her family if *I* show up.

We duck into the hair and makeup room.

Vintage bulbs glitter around rectangular mirrors. A woman with white and blue split-tone hair washes makeup brushes in the sink, next to the restrooms. Foamy shampoo coats her fingers.

She glances up at us over blocky rimmed, pink glasses.

"Hi, can I help you?"

I explain the situation from the practice room.

"I guess what we're trying to figure out is, is it possible to put prosthetics on skin that has been burned?"

"Depends."

She shoves her hands underneath a power dryer. Hums plague the air for the next several seconds. She gives up on the drying efforts and pats her hands on her jeans.

"Does the skin hurt if you touch it?"

I glance at Eric. He shakes his head.

The hair and makeup woman approaches him, talons outstretched. I catch a whiff of hairspray as she passes me. Her arms seize back and she motions to her own face. "Do you mind if I—?"

Eric sucks in a long breath and lets it out, until all of him deflates.

"Yes, go ahead."

With ginger movements, she peels off the mask. Keeps her expression cool, stony. This causes Eric's shoulders to relax. If anyone got the "don't judge others" principle down, it was theater people.

She asks permission once more to touch his face, and he allows her.

Doesn't wince as her fingers move up and down the grooves.

Then she hands him back the mask. In a hasty motion, he slips the thing back onto his face.

"Yes, it *is* possible to do prosthetics. But we'll probably have to do a few practice runs and send instructions to the hair and makeup crew at the theaters you'll perform *Phantom* in. Also." She motioned at the mask. "You're going to have to get a new one made, to fit the contouring. We can probably make a cast here."

She informs me all about petroleum jelly and the benefits of creating a bloody look on stage. I walk away from the conversation knowing way too much about foam latex.

Eric laces his hand in mine in the hallway and doesn't let go until Antonia makes us run through the scene again.

In the hotel lobby that evening, our group makes plans to check out a Cajun restaurant in the area. Meg goes on and on about the boudin in the elevator ride upstairs.

"Also, Miss Maid of Honor." She wags her fingers at me as we step off. We dodge around a silver room service tray outside someone's door. Seafood scents from it gurgle my stomach. "We still have a few details to work out about the wedding. Thought of a few things after the bus ride."

"I'm your maid of honor now?"

"Chica, why did you think we were going over details on the bus ride?"

I shrug, and she cackles.

"Don't you want someone else to be your maid of honor? You have a million family members in this troupe, you know."

Sisters in my extended family would kill if they didn't get the coveted "maid" or "matron of honor" title.

"Oh, Tina." She squeezes my elbow and digs into her pockets for her key card. "Don't you know that you're practically a Daaé by this point?"

That sours my stomach.

Meg vanishes into her room, and I enter mine. My heart wilts against my ribcage, like a popped balloon, when I see it.

Three items now rest on my dresser. A rose, a note...and a small box?

Waves of nausea hit me, and suddenly Cajun sounds like the worst idea in the world.

Per tradition when dealing with Roger's—or whoever's—note. Someone could've slipped out during rehearsal to stick these items in my room. During lunch today, everyone took a ride back to the hotel to check out the restaurant's options downstairs. Plenty of people excused themselves to use the restroom then.

Fingers shake as I hold up the letter to me.

"When a woman has seen me, as you have, she belongs to me. She loves me forever."

A *Phantom* quote, probably from the book, no doubt. Like the others. No energy swirls in me to fact-check on Google.

My pulse spikes as I turn my attention to the small box. I slide it out of its case. Velvet brushes my fingertips.

This can't be good.

I flip open the lid and gasp.

An engagement ring with a ruby red stone encircled with diamonds rests inside. In the fabric of the box, gold letters etch out, in cursive.

"*Be mine.*"

CHAPTER 24

S o yeah, we don't put *that* on.

For one, I can't get engaged to someone if I don't know who that someone is.

Secondly, I can't get engaged in general. I'm *eighteen* and not ready for that.

Tremors overtake my arms. I set the box down and return to the note. Air from the AC unit cools my flaming cheeks.

"When a woman has seen me, as you have, she belongs to me. She loves me forever.'"

Eric.

I know it in my gut that this refers to Eric.

Much as I like to yell at Raph for his hunches—as they make poor detective work—I can't deny the intuitive feeling that someone wants me to get engaged to Eric Daaé.

Screw it.

I punch the quote into Google. Sure enough, it hails from the novel version of *Phantom,* and not the opera.

Raph's warning rests in the back of my mind. What if Eric had been leaving all of these notes? Known to slip around the theater like a vapor, he could steal keycards, roses, trail mix brownies from the kitchens—the non-allergy-friendly kind.

Deep breath.

Easy there, girl. You can't jump to conclusions without enough evidence first.

Sure, Eric didn't like Carmen. And sure, he liked me a lot, enough to tell me he'd take care of certain situations. That didn't make him a murderer.

Auditory memory blurs back to the night of my and Raph's fight.

"Most serial killer's spouses don't suspect them, you know."

Did I fall into that category?

I shake my head and glimpse the quote again. Something tells me I need to read up on the original *Phantom* book, to figure out what I've been missing.

A knock at the door forces a sharp gasp out of my throat. I stuff the items into the top drawer of the dresser, next to my socks, and race to the door. Meg stands in the frame when I open it.

"Hey, we're ready to head out for dinner. You coming with?"

Ants crawl under my skin. After the encounter with the rose and the ring, I don't think I want to people for a few hours. "Actually, do you know if there's a library nearby? Might want to do some research for the play. Tablework, you know."

She surveys me for a second.

"Okey-dokey then. I think there's actually one a few blocks away. Need your chaperone to get you there safely?"

Ah yes, Raph. Even though he's accompanied us on tour, he feels more and more distant. Unlike our community theater, he can't join the cast in most activities—except for meals.

Am I pushing him away?

If so, why? Because the Daaé family has enveloped me as one of their own? And excluded him?

Often, in co-op, we talked about people drifting away after graduation. Had Raph and I started this? We dreaded if this would happen, swore to each other that we'd maintain our friendship forever.

And if Eric and I stay together, will that forever shove my best friend away?

No wonder he felt prickles of anger around Eric. I'd get frustrated, too, if someone stole my friend from me.

Despite myself, I force a smile. "I'm going to be fine. Location's shared with him, so he'll know where I am."

"Suit yourself. Make sure to eat something though. Rehearsals are going to be brutal for the next few weeks."

Tell me about it. Soreness coats my muscles, laces my marrow. Not a single part of me doesn't ache for sleep.

I give the group ten minutes to load up on the bus and head to the restaurant. Then I bolt downstairs. Sun bakes my calves on the sidewalk as I follow my GPS to the library.

Squat brick buildings greet me as I traverse the streets. Everything about this place reads small town, much like where I hail from. It tickles me that they stuck a large opera house in this place, but then I think of Blossom Music Center in Ohio. Literally in the middle of the Metro Parks, smack in the middle of nowhere, famous artists perform concerts at that venue.

Glass doors glitter in the sunshine as I pad up the slanted sidewalk to the library entrance.

Everything about the building looks new. A quick Google search tells me that up until a couple years ago, the town only had a parish library to its name.

Metal singes my hands as I yank open the door and step inside. A gust of AC causes an involuntary gasp.

The library's hours are plastered on both sides of the glass door. I have less than an hour.

Wasting no time, I charge toward a circular desk of computers and plug the title into the database. Top floor, classics section, got it.

Footsteps pound up the carpeted stairs to the second floor. I mill through a labyrinth of shelves until I pinpoint the black cover. My finger nudges it out and I run my hands up the plastic on top of the cover.

Neck craning to the right, I spot a study room. No one inside.

I shut myself inside and flick on the lights. Rolling chairs conference around a polished, round table. Above them, a TV is hoisted onto the wall. And on the other wall, a whiteboard contains the ghost etchings of meetings past. Someone drew Garfield the cat in green Expo marker.

The chair nearest to that board calls my name. I park in it and open the book.

"It was the evening in which MM. Debienne and Poligny—"

Buzzes erupt from my bag. Butterflying the book on the table, I open my phone and see a new email from an unknown address. "OperaLife777@gmail.com."

Someone from the cast?

The subject line reads: CHOOSE

Not foreboding at all.

When I click on the message, no paragraph body exists inside of the email. Instead, two pictures of flower bouquets—red and gold in tones—appear on screen. Huh, so Meg couldn't wait to talk with me about wedding stuff after all.

After I save the email address in my contacts under Meg, I hit reply.

"Pretty sure you wanted to go with a different color scheme, but I like the second bouquet. The red and gold roses are going to catch everyone's eyes as you go down the aisle. Excited :)"

Send.

Okay, time to return to the book.

"—the managers of the Opera were giving a last gala perfor-mance—"

Once again, my phone vibrates. A groan passes through my nostrils as I pull up another email from Meg, same subject line. This time, two photographs of cakes appear. One with a golden drip down the side. Another with piped scarlet roses.

Once more, I reply.

*"So, Meg, you *do* realize that we're going to be spending a couple more weeks in rehearsals together, right? We have plenty of time when we're in person to talk over these. But if you must know, I like*

the drip cake. I don't think I've ever seen one done in gold piping before. But seriously, girl, we can talk another time."

A whoosh sounds from my phone as the email zips off to its destination. No sooner do I pick up the book than yet another message from Meg plops into my inbox.

Now, it strikes me as strange she wouldn't text me. Most of the time, she would send messages in our group text. On rare occasions, individual texts to me.

Could've caught on to the fact that I tend to check emails more, and put most texts on mute, after the Carmen situation.

CHOOSE.

Two pictures of wedding dresses inhabit the body of the email. Odd, because these look nothing like the styles she showed me on the bus. Way too old-fashioned for Meg, these gowns boast long trumpet sleeves, ruffles, and lace in just about every place.

Brides, stressed, changed their minds, though.

Once again, I reply.

"A forewarning, but I'm about to turn my phone on mute. Feel free to talk with me about all of this stuff at the hotel. In terms of the dresses, they're both beautiful. I think the one with the flowy sleeves catches my eye the most. Makes me think of a pirate :) if that's not what you're going for, though, pick the other one. Either way, they'd both look beautiful on you. Okay, must get back to reading!"

Before the email even sends, I put my phone on Do Not Disturb mode and check the clock.

Dang, only fifty minutes left. No way can I get through this whole book before the library closes. Even if I got a library card with this place—and most wanted you to live in the area before you could do that—rehearsals for the rest of the week would allow for little reading time.

I shut the book on the table and thumb my chin.

"Maybe there's an article online that summarizes the differences between the play and book?"

Pulling up Google, I type, "difference between phantom of opera book and opera." Results blitz my screen in an instant.

Scents from the whiteboard cleaner cause my head to spin as I scroll. Three entries down, I spy a clickbait title. "10 Reasons You Should Read 'Phantom of the Opera' before You See It."

What can I say? I like lists.

My thumb taps the article. It takes several seconds to load, thanks to the number of gifs and images contained in the article. I read.

10 Reasons You Should Read 'Phantom of the Opera' before You See It

Marissa Dunkerly

I don't know about you guys, but when I first saw Phantom, I was like whaaaaaat? And when Christine sang, again, whaaaaat? And when that chandelier came down, you guessed, it, whaaaat?

<gif from Phantom of the Opera movie 2004 film, where chandelier crashes in the theater>

But also, after I got over my fangirling of the phantom and the huge theater the opera was taking place in, I realized that a lot of the opera didn't make a whole lot of sense. I don't know about you, but what was a sixteen-year-old girl doing with some masked forty-year-old man? And why was he trying to get her to marry him? And literally, why was Madame Giry all for the phantom's antics? Is it because he's hot? Well, until you unmask him...

It could've been because I had several drinks during intermission, so the second half didn't compute in my mind. But after a friend recommended I read the book to understand the "context" my brain was blown, y'all.

<gif of a girl falling asleep while reading>

Now, I know, I know. Reading is BORING. You are probably scrolling down this article to get to the good stuff, am I right? Hang with me here, because this book will keep you reading nonstop. It was almost like when I was in fifth grade and read "Percy Jackson" and was an avid bookworm, until my high school English teachers forced me to read boring stuff like "Wuthering Heights" and "The Scarlet Letter."

WARNING: The book is pretty different from the opera. So know that if you read first and then see the opera after that, you will run into variations.

With that in mind, let's begin with the 10 reasons why you should read the book before you go to see the opera (again).

<gif of girl bouncing up and down and saying, "I'm so pumped!">

1. The Phantoms Are Different

Like, legit, in the opera he was hurt in a fire, and that's how half of his face is left deformed. And he definitely is supposed to be a sympathetic character. I mean, helloooo? With a choice between this super-hot mysterious guy who writes music—and blah Raul—we know who we'd choose.

But in the book, he not only was deformed since birth…but is legit evil. Like, he kills for fun and looks like a fricken skeleton.

It makes me wonder why Andrew Lloyd Webber went the direction he did for the opera, but hey, ya girl is not complaining.

<gif of woman fanning herself and collapsing in a chair>

2. Christine Doesn't Love the Phantom in the Book

In the play, they HEAVILY imply that the Phantom and Christine get it on, if you know what I mean.

<gif of woman shimmying shoulders>

But in the book? Not the case at all. Christine feels sorry for the Phantom in the book, because he's gone through hard stuff and all that. Still, she never wants to get with him.

In fact, every time he kidnaps her, she pretends to flirt, just to get out of situations with him. And honestly #myhero.

Which leads me to my next point.

3. Christine Has *Agency*

If you watch the opera, you may be thinking, "Why is Christine doing literally nothing?" She gets led into the magic underground lair of the Phantom, questions nothing.

Is forced to almost marry the guy, or he'll kill Raul. Her only real *hero* moment is she's willing to sacrifice herself to save her friend. And as much as I would like to rant about how they never give female characters anything interesting to do in these types of shows, I digress, because…

The Christine in the book is now who I want to be when I grow up.

She's clever. She evades the Phantom all the time, tries to uncover the mystery of him and the deaths that take place in the opera. She *does* things. And with a misogynistic boyfriend like Raul, I might add.

My eyes glaze as I scan through the rest of the article, which spends way too much time ranting about how the mask could even stay on the Phantom's face in the first place on stage.

My attention keeps darting back to the first three points. Two thoughts pop into my head.

One: Is Eric misunderstood, or, like Raph thinks, perfectly understood? What if he did have something to do with the roses and the deaths?

Two: Am I like the Christine in the play or the book? Do I just let things happen to me?

The second one twists my stomach. So far, I've been absent when any of the mysterious deaths took place. And I didn't do anything about the roses in my room.

I place the book on a cart by the nonfiction section. A label plastered to it reads, "Please do not return the books to the shelves. Put any books you've finished onto this cart. One of our workers will take it from here!"

Temperatures outside dropped a few degrees since my visit at the library.

I rush back to the hotel and return to my room. Soon as I step inside and slump onto my bed, a knock raps against the door.

In an automatic motion, I open it. No surprise, I find Meg perched with her fist raised.

"Hey, girl, missed you at the restaurant." She holds up a Styrofoam box. Strong scents of Cajun seasoning waft from the container. "Figured you were hyper focusing on work and forgot to eat."

She roves to the mini fridge in my room and slides the food onto the top shelf.

When she bangs the door shut, she heads to the snack fridge on the other side of the room and nudges out a sparkling water.

"Want anything? It's on the troupe, of course."

Dryness parches my tongue. "Maybe one of the lemonades."

"You got it."

She hands me a glass bottle, cool to the touch. Thumb grazes the "sparkling" label on mine. Pink bubbly lemonade? *Don't mind if I do.* Steam wisps from the bottle neck as I twist the cap off.

Citric fizz burns my throat, and I love every minute of it.

Meg lets out an 'ahh' after a long swing. "You missed the catfight at the restaurant."

"Between who?"

"Your boyfriend and your chaperone."

Rocks plummet into my stomach. Great, Raph and Eric now hated each other?

"What happened?"

Meg slams herself back against my bed, glances up at the ceiling.

"Well, it started off with the fact that Eric couldn't get off his phone. Guess the guy's helpless in social situations if you're not there."

Someone else also couldn't seem to get off hers.

I bite back the comment. Meg and I can address the emails later after she finishes this story.

"I guess it was bugging Raph, or something. Maybe Eric was texting you? In either case, Raph started flicking his oysters at Eric. Mind you, not the shells, but the little goopy things found inside."

Good grief, Raph, why?

Shielding my face with my fingers, as though watching the scene play before my eyes, I groan.

"This, obviously, upset Eric. He slammed his chair back and said he'd bash Raph's head in if he did something like that again."

Cold spikes my veins.

"Excuse me? Bash his head in?"

"You know how it gets when you put testosterone with testosterone. I think Karim even threatened to do some guy in when he threatened me on the streets of Paris last year."

Eric doesn't strike me as the type to launch a fist at anyone.

"Anyway, they were facing each other off, cowboy style. And not going to lie, it was so hard not to laugh in the moment, because they were both being extremely dramatic. At this point, Antonia broke up the fight and said that concussions were no joking matter."

My lips twitch. "She did?"

"Yeah, I guess some prima donna, back in Antonia's early opera days, landed herself in a coma because she smacked her head too hard against a column in the theater. Guess it was a labyrinth, and if you turned the wrong way too fast, you could run into something."

Coma, huh?

Plenty of true crime podcasts talked about head injuries. I suppose if you, or someone else, knocked your head hard enough, you could end up out for days. Weeks, even.

"Anyway, she finished off the time with a warning that we need to develop spatial awareness at future theaters and yada yada yada. Point is, please don't miss out on our next outing, or the boys are going to get into a fight."

Cupping a knee with my palm, the one without the bottle in hand, I exhale long, hard.

"This is so much extra stress on top of everything."

"On top of learning Phantom, you mean?"

"Yes, and—" I eye my top drawer. Where the rose and notes are housed. "No."

"What do you mean?"

Should I tell her? About the notes and the threats. What if she caused them?

Images flicker back to the article by Marissa. About how she believed Christine in the opera had little agency. Maybe, by telling Meg, I could take control of the situation. And if Meg turns out to be a killer...cross that bridge when we arrive at it, right?

Of all the people to trust in this group—Eric and Meg topped my list.

"Actually, Meg, there's been something really weird happening. And, I'm not sure how to say it." My voice lowered to a whisper on the tail end of that sentence.

She curls herself up into a sitting position once more. "What do you mean?"

The tone doesn't come out as cold or a warning. Safe so far.

"You know how Carmen passed suddenly? And we're all pretty sure it's because the chefs didn't double-check to make sure the food was safe for her allergy? At least, that's what the autopsy said."

Roger produced proof that they had—in fact—placed her allergen sheet in the kitchens, and the culinary artists couldn't have ignored it.

Part of me wondered if they switched it out with a falsified sheet, and changed it back again, once the murderer placed the brownie in her changing room.

It also struck me that perhaps Roger could've paid off the pathologist, to fake the autopsy, if poison got involved. Money could do a lot of things—even create liars.

"Yeah, chica, what about it?"

Again, non-threatening tone.

"The night before, at the ball, she mentioned something about receiving a note from someone. Like a threatening kind of note, and," I lift myself from the bed and head to the top drawer. "At first, she thought it was from me. My first thought was that maybe she was making it up to be dramatic. She didn't show us any screenshots or anything—"

Fingers graze the top of the drawer as they curl around it.

"Now, I'm not so sure, because—"

I yank open the drawer and glimpse inside. Socks stare at me. But no rose, no ring. No note.

Someone took them when I left for the library.

A shadow hovers beside me, as Meg peers into the drawer.

"Socks? Oh yes, very scary." She reaches in and pulls out a pair. "Oh, this is adorable. You have the days of the week on these. Do you ever try to mess with people and wear the Friday ones on a Tuesday?"

She giggles and tosses it back onto the pile of footwear.

"Sorry, still slap happy from the restaurant. What was it you wanted to tell me?"

I bang the drawer shut and stagger back, off balance. Without evidence, Meg'll probably think I've gone insane. Although she did spot the rose during the night of the ball.

Hesitation seizes my throat. Maybe I don't trust her as much as I think. Or maybe the missing items are a blessing, telling me to shut up and keep waiting for more evidence.

"Nothing, Meg. Nothing."

CHAPTER 25

For a week, nothing happens.

After Louisiana, Dallas, Texas embraces us like the breath of fresh air we need—granted, a breath full of humidity and green pollen that could kill any severe asthmatic.

The opera draws together well. So well, in fact, that Antonia, on our last rehearsal day in Dallas, tells me and Eric to end scene work early and help the cast finish the set. We spot Raph on stage, whirring an electric drill.

He turns and leers at Eric.

Although the two have not exchanged more than a few sentences since the restaurant, tension rubber bands them together any time they step into a room. Soon, the band'll snap them together, and they'll start throwing fists.

"Bet I can screw nails faster than you." He clicks the trigger on the electric drill twice to mean business.

Sawdust litters the stage floor. Lights illuminate the several tiers of balconies. Too bad we didn't perform *Schicchi* here. I can imagine myself in an aria, staring out at the large glass chandelier that hangs from the ceiling.

In my periphery, Eric bunches his fists.

Oh goodness, not now.

"Hey." I squeeze his arm, and hiss. "Not here."

Before he can object, I drag him backstage, through the hallway, and into a practice room.

"Look." I jab a finger at his nose. "I don't care how you and Raph feel toward one another. I'm not having my best friend and boyfriend fight over who can build set pieces faster. One of you is going to put out someone's eye if you do that."

He blinks several times at me.

Then sits on a piano bench and leans his back against a cinderblock wall.

"Sorry."

"You guys only have to deal with each other for a few more weeks. Think you can handle that?"

"Well that's the thing, Tina. It might be *more* than a few more weeks?"

My eyebrows scrunch. "What do you mean?"

He extends his hand. We lace our fingers together, and he leads me onto the second floor, into a room full of Mac computers. When he slides into a chair, the bright computer light highlights the contours of his mask. Today, he's gone for a navy blue one, in full support of the Dallas Cowboys.

Even white stars bedeck his cheekbones.

He punches in the login info and pulls up an email. Not his email. I can tell by the subject lines in the inbox.

"Dress Fitting for Christine"

"Programs for the Colorado Springs Performance"

"Changes to the Lighting Cues for the Dress Run"

My palms rest on the desk as I lean forward to make sure I read everything right.

"Eric?"

"Mm?" He taps the Drafts folder.

"Why are you in the manager's inbox?"

He leans back in the seat. Lights from the computer flick beams onto various objects on the desk—a glass paperweight angel, a face-down butterflied book, an emptied coffee mug.

"When you're backstage as much as I used to be in the theater, you get really good at noticing things, collecting things. Like when Richard would put sticky notes on his computer to remind him of usernames and passwords. And like how Roger apparently didn't change them from his predecessor."

Chills run up and down my back.

All this time, I suspected Karim of sending emails from that inbox. As the unofficial social media manager for the company, he knew his way around technology.

But so did Eric.

How many other signs have I been ignoring?

The thought plagues me—what if Raph guessed right about Eric?

"Anyway, I'm not in here to discuss the really poor security measures that our managers have implemented on their technology. Let's just say, if I wanted to change where we were staying in a hotel, I could do it."

He winks at me. I can't tell what expression I give back to him, but not a warm one. Because his shoulders hike to his ears. He returns his stare to the computer.

"You're under the impression that you and Raph are done here at the end of August. But as far as I can tell, Mom loves you as a singer and may ask you to stay with the troupe longer. Like Karim."

This causes my legs to wobble. I balance myself on the desk's surface.

Can I even say no to that? I'd worried about what would happen if I turned down three months with this group. What about forever?

"And she and Roger have absolutely loved the photos Raph has been taking on dress runs and during show nights. He's younger, cheaper than those we've hired before. And does a much better job. Here." He taps on an email in the Drafts folder. "See for yourself. Roger's probably planning to send this out, sometime in August."

Dear Raph,

Antonia and I, as well as the rest of the Daaé Troupe cast and crew, have been extremely grateful for your work. You are incredibly talented, especially for someone of your age.

We have spoken with the Board of Directors, and amongst ourselves, and all agree that we would love to have you on our staff full-time. This would include taking over responsibilities as our social media manager. As much as we appreciate Karim's work, and the work of several college interns who work with us on that side, we would like to combine the role of photographer and social media manager into one.

I have attached an overview of the offer, including an offer for a salary, as well as expectations for the role.

Please let us know as soon as you are able to about your decision, and we look forward to receiving the rest of your work this season with the Phantom performances.

Roger hadn't signed the email yet, nor attached any sheets to the message. But I imagine they'll offer him a lot. An amount he can't refuse.

I catch Eric staring at me, to gauge my reaction.

Keeping my expression steady, I press my eyes onto the angel paperweight on the desk. "Raph might not accept it, you know."

"He'd be an idiot not to."

Indeed. I want to sabotage this for him, so he doesn't feel like he has to spend any more time with this family. One wrong move and Raph could end up like Carmen or Richard.

"Why do you hate him so much?"

Eric shuts down the computer. Blackout, as the darkness shrouds us, shrouds him.

"I don't hate him. It's just, when he looks at me. It's like he's looking for something. Something bad. Like he's waiting for me to screw up."

Suspecting someone of murder could do that to a person.

"He's just overprotective." I lean against the wall and triangle one of my legs. The stance reminds me of a flamingo. "And besides, even if someone thinks you've done something terrible, if you didn't do it, there's nothing to feel guilty about, right?"

His silhouette hunches underneath the words.

Then he speaks. "You wouldn't get it."

"Eric."

"Come on, let's go back to helping with the set."

And we do. Once again, the week finishes off with a hush. We hop onto the tour bus and head toward St. Louis.

It's been weird not performing in cities, and instead, practicing in them. Because of what happened with Carmen, we needed to hold off on the rest of our shows. But we did have to go from theater to theater, based on how our schedule was booked.

Plenty of other troupes would perform in the theaters we'd been residing in—so we didn't want to get in their way. Besides, Antonia insisted that traveling to the different theaters—even if we wouldn't perform in them—would get us used to putting on operas in different spaces.

Every theater felt different. Had a unique soul, a unique flavor. And it took a few moments to adjust to the new atmosphere.

During our first night in St. Louis, we pack in all the pit stops we can. With tech and dress week ahead, Roger'll give us very little free time to spare.

Raph photographs us at the Gateway Arch, and we make our way up and down the exhibits at the zoo. Giraffes lick food out of our hands with their long tongues, and Meg forces Karim to buy her a manatee stuffed animal from the gift shop. She nuzzles it under her chin the whole way back to the hotel.

The next day, we arrive at the theater, and I feel as though someone has transported me back to the 1800s or early 1900s. Gold detailing covers every inch of the walls. Arches form above box seats that hover above the rows of the audience. Part of me wishes I could perch in one of those and watch a show.

Soon as the morning starts, and we do our stretches, Antonia pulls me into the costume shop for a fitting. A woman, with pins stuck in her teeth, waves at me.

"Roger arranged for us to rent costumes from this theater." Antonia leans her arm on top of a Z-rack, full of large dresses. "We'll take them with us to the four performance spaces for *Phantom*. Figured we could get some shots of you all doing a dress run, here, beforehand though. For marketing purposes."

"Sounds like a plan."

She leaves me in the capable hands of the dress lady, who leads me to one of the farthest dress racks. Dress lady takes the pins out of her mouth and sticks them on a pin cushion strapped to her wrist.

"I figure we'll get you to try on the wedding dress first, since it's the hardest one to get into. You'll have people helping you backstage with the change."

Her fist clamps onto a hanger, and she pulls a dress off of the rack.

Chills fill my lungs until I can't breathe.

"That's—"

I stop myself short.

The dress from the email. The one with the subject line "CHOOSE."

Meg didn't send those messages to me, did she? Someone had wanted me to pick out the dress from the show. And what about the bouquets and the cakes? Would those make an appearance in the show?

Maybe they'd wanted Christine to hold a bouquet for the show. But a cake seems overkill, unless they plan to have one at a cast party after the closing night performance.

Also, since when did theaters ever let the actors get to pick out the outfits? Far as I could tell, they'll hand you a dress from a rack, and you'd say, "Thanks, I love it."

Dress lady stares me down.

Got it, gotta finish my thought.

"—that's lovely, can't wait to put it on."

After I shed my clothes, except for my undergarments, I step into the dress. My hands hold up the bodice as she laces me into the corset. Boning tightens against my ribs. It'll be tricky to muster any breath support in this thing because she's tied it tight.

"How does that look?"

She leads me to a full-sized mirror. Billowing trumpet sleeves obscure my hands.

"Umm, great. Thanks."

"Tina." A breathy voice pants at the door. Meg clasps the frame for support, color in her face drained.

I gather the skirts in my hands and rush over to her.

"What's going on?"

"Follow me. Hurry."

Meg races off in the direction of the auditorium. I flick a glance back at dress lady, and she shrugs. "Make sure it doesn't drag against the ground."

I hoist the hemline as high as it can go, bunched in my fists, and charge after Meg. Wheezing breaths overtake me before I step onto the stage. Corsets and running away do not make a good combo.

When I step onto the stage, I see the group huddled around the seats. All the people called to rehearsal early—Roger, Karim, Meg, Antonia, and Eric. They bubble around a figure on the floor.

A sharp gasp cuts my throat. Rushing to the front of the stage, I kneel. A long drop will land me in the pit. But even from where I sit, I recognize him right away.

Raph, unconscious.

Or dead?

Please, God, no, don't let him be dead.

Raph's legs and arms form jagged angles. Could've broken all of his limbs, with what looks like a fall. Or a push.

Just like Richard on the bridge.

Tremors overtake my voice. Lip quivers. "Is he—?"

"Still breathing," Meg says. "But out of it. Ambulance is on its way."

"What happened?"

"A blackout."

This comes from Karim. Every once in a while, the tech booth will call for a blackout, to practice lighting cues. They always inform the singers when this will take place, and the pitch darkness can shroud the theater for up to a minute.

Meg approaches the stage.

"They didn't call it from the tech booth. Or at least, we couldn't hear it. It got dark for a long time. Then we heard something like a smack and someone fall." She gestures up at one of the booths, several yards above the audience. "Raph must've hit his head against one of those columns up there when he couldn't see and fell."

Tears sparkle in her eyes.

Everyone blinks away moisture except for Eric, who slumps into his hoodie.

He did this, didn't he?

He did all of it.

The blackout gave him plenty of time to run up into the box seats, deliver a blow to Raph's head, send him over the balcony's edge, and return to his spot in the auditorium.

It takes ages for the ambulance to arrive. Meg herds me onto the tour bus, which makes a pit stop at the hospital. Even though I beg them, they don't let me onto the ambulance with him. Maybe there's a family-only rule.

When we reach the hospital, Meg squeezes my shoulder. "Most of the group is back at the hotel. We're going to let them know, okay? And then we'll be right back with more people. Antonia's calling his emergency contact."

It's now that I realize I'm still in the dress from the show. The costumer will probably kill me, but I don't care.

Words don't come. So I bobble my chin and stumble off the bus.

The ground floor smells of broccoli cheddar soup from one of the hospital restaurants. Teddy bears greet me as I pass by them on the way to the elevators. Once Antonia gets his room number, she texts it to me.

After I check in, and get the go-ahead a good hour later to visit him, I head upstairs.

One of the doctors in the room speaks with me. Words don't register, but I catch pieces like "acute trauma to the head" "broken bones" and "possible coma."

So Eric really did bash his head in, didn't he?

All for what? Because he couldn't stand the fact that Raph liked to protect me? Because Raph suspected him all this time?

When the doctor leaves the room and clicks off the lights, beams from the hallway our only source of illumination, I grip the bars on the bedside. Fight back tears.

"Oh, Raph, I was so stupid. Why didn't I believe you?"

A machine clamps to his forefinger. I grab his hand and rub my thumb up and down the skin.

"I'm going to nail this guy, okay? Gonna make him come out of the shadows one way or another. You were sent here to protect me, and I'm going to return the favor."

His skin sinks into his skull. No surprise that he doesn't respond.

After a while, the doctors ask me to leave, and I head downstairs to the restaurant. I force myself to eat a flaky croissant and wait. Meg and Karim arrive within the hour and find me at the two-person table.

"Hey, girl. The bus is making round trips back and forth to the hotel since only a certain amount of people are allowed to visit him at one time." Her hand clasps my shoulder. "Why don't you head back? Get a shower, get some sleep, and then you can come back."

My jaw sinks to protest, but she throws up a hand.

"We'll let you know if something serious changes, okay? But right now, you need to take care of you."

Unable to formulate thoughts, I nod and follow her back to the bus. She waves me off in the drop-off spot in the hospital parking lot. Rumbles on the road do little to break through the numbness in my skin.

When I, the only passenger, disembark from the bus, a cluster of singers steps on. As they do, they squeeze me into side hugs and I hear the word "sorry" more times than I think I ever want to again.

I step onto the elevator and head to my room.

It takes me several moments to dig through my pockets and procure the key card to the room. Limbs don't want to work today.

A green light lets me know I can step inside.

Cool gusts of air suck the oxygen out of my lungs. Lights flicked off. I think I'll take Meg up on her advice to get some sleep.

Drowsiness weighs on my eyelids, and I drift off into darkness. Can't tell how long I went out like a light, but I bolt up in bed and spot something on my dresser.

"Please. Not now," I whisper.

Sheets crumple around me as I get out of bed and flick on the lights. Sure enough, the ring box—the one that went missing two weeks back—sits open-faced. Jewels glimmer in the room lighting.

No rose this time, but still an anonymous note.

"He loved her so much that it <u>almost</u> took his breath away.'"

Breath away.

He underlined almost.

My mind first races to jealousy. Did Eric think that Raph and I had something going on between us? And so he tried to take him out, to get him out of the picture?

Hold on, why *did* he underline that word?

Almost, almost, almost, almost...

Got it. Eric knew the blow to the head likely wouldn't kill Raph. But it would serve as a warning to me. If I didn't put on that ring...

Crimson, the jewel glowers at me.

"Is Eric seriously forcing me to *marry* him?" Sure, yes, I'd reached adulthood. He, being two years my senior, wouldn't make it as weird as the Phantom and Christine age gap in the opera.

But to go as far as to succeed in killing off two other people, attempting a third?

I rub my temples and perch on the edge of my bed. "Why would he want to kill Richard, though?"

Carmen made total sense. She'd given him plenty of motive to destroy her.

But Richard?

A groan through my fingertips. "I don't have enough evidence to nail the guy."

Still, I made a promise to Raph on his hospital bed. Where the monitors beeped, and I held my breath at every note, listening for each sign and sound of life.

"Maybe." I suck in a breath. "Maybe I don't need all the evidence. I have enough to draw him out and get him to confess."

Bluff.

So many detectives in books do it. They have a hunch and enough evidence to make the accused spill the rest.

For now, though…

I glimpse the ring. Yes, I did promise Raph I'd protect him.

And Eric has made it clear that if I don't go along with his little game, he'll do far worse to my friend. Fingers run up and down my knees.

"Okay, girl, you can do this. You can fake an engagement for a few weeks."

Pulse pounds in my fingertips as I rise from the bed and approach the box. My index finger curls around the ring and I place it into my palm.

"All right, Tina." I slip the ring onto the correct finger. "You are officially a serial killer's fiancée."

CHAPTER 26

T rue to his word, Eric doesn't touch Raph for the rest of the week.

During our outings, I make sure Meg and Karim lie in close distance. Allow for minimal physical contact, so Eric doesn't raise questions. An arm around the shoulder? Fine. A kiss? I duck out of the way and complain about an oncoming headache.

Roger manages to find a local photographer to shoot the dress run, and Antonia calls "hold" whenever she wants to capture a still photograph.

"Tina, you're way too far away from Eric's face in this shot. Get a little closer, like we practiced."

Grimacing, I place my forehead centimeters away from him.

"Thank you, now hold that pose."

We hit the road to Colorado, a day early. Antonia says the cast could use a pick-me-up and schedules us for an afternoon in Garden of the Gods in the Springs. Purple mountains fade in and out of clouds on the bus ride there.

When we reach the garden, Eric clasps my hand in his and tugs me off of the vehicle before the others can join us. Red dirt kicks up underneath his shoes. Clouds of dust form behind us as we weave around vermillion rock structures. At long last, he winds us in a labyrinth of stones and stops us underneath two camel-shaped ones kissing.

"Eric." I pant. "What was that?"

"You've been surrounded by people lately, and I figure you'd need some time alone."

Alone with him? *Way to fit the serial killer stereotypes, Eric.*

"Thanks." I release my hand and wipe the sweat onto my pants. "Sorry, clammy palms." I don't reach for his outstretched fingers again. "This whole Raph thing's been a lot. I'm just glad that his mom's there with him now."

I made certain that I didn't leave St. Louis until I knew he had an angel of protection hovering over him. That woman could make walls peel with her angry stare. Neighbors would walk their dogs across the street, for fear of what she would do to them if their puppies happened to relieve themselves on her well-manicured lawn.

Plus, I couldn't reveal to Eric what I know until we got several states away from Raph. No leverage equals no need for me to stay engaged to this creep.

"You doing okay?" Although half of his face melts in concern, I can read the words between the words.

You've been distant from me lately.

You haven't kissed me since the incident.

You suspect me, don't you?

I clasp my hands.

Much as I need to keep acting the part, my skin crawls any time I make physical contact with him now.

"Yeah, just needing time to process." I make an obvious motion of twisting the ring around my finger. He doesn't stare at it.

No one in the troupe has acknowledged the new piece of jewelry. This confirms my thoughts that everyone either plays a hand in the "accidents" that take place—or turns a blind eye when something shady goes down.

"Well, if you need anyone to talk to—"

"Guys." Meg's voice cuts off Eric's. She pants and leans against a rock. A family behind her poses for a picture. Probably to capture the kissing camels in the background. "You can't just run off like that. It's a maze in here."

Think that's the point, Meg.

"I had a friend once get lost near the Three Graces, and, girl," She motions to her nose. "You're bleeding."

Metallic liquid pools into my mouth. By reflex, my fingers reach up to my nose. Sure enough, when I pull them away, scarlet glistens on my fingertips.

"You." Meg jabs a finger at Eric. "Go be a good boyfriend and get a first aid kit from the bus. You, Karim." He hovers behind her. "Go join him. For...moral support. And you, Tina." She pinches her nose. "Do this, and breathe out of your mouth for the next few minutes."

Eric's jaw sinks in a protest, but one glimpse of Meg's glare springs him into action. He and Karim sprint off. Dust kicks up behind them, blurring the tourist family.

Meg grabs the elbow of my free arm and leads me to flat rocks we can sit on. She parks on the end of one and pats the space beside her.

"Colorado has a much drier climate than Ohio, so this happens all the time. Good thing you're getting this now and not during the preview performance tomorrow."

Not sure how getting a nosebleed once will prevent future ones, but we can hope so.

"Also, figured I'd send the guys to the bus. You look like you need space from a certain clingy boyfriend."

"Thanks." I wince at how my words come out, through having to plug my nose. "He's not been super understanding about this whole Raph situation."

"Boy's been locked in opera houses his whole life, so he hasn't picked up on a ton of social cues. Don't worry, I'll make sure to yell at him later for being insensitive."

Yes, because I'm sure a scolding will take care of his murderous tendencies.

"But I also want to check in on you. Tina. You look like you've been seeing a ghost these past few days. And yes, that was slightly a pun, given the opera we're performing."

"I—"

Hesitate.

Although Meg didn't commit the murders, as far as my knowledge goes, I don't know who she sides with. Me or Eric.

Doesn't hurt to test the waters.

Time to weigh each word. "Do you ever feel like something bad's about to go down? And that if it does, you will have no control over the situation?"

She locks eyes with me for several moments. Irises darting back and forth.

Then she nods. "We've been hit by a lot of bad luck this summer. It's definitely natural to feel like something bad is coming."

Blood from my nose sputters onto my left hand, the one with the ring finger. Although the skin has gotten slippery, I pinch my nose tighter.

"No, like, Meg, I'm pretty sure something bad is going to happen. Soon."

Eric never put a deadline on the engagement. Something tells me he won't want to wait long.

"And there's something you can do to prevent it?"

"There's—" I pause. "A possibility I can. But I have to play it right."

Birds twitter in nearby bushes as she soaks in the words. Draws her knees against her chest and hugs them tight.

"Then, Tina, I think you need to do whatever it is you need to do."

I blink. "Really?"

"Yeah. Trust me, been in that situation before, and found out way too late. Once it's out of your control"—she shoots her arm straight forward and releases her fists into an open hand gesture. Like tossing sand to the wind—"then it's out of your control. Might as well throw the first punch before they can."

That would mean sometime this week, I'd have to call out Eric. Before Meg's elopement, and before he could get away with any more murders.

Fear stabs my skin like a needle.

"Meg, I—when I do it. Go confront the bad, can I let you know? That way I'll feel a little safer?"

Her expression softens. "Of course. It's a scary world out there. Maybe we even come up with a code word, so no one else can figure out what we're talking about?"

How did she—?

Does she know what I'm actually referring to? Like her part in the play, Madame Giry, does she have one foot in Christine's territory, and one in the Phantom's? Maybe he let her into pieces of his plan before he enacted it.

Maybe he also threatened her too, to ensure her silence.

Blood dries inside my nostrils. I can feel the clots forming. Any minute now, and the boys will return.

"What's a code word you think will be good?"

"Hmm." She rubs a thumb under her chin. "Maybe something like, 'the roses are blooming.'"

"'The roses are blooming.' Why?"

"Because there's a rose used in the play. No one will question it. Probably will dig a finger into their earwax to make sure they heard you right –since no one talks that way, but it's a quirky enough sentence that I'll know. Also."

She leans in, breath carrying the essence of a sports drink she chugged on the bus. Needed the electrolytes before hiking with us on the dusty trails.

"If you can, get it in front of a camera. Otherwise, it's your word against theirs."

Cameras. Didn't Karim station those all around the theater to capture B-roll for the social media pages? If I could get Eric to meet with me, anywhere but the dressing rooms, we could nail a surefire confession on tape.

Eric knew about the cameras though, right?

The only people who didn't seem to pay attention to those were on staff, like Roger and Antonia.

Maybe I could sneak a phone and turn on the voice recording app.

Two minutes later, the boys return with wads of gauze. I shove them up my nose to collect the rest of the body fluids. When the dizziness from loss of blood eases, we traverse the rest of the grounds together.

We pause to snap photos of mule deer and their jagged horns when we spot them in a cluster of bushes. Thick, white clouds cast shadows on the ground.

That evening, we stop by a Greek restaurant. Eric and I don't share any words over the pita and hummus. As Karim goes on and on about how he swears he spotted a bobcat on the ledge of one of the rock structures, Eric doesn't keep his stare off of me.

Sparks form in his pupils. A challenge.

I hope mine flint back.

When we return to the hotel, I race to the elevator and ride up the shaft alone, before Eric can pull me to the side again, as he'd done in the Garden of the Gods. Shutting myself into my room, I double-lock the door and shove my heavy suitcase against it for good measure.

Having learned that Eric has access to all the emails answers the keycard question. He logged in, using Roger's information, and asked for extra room keys. Then collected them from Roger or the front desk at one point. He had a habit of pilfering, so I wouldn't put it past him to sneak those away without anyone else's notice.

Did the troupe hide him away for this reason?

Did they suspect him of dangerous acts in the past?

Could he really have gotten those burns from Scouts, or from something far more sinister?

Like Meg encouraged me to do, I'll beat him to the punch.

For courage, I race to my fridge and pull out a bag of peanut M&Ms. Slipping a yellow one into my mouth, I open my email on my phone and type out a message to the manager's email.

Although I have no idea how often Roger checks the in-box—based on the number of bolded messages I saw in the office, not many.

If Eric spotted a draft email to Raph, offering him a full-time position, he'd probably spy something from me before our manager did.

Shaky fingers grip the side of my phone.

Okay, girl, time for the punch.

I type in the subject first. "To the person who has been writing me notes <3"

Then the body of the email. Something tells me this'll go to spam, which I have no doubt, Eric also checks. The person behind these murders appears to be thorough.

Dear Secret Admirer,

I just want to say I've been getting your notes, and I absolutely love them <smiling face surrounded by hearts emoji>

Although I must say, Secret Admirer, that you're no longer a secret <gasp emoji>

In fact, I know all of your dirty little secrets. So let's just stop this cat-and-mouse game and be straightforward about everything.

You and me, meet in private to discuss this. I'll keep your secrets safe if you stop threatening to take out my loved ones, okay? <heart emoji>

I expect us to meet sometime before the performances. Will give you before the end of the preview tomorrow to confess.

If not, I'll share all your secrets with the world. I know that tons of people have been knocking down your inbox for interviews.

And let's just say, they're going to be very anxious to hear from the prima donna, all about you.

Do we have a deal?

Sincerely,

The Girl You Shouldn't Have Messed With

Before I can let regret twist my stomach into knots, I hit send. Whoosh goes the email.

Tension spikes my temples and I collapse into my bed.

Darkness overcomes me, and chimes from my phone alarm wake me the next day. *Shoot, forgot to charge the sucker last night.* The battery mopes, at a weak five percent.

At least the murderer didn't slip into my room last night and slit my throat.

Maybe they'll take me up on my offer to meet. If not...

Gotta keep my promise then. Instead of meeting the group over a bowl of oatmeal downstairs, I draft an email to potential interviewers.

Hello!

My name is Tina, and you may have possibly heard of me. I've been blessed to work with the Daaé family troupe this past summer, and it certainly has been quite the experience.

I know the family isn't often up for interviews, but I'd love to share what I've discovered these past few months.

Please let me know any other details you'd need from me before we can schedule an interview.

Thanks!

Tina

When I click to save the draft, a thought strikes me. Why would he even get a social media account in the first place? No doubt he posted the videos to out himself to the world. Even though he pretended someone else uploaded them without his permission.

But people hounded him for mask reveals, for him to expose the secrets of the family.

Why risk it?

Of course, plenty of influencers got outed as scammers, abusers, and all sorts of horrible things. Fame came at a price; it always does.

From my bag, I grab a granola bar and force myself to down it. Although my stomach sours, I can't risk any health issues today. What the killer wouldn't do if I passed out on the spot.

Several tiers of crimson seats await us as we step into the auditorium in the afternoon. Although most opera houses blasted the AC, the chill in here feels different today. Deadly. Corpse-like.

Almost like someone had stuffed a bunch of ghosts into the vents, their vapors causing goosebumps to ripple up and down our skin.

Antonia leads us through stretches on stage and meets with us individually for director's notes. She has none for me tonight except, "You're going to be a brilliant Christine. I've always known you've had this in you."

After vocal warm-ups, women sponge my face full of foundation in the hair and makeup chair. Buzzing fills my ears, my veins, my nerves. What if the killer didn't see the email? What if Roger spotted the message instead and deleted it?

Should I drop a note in Eric's dressing room?

I shut my eyes and formulate what the message will say as they daub my eyes with shadow. They ease the wig onto my capped skull, and sweat breaks out on my upper lip from the heat of the lights and the hair.

"Whew." I fan myself. "Mind if I step into my dressing room?" I grab the tube of lipstick. "I can finish it in there, just feeling hot."

Meg, in the seat next to me, frowns as a woman contours her cheeks. "Are the roses blooming, chica?"

"If not, we're going to make them tonight."

Her face doesn't move, thanks to the hair and makeup artist. But I do see her eyebrows arch. "Okay, well, be careful. Remember what I said."

Get it on film.

"You got it."

Breezes from my stride cool my cheeks and neck. I enter my dressing room and pause, two steps in. A single red rose awaits on the table. In the mirror's reflection, a single black string, in a bow, chokes the stem.

My secret admirer made another appearance.

I shut the door behind me and go to the note, stationed next to Lenny, on the desk. Eric must've slipped out during my director's meeting.

The note reads:

"Deal. Meet me downstairs the minute you read this. No other people. No phones. Or else. Rip this note several times and throw it in the trash. If you take any pictures of it on your cell phone, I will know."

No phone. That means no voice recording device.

I have to hope Eric forgets about the camera in the basement. *If* Karim managed to get one down there in time. By now, he could've given up at the lack of B-roll that happened in the nether regions of the opera house.

Fear prickles my veins, and I swallow bile. Granola bar was a bad idea.

Can't back out now, camera or not. The killer knows I've "figured it out" and intends to speak with me either way.

If I don't go downstairs, he'll call my bluff.

And do who knows what to Raph...or others.

My preshow robe sticks to my chest like a second skin. No wonder sweat pours from me. With shaky hands, I tear the note and toss it into the bin stationed by the door. My heart droops as I do so. One piece of solid evidence, gone.

But I gotta compromise, right? To get the killer to work with me.

I wick the dew off my lips and charge into the hallway. Gonna meet a killer in the next thirty seconds. As I wind down the staircase into the basement, the orchestra tunes above me. They do that about forty minutes before the show. That means I have about ten or so to wrangle a confession out of Eric.

Light floods the basement. *Weird.* He likes to hide in darkness.

When my shoes hit the sawdusty ground, I squint through the large set pieces. Then I see a figure, with their back turned to me.

They turn around and a gasp squeezes my gut.

"Hello, darling."

It's Antonia.

CHAPTER 27

"**Y**ou seem surprised."

My features slacken, and my thoughts race. If I give away the fact that I did *not* in fact predict the killer, she'll clam up.

Eyes rove the room for the camera. I spot it hoisted on a box. Tankards, probably excess from the props loft, cover the sides and back of it, hiding it in the rows. Meg must've tipped Karim off to shield the recording device.

Or Karim, just by nature, had a weird setup when it came to recording videos. Maybe to get candid reels of the cast.

I pace toward her, straightening my spine.

Every inch of me screams to dart up the staircase, but I can't reveal my fear. Not in front of her.

"I think the only thing that surprises me, Antonia, is that you took me up on my deal. Glad you got the email."

Whoo, my voice comes out cooler than an Ohio winter storm. I lean against a chimney set piece and triangle my leg. Cross my arms.

"Surprised it didn't go to spam with all the emojis." Tassels on her shawl sway as she paces between two large Ancient Greek-style statues. "You wanted to talk, let's talk."

"Yes, let's."

Enough to get her to say the words, "I, Antonia, murdered Richard Armand, Carmen Driver, and attempted to kill Tina's best friend Raphael."

Good luck with that, girl.

"Why don't you start with admitting what you did, Antonia, and we'll go from there. Per the deal."

The email to her mentioned a confession.

Her chin juts upward, and she curves a smile at me. "You're a clever girl. Why don't you tell me what you discovered?"

Bluff, called.

Improvisational exercises spring to life in the back of my mind. *Community theater, don't let me down now.*

"Fine, I will. Let's start with Richard and why you killed him."

Thumbs curve into my pockets as I shove myself from the chimney and start my own pace. Her and my walks intersect. She stills and watches me.

"You didn't just fire Richard because he'd been dropping the ball of different things. A missing helm and missing maestro really aren't enough to fire some guy you'd been working with for years. Richard did something that made you want to cut ties right away."

"Oh indeed?" She perches a brow. "Do tell what that was?"

Thoughts race in my skull until my temples pound with a headache. Didn't someone mention something about him insisting on them hiring Carmen?

"He hired Carmen, to sabotage you."

She claps in mock applause.

"Oh, my dear, you *are* clever. Why was that sabotage, exactly?"

"Because—she wasn't just an opera prodigy, was she? Eric and she spent lots of time together. He thought she was wanting to get with him. But Richard told her to buddy up with Eric to get all the family secrets. Richard knew he was in too deep to share, didn't he? If someone new stepped in and made an exit before it was too late, she could get the news out to whoever she liked, couldn't she."

Oh, *Eric*.

Can't believe I suspected him. All for what? Because I got some impression that he and the *Phantom* from the book shared the same personalities?

"So you fired him. Not killed him at first. Because he'd been such a help over the years, acting like a second father to Eric. You have a soft spot for your son, don't you?"

Her long red talons grasp a necklace, nearest to her jutting collarbone.

She keeps her neck hunched to the ground.

"Indeed, a mother's bond with her son is strong, no matter what the situation."

"But firing wasn't enough for Richard, was it? Because he followed us on various tour stops. Probably to threaten you for trying to silence him. You had to do something about it, Antonia, didn't you?"

Her features harden, but somehow, she still keeps her smile.

That grin sends goosebumps up my arms. She knows something I don't.

"So then, tell me what I did, Tina."

"When we made a stop in Gatlinburg, you realized there was a suspension bridge next to the aquarium. Luck would have it that it rained that day. So you told Richard to meet you there. You placed a sign by the bridge saying it was closed due to it being slippery."

I don't have confirmation that anyone emailed Richard. For all we know, maybe she found him on the bridge and enacted the plan. But for someone as thorough as her, she'd want all the right pieces in place.

"And then, what? I threw him off?"

She laughs and straightens her arms.

"Darling, I haven't done push-ups in years. And even with those rigorous workouts they make the prima donnas do, we couldn't lift a man of that weight."

Sores of workouts past pain my muscles. Yes, even Meg couldn't chuck a full-sized man into a forest below.

Back in the hotel, Raph and I speculated about how if Meg did that, she'd need to take Karim alongside her to finish the job.

"No, you hired it out."

"Oh, did I now?" Her body goes slack, though.

"You did. Since, as director, you have a habit of hiring and firing people, you'd have no issue with making sure someone finished the job for you." I wonder why I ever thought Richard or Roger had this sort of power. "And you made sure you personally had an alibi for the aquarium. The pictures and the timestamps. You knew I'd check them."

She simpers but doesn't reply.

"And you knew one of us would check Roger's phone. It makes him look extremely guilty if Annika's signature thumbprint was seen in every photo. Would make me think that he handed it off to her and went off to commit a murder, wouldn't it?"

In fact, now that I think of it, Antonia seemed to place the blame on others any chance she got.

Ship's helm? Found it in Meg's house. The one Antonia bought for the couple. It would make sense that she could make a copy of the keys. Just like she did for the hotels, to slip in and out of my and Carmen's room.

Technology? Pretended to be horrible at it. So I could suspect Karim of hacking into the email accounts. Maybe she'd even drafted that email, knowing Eric popped into the emails often and would show me that.

Roses? All of the quotes came from *Phantom of the Opera* and used "he" pronouns. Of course, I'd put two and two together and blame Eric for all the deaths.

Antonia played her cards well.

Like me, she worked everything like a diplomat. Thought about how others would take the information and used that to her advantage.

"And if you made the death look like a suicide or a slip, then people wouldn't look too hard into it, would they?"

She roams to an angel statue. Shadows from the wings obscure her expression.

"Interesting take, I suppose. But that only accounts for one death. What about Carmen?"

It made obvious sense why the mom of Eric would want to rip off the head of Eric's ex. With all of her superfans, though, why take the risk? Someone in the hair and makeup room mentioned security had to flag down several of Carmen's fans outside of the opera house. They tracked us down to Colorado, convinced one of us offed her on purpose.

They'd be right, of course.

"Carmen was—"

I couldn't read her expression from the tech booth during Carmen's audition, but no Antonia in her right mind would bring back the girl who tried to squeak all the family secrets out of Eric.

"—she was an unexpected person you had to deal with. You didn't think she'd show up for auditions or try to take the parts. When you hired me, you figured I was young, green, grateful for the opportunity and wouldn't look as hard into the family secrets, didn't you?"

"We didn't expect her to return for auditions, no."

"But she was greedy. Wanted the money she was promised. Enough to throw herself back into a dangerous situation, thinking her fans would have her back and protect her. You had to get rid of her, though, didn't you? She was a loose end."

And unmasking Eric in the hotel hallway didn't help her case.

"Ah, I also killed her, did I? Do tell how I got away with that."

"Easy. She had an acute peanut allergy. But you didn't just kill her with peanuts, did you? Because a few bites into that brownie, she would've suspected she'd eaten something she couldn't and went for her EpiPen."

Shoot, the EpiPen. Why didn't I think of that earlier?Maybe someone had gotten a hold of it and stashed it away, or maybe—

"She figured that she'd just eaten something bad that didn't have peanuts. The reactions between certain poisons and allergens are very similar. So she asked to be taken back to the hotel, instead of the hospital. And the poison killed her off there, didn't it?"

For all we know, Antonia could've slipped into her room and given her another dose during one of the acts.

"They didn't find it in the autopsy because they weren't looking for it. She'd digested trace amounts of peanuts, and that was enough for them. In either case, she ate a poisoned treat—in one way or another—and you could blame the kitchens for negligence on their part. For failing to read her health information sheet carefully."

Seconds of silence swallow us whole.

Then she speaks. She sits on the base of the angel statue.

"So that must be how you think I killed her. But tell me, what about your friend, Raph? I treated him well. Praised his photographs. Even wanted to hire him full-time."

"You did."

I falter. So she did. The main reason I didn't think she'd committed the murders. Raph spoke so well of her.

"You did, but you needed to get to me. Because I wasn't wearing this." I hold up my left hand. Jewels glitter in the wan basement lights. "I wasn't cooperating. You wanted me to marry your son. To shut me up, tie up another loose end. Because once you're a part of the Daaés, you have to keep your silence. Or else."

Or else other Raphs would meet their end.

Meg, Karim, others—they probably knew more than they let on. Hence Meg's warning to me in the first email I ever received from her.

"Careful, darling." Antonia lifts herself from the base of the statue. "It's dangerous to play with fire."

Fire. Like how half of Eric's face went caput in flames.

And his dad...

Shoot, his dad. He died in a fire too, didn't he?

Wanna bet Antonia had something to do with that?

"You would know all about fire, wouldn't you, Antonia?"

It's a bold accusation, I admit. It freezes her in place, and all spark has vanished from her pupils.

"He told you about what really happened with his father?"

Lord knows I can't lie, but I stare her right in the face. No shifting eyes, no change of voice. "As a matter of fact, he did. I know it wasn't from a camping accident, Antonia."

A hiss flees her lips. Perhaps from a secret she made Eric swear never to tell.

She buckles. Blinking several times. Then she regains her balance.

"I told him not to go inside. When he got back from his trip, after the Scouts kicked embers into his eyes...I told him not to go into the house. He didn't listen to me anyway. I didn't know he was going to slip on the puddle."

The puddle?

Wouldn't most puddles put out fires unless they were made of...ohhhhhh.

Gasoline.

Antonia burned her husband alive. Waited for him to go upstairs, probably flicked on the gas, lit some candles, and poured some gasoline by the stove. Fire department wouldn't detect arson if they spotted the other factors that would make the house go up in flames.

Eric must've run in, slipped, gotten some lighting fluid on his face.

And when the house ignited...

So did half of Eric's face.

"You look surprised again, dear."

"Just—sad."

Not a lie. His mother murdered his father, for whatever reason. Maybe he, too, had learned too many secrets.

Eric lost his father and any touch with civilization after that day. No wonder Antonia buried him away. One more loose end to snuff out, so no one could suspect ill will from the family.

Couldn't bring herself to kill Eric, though.

Like I said earlier, soft spot for him.

"Well, I suppose that won't do. Sadness is not to be had twenty minutes before curtain. I expect to have a cheery bride when we head to the courthouse tomorrow."

All air sucks from out of the room.

"Excuse me, what?"

"The original plan had been to have a double wedding in Vegas, along with Karim and Meg. Thank you for your swift responses to my emails, by the way."

The CHOOSE messages.

Shoot, shoot, shoot.

"You, my dear, you are far too clever for your own good, and it would be a shame to see you marry into any other family. Right before the performance, tomorrow, we'll get the paperwork assigned and make it official."

Heels tap as she advances toward me. It takes everything inside of me not to flinch.

She takes my left hand in hers and squeezes.

"Toi, toi, toi, darling—"

The opera equivalent of "break a leg." My body slackens. Holy crap, she's going to force me to marry Eric tomorrow. But what if—

"What if he refuses?"

"He's been warned about the consequences of going against what's best for him. Definitely learned in the past." Meaning his father in the fire. "And there's a certain angel he won't want to get to heaven just yet."

She cocks her head and releases me.

Shoot, she means me.

They'll kill me if Eric doesn't agree to the marriage. And he knows it.

"Speaking of warnings." Her nostrils flare. "I'm sure you're a clever enough girl to know that sharing this information with anyone else would be most unfortunate. Good luck, darling. And best get into costume. Preview performance starts soon."

She marches off toward the staircase. Even in the midst of the musical notes from upstairs, I can hear every step echo.

Tears blur my vision as I follow, minutes later, into the costume room.

As the ladies lace me into my first outfit, Eric surfaces in my periphery. He races to me, grasps my hand in his.

"What's wrong?"

Antonia's caution niggles the back of my skull. Would she finish the job on Raph if I told? Does Eric already know?

"Nothing, just nervous."

"Your cheeks are like roses." His hand grazes them. "Blooming."

"Guess the hair and makeup room put on a lot of blush and—"

I freeze. How did he find out that secret code? Before I can ask, he scampers off and I join the rest of the crew backstage. Antonia goes on for a curtain speech, informing the audience that Eric's face is in fact contoured, and they wouldn't see his true face tonight.

"As far as masks go, we can only allow ourselves to lift them with people we trust. With that in mind, we are pleased to present *The Phantom of the Opera*."

Music and scenes blur in my mind. I pass through them on autopilot. One thought plagues me the whole time. *I'll be someone's bride tomorrow.*

Speaking of brides, we reach the scene where they strap me into the wedding dress. Will I wear this one tomorrow? Does Antonia have a gold and red bouquet of roses at the ready, a drip cake too?

I stagger onto the stage to sing at the Phantom to stop choking Raul with a rope.

He holds up a hand, to silence me. Wait a minute, Eric, this isn't part of the blocking.

Voice dies in my throat, and he points upward. A screen rolls down over the stage. Projections from the tech booth beam blue light onto it. Moments later, a grainy version of my voice sounds from the speakers.

"Why don't you start with admitting what you did, Antonia, and we'll go from there. Per the deal."

My eyes widen.

Karim got to the videos. Considering we're now close to the end of the show, he must've reviewed them during intermission.

I rush to the front of the stage as the sound continues. When I glance upward, I see the video has been posted on Karim's Facebook page. I crane my neck back at Eric, and half of his lip twitches.

So I had guessed right, sort of. The family was in on something. But maybe it was to out Antonia.

As I sprint back to Eric, to launch into his chest and bury myself there, something flickers in my periphery. Flames.

Fire consumes the red curtains.

Antonia said not to play with fire. We expose her; we get burned.

Eric snatches my hand, and we sprint out the backstage exit on the other side of the stage. Cast and crew surge behind us. I hope and pray the audience manages to escape the building.

We rush to the parking lot and huddle next to parked cars. A fire truck blares its horn and shields the building from our view. I sit and cradle myself into Eric beside me.

"Anyone know where Antonia went?" Karim asks this.

We all shake our heads.

Fire, a clever distraction. She probably made an exit somewhere out the other end of the building. We can hope the police track her down. Shouldn't take them much time.

Silence overtakes us as the crowd rushes to their cars. We find a spot in the dirt, away from the reversing vehicles, and form little sand turtles to pass the time and get our minds off of whatever the heck just happened.

"So." I poke eyes into the turtle's head. "Anyone else want to explain to me what just happened?"

CHAPTER 28

"First of all, Karim and I aren't in love."

Meg squeezes Karim's shoulder, then returns to adding lines to the turtle's shell.

"You aren't?"

That could explain why Meg seemed to be okay with Karim's "cheating."

"No, Karim, he—"

"Auditioned to be a part of the company for three months." Karim tucks his feet underneath his legs in crisscross applesauce. "But Antonia had started to worry that I was learning a little bit too much. So she…"

He breaks off.

"Set us up together." Meg finishes for him. "Karim has a lot of family and friends back home. Has a big heart. And let's just say, he didn't want them to meet their end soon, so he agreed to the marriage."

She starts to work on the turtle's legs. Hands smooth out the sand to form even triangles.

"Of course, Karim and I weren't having it. Antonia mentioned something like a year-long engagement, so we got to work, trying to figure out ways to get a confession out of her."

Hence why Karim stationed so many cameras around the theater.

I imagine the painstaking hours it takes him to go through all of the videos, in the hopes that Antonia slipped up and spoke out of turn.

"She wasn't cooperating. And so we decided to do two things. One—"

Meg throws up her index finger. Dust powders her skin.

"—we figured out that Eric here was recording videos. He's been Antonia's best-kept secret. But if he were to get online and the world could see him, she'd have to handle the PR. Maybe something that catastrophic could cause her to slip up and confess."

It must not have, though.

Antonia took the videos in stride and allowed her son to join the group.

"And two—we told Richard to hire a mole."

Up went the second finger, to represent Carmen.

"We'd been sensing, for a while, that he was getting more and more uneasy about Antonia. Although he was the keep-your-head-low kind of guy, we could tell he knew more than he let on. It was too late for him, but not too late for anyone he hired."

Lace from my wedding dress billows in the wind.

Every inch of me wants to tear it off. Children linger nearby, next to their cars. Can't scar them for life, so we'll keep the clothes on. They wave at us, and we return the gesture.

A few couples stop by and ask us to sign the programs. Telling us "good job" and "it's a shame we couldn't see the rest."

Once they leave, Meg continues.

"Of course, Carmen chickened out. So we figured, there went that plan. And then you stepped in."

Me.

"Was I bait, then?"

Fire ants run up and down my skin at the thought of that. Did Meg and Karim purposely withhold info from me so I could get myself into almost point-of-no-return territory?

"Oh, girl, of course not. At first, I'd even told you to keep your head down. But you couldn't help yourself. You were such a little Nancy Drew, that we couldn't stop you. So we decided that if anyone could tease information out of Antonia, it was you."

"Why didn't you just tell her that then?"

Red inches up Eric's neck. They must've kept him out of the loop too. And after what happened with his dad, Eric probably stayed as far away from family secrets as he could.

Meg crosses her arms. "Antonia made us swear to secrecy. So we couldn't exactly go up to Tina and be like, 'Yeah so Aunt Antonia has been murdering all the people. Want to record a confession from her for us?'"

"But—"

Karim lifts a finger before working on the turtle tail.

"—we could try and get her to ask us for help."

"Hence why I was trying to hang with you all the time, chica. Not just because you're good company, but because I wanted you to trust me. Of course, Antonia threw a whole wrench into that by making it seem like Karim and I actually had something to do with the murders."

I think back to the first day at the Cleveland opera house. How Meg passed out, and I thought she'd faked fainting to steal the ship's helm.

"What exactly is the medical condition you deal with, Meg?"

And why hadn't I asked this before?

"POTS. Basically, my blood doesn't circulate right. So I can get dizzy, nauseous, or faint a lot—especially if I push myself too much. Also the reason why I want to get out of opera. It's a lot on the body, and the opera world is really terrible for people with disabilities."

POTS. Hmm, would have to look up that one.

Shame on me for ever thinking she'd faked an invisible illness.

"And I can see you looking upset that I didn't share it with you. Antonia's the suck-it-up type, so I don't think she even believed my disease was real in the first place. I didn't talk about it for those reasons."

Red lights from the fire truck continue to whir in circles. Although, by now, the sirens have died.

"Guys, I—" My voice cracks. "I didn't get a clear confession from her. She basically made me tell her what she did."

"Oh, we know." Karim holds up his phone. "But it was apparently enough to make her freak out and try to burn down a theater. Not a good look for her."

If they nabbed her, maybe they could pull us in for questioning.

I wipe the sand off of my fingertips and rise to get the grains out of the dress.

"So, what do we do now?"

Unease lingers in my gut. What if she finds us and murders us in our sleep?

Could she risk it with her pseudo-confession floating around? Or would she let us go this time around?

"Wait," Meg says. "And hope justice prevails. I'm sure we're going to be heading back to Ohio within the coming weeks, though. And maybe, just maybe, after all of this, we can stay good friends."

Without a doubt.

Eric motions me to join him several feet away from Karim and Meg. Tucks me into a hug.

"I completely understand if you'd want to break all ties with us, though."

"You? Are you kidding?" I break off and cup his chin. "What's the point of a boyfriend if he doesn't have a psychopathic mom?"

This makes him chuckle. And we re-embrace.

"Although, I think I may just need a few days to myself, Eric. To process. Then maybe we can find a time to get together and pick up where we left off."

"That's more than fair. I think I have one more piece of business I need to take care of myself."

Before I can ask what, Meg shrieks.

I break away and turn to her. Mirth explodes in her expression. She holds up her phone.

"Guys, I got a text. Raph just woke up."

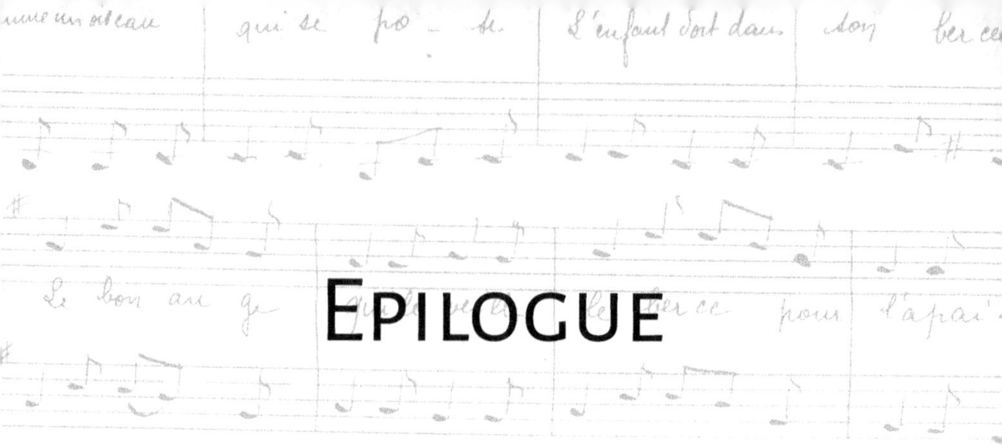

EPILOGUE

I t takes more than a few days to process.

Some time, during the night of the preview performance, the police track down Antonia. A stage manager caught her in the act of setting the curtains on fire. For the first time, she didn't hire out someone to do her dirty work.

When I reconnect with Raph on a FaceTime call, he explains that something smacked him in the back of his head, and the next thing he knew, he woke up in the hospital.

Maybe Antonia did have a personal hand in that one. She could've run into the theater box and whacked him on the head with an oar or something. But something tells me she could've also asked someone else to do it.

After the police take us in for some questioning, I return home. Mom greets me at the airport with a boa constrictor hug and tells me I cannot leave the house for any reason for the next few days.

She says "kidding," but not totally sure if she is.

For the next few days, I catch up on shows I've missed binging and babysit the kids.

Three weeks after the whole ordeal—into the start of my gap year—a package arrives on our front step, addressed to me.

I tear open the casing and a paper box, tied up with strings, sits in my hand. A note is attached to it. My breath hitches. *Please tell me Antonia didn't make a prison break.*

The note:

"Do not open this box until you watch the recent video I uploaded. Miss you. Hope to see you soon."

I tuck myself into my bedroom and pull open my phone.

For the first time ever, I download the video app and create a username. Mom will kill me because she absolutely hates this social media platform in particular. But she'll have to deal.

I escaped a murderer and a wedding this summer. Something tells me I can handle a lecture.

I find his profile, follow him, and tap on the newest video.

"Hey, guys. Sorry that I've been gone for the past few weeks. As I'm sure you've been seeing tons of videos about it, a certain leak from one of our productions has put my mom under hot water."

Understatement of the year. Jail time meant a little more than "hot water" in my mind.

"And after that whole ordeal, I've been thinking a lot about my relationship with her. And how she encouraged me to hide. For the longest time, I thought I deserved to be tucked away, invisible."

I sink into a beanbag chair.

"After you guys, and a certain amazing soprano walked into my life, I think I've been able to see past those lies. Secrets belong to us. But in due time, they're worth sharing. We're worth sharing. So."

He sets his phone onto a sturdy surface and unhooks the mask from his face. I gasp. Already the video has gotten millions of views. He uploaded this a few days before, probably when he sent the package off to me.

"Hello, world. This is me. All of me."

The video stops. I glance down at the paper package in my lip. Fingers reach for the strings and untie the knot. As I unfold the paper, I flip open the lid to a velvety box underneath.

"Eric, you better not be giving me a ring—" Or roses. Lord knows I cannot take a look at a rose bush without resisting the urge to vomit.

My words cut off. There are two items at the bottom of the box.

A paperweight angel.

And...

I run a finger up and down the chain. "You son of a gun, you did it."

And the Kintsugi necklace.

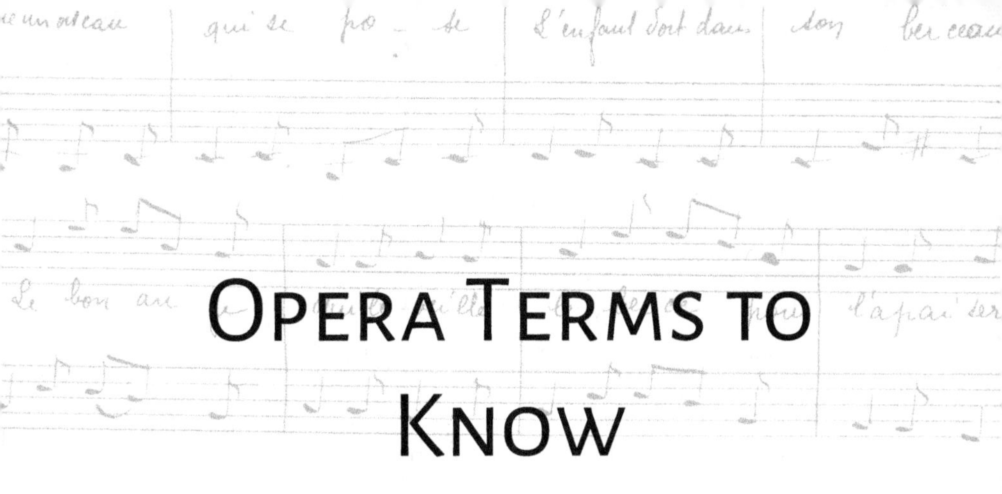

Opera Terms to Know

Although you can probably figure out from the context of passages what certain words mean, I figured it may help to have a glossary of terms. Especially if you were as excited to explore the world of opera as I was.

Alto - One of the lower voice parts for a female in opera. There are not many leading roles that are altos, but you'll find many supporting roles who are.

Archives - Contained in some theaters, they will have a room dedicated to papers, photographs, and other important memorabilia pertaining to that particular opera house.

Aria - A piece for a specific voice part (soprano, alto, etc.).

Ballet Master/Mistress - Someone who instructs the dancers on the choreography for the show. The actors and dancers will be trained by different people. It's important for the actors to know the score, and for the dancers to know the dances. Actors will learn choreography, but nowhere near as rigorous as those of the dancers (in most cases).

Baritone - A middle-voice part for men. It's between tenor and bass.

Bass - The lowest voice part for men, known for deep, low notes.

Box Office Assistant - The person responsible for selling and managing ticket sales for an opera house. Opera tickets for professional theater, at the low end, are probably going to go for about $50. And the higher-end ones can be in the hundreds. Operas can seat thousands of patrons, so an opera house can make quite a bit of money in one night, if it has a full house.

Cadenza - A part in the music where the singer has the opportunity to ad-lib and really show off what they can do.

Chaîné - A ballet spin that requires twirling twice and then lifting one leg in a triangle shape.

Contralto - The lowest voice part for women in opera. These roles are really rare to find. Women can often sing men's voice parts as well when they play the role of a man in an opera.

Costume Shop - Where all the costumes for different shows are housed. Many actors will wear the same outfits (certain voice parts tend to require certain body types—although, thankfully, there are exceptions). Larger theaters will also have a separate room dedicated to creating the costumes.

Director - Much like theater, opera also has these. They will work with the singers to put on a believable performance, and will often meet with leading roles ahead of time one-on-one before a show.

Diva/Prima Donna: In opera, this usually has positive connotations. It means the lead female soprano lead in a show. At more professional opera houses, she'll get her own dressing room and tends to get preferential treatment.

Dress Run - A dress rehearsal, usually a day before the show. Although sometimes the day of a show, you may do a dress run too. Some opera houses also have preview performances. The actors will do a dress rehearsal for an audience who pays for discounted tickets.

Fortissimo - As loud as you can possibly sing/play a note. So basically, an impossible standard in music.

Libretto - The text of the opera. Think of it as an opera script. Actors will mark this up with highlighter, stickers, tabs, and pencils (most likely marking the double-consonants in other languages).

Lip Trills - A type of vocal warm-up where you raspberry your lips while singing notes. In opera, it's extremely important to loosen the tongue, jaw, lips, and to relieve tension in the throat and lymph nodes.

Maestro - A composer or a conductor. Often also be a teacher of music.

Manager - Every major opera company has one (or more) of these. They tend to have a base of operations in one theater—unlike the managers in this book who travel with a troupe. They are in charge of making sure everything is in place and runs smoothly.

Master Carpenter - The person in charge of constructing the scenery in a show. If there are moving parts, they are also in charge of engineering those. They operate under the direction of the technical director.

Mezzo - Otherwise known as a second soprano. One of the higher voice parts for women.

Orchestra - All professional shows will have one of these. They play in the orchestra pit, and during intermission, will often hang in the orchestra lounge.

Pianissimo - Really soft notes. Basically near-impossible for opera singers to hit. We have to think that some opera houses won't even mic the singers, so you have to have incredible projection abilities.

Props Mezzanine - It may go by other names, such as props storage, but it will always have props in the name. Props of all kinds are stored, often by category, in this place. If a theater is large enough, they may have an additional basement storage area for the larger props.

Scene/Scenic Shop - Where set pieces are made. You're going to find a lot of circular saws and protective eye gear back here. If there isn't a separate room dedicated to it, props may also be assembled and painted here.

Singing Straw – Singers will dip this straw into a few centimeters of water and sing solfege into the straw. This helps to relieve tension in the throat and gives them a smoother voice. Actors may sometimes even operate a humidifier or a stream inhaler.

Solfege - Do, re, mi, fa, sol, la, ti, do. Every note is given a name. And if we want to get really fancy, we can mention the ones on the chromatic scale (do, ti, te, la, le, sol, se, fa, mi, me, re, rah, do).

Soprano - The highest voice part for women, and in opera, they tend to be the leads.

Soubrette - A soprano with a slightly weaker or less developed voice. Her sound is going to be less full. There are many parts written for this type of voice. As sopranos develop their voices, they may get propelled into some of the categories with a little more power behind the voice such as Lyric Soprano or Dramatic Coloratura.

Stage Manager - Much like theater, you'll find these people backstage, making sure singers are entering on time, and that everything is running smoothly during the show. They're probably also dancing backstage and imitating what you are doing on stage. It can't be helped.

Supernumerary - People who fill the non-speaking background roles.

Supertitles - If an opera is in a different language than that the audience members speak, they may put subtitles on a screen above the stage.

Tablework - A theater term, although applicable to the world of opera. Actors will research their parts and the context of the play, to better understand their characters and the world they live in. Authors of books do this too. Sadly, actors and authors don't get to show everything they learn in the process, but tablework is still important nevertheless.

Technical Director - This person is in charge of several departments. They make sure that lighting, scenery, and carpentry are all in place. They also make sure that the company equipment is well cared for and up to date.

Tenor - The highest voice part for men. They often operate something known as a falsetto. Boys are lucky because they have a chest voice, head voice, and falsetto. Girls only have the chest voice and head voice.

Toi, Toi, Toi - The opera equivalent of "break a leg."

Trouser Role - When a woman is asked to perform the role of a man. This can happen pretty frequently in the world of opera.

Wig Shop - What it sounds like. Utmost care goes into the hair accessories of each show. Actors will often put on wig caps, or wig wraps (what looks like plastic wrap in some photos) and then will wear the wigs for each show. Sometimes actors are allowed to wear their natural hair for shows, but in professional companies, this is rarer.

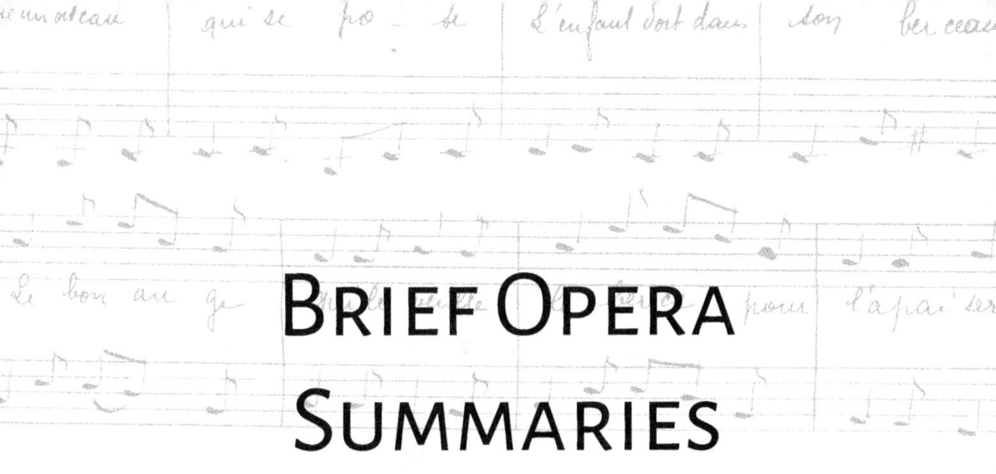

BRIEF OPERA SUMMARIES

Tina ultimately performs in three different operas. Although you can probably figure out from the context of the book what's generally happening in these, I'll provide some brief synopses below. I highly recommend checking out performances of these.

The Pirates of Penzance: It's Frederick's twenty-first birthday. He's been an indentured servant to pirates all of these years, since his nursery maid misheard his father's request to apprentice him to a "pilot" instead of "pirate." He cuts off all ties with the pirates and seeks to end them when he gets a chance. He meets Mabel, who offers to marry him. Mabel's father brought her and her sisters to the same island Frederick is on. When the pirates attempt to capture Mabel's sisters, their father (after the "Modern Major General" song) tells them he's an orphan. This tugs at the pirates' heartstrings because they, too, are orphans. They attempt to find a loophole to make Frederick a pirate again, so he can help to wreak revenge on the father—who is not, in fact, an orphan. It's revealed at the end of the play that the pirates were born from noble families. All is amended, and Frederick gets to be with Mabel.

Gianni Schicchi: A very rich man, Buoso, dies at the beginning of the opera. His family expects to receive a lot of riches out of his will. When they look at the will, they realize he's decided to donate it all to the church. Incensed, they ask the trickster Gianni Schicchi to impersonate Buoso when the notary arrives. At first Gianni refuses. But his daughter, Lauretta, pleads with him. She's in love with Buoso's nephew, and cannot be with him, unless he happens to fall into money. Gianni Schicchi goes through with the plan and manages to trick the notary. He gives the family some minor gifts, but tells the notary to give the majority of the inheritance to his "good friend Gianni Schicchi." Lauretta is now a rich daughter and can marry the love of her life. Gianni Schicchi's story stems from a character from Dante's Divine Comedy.

Phantom of the Opera - What this book makes several nods and parallels to. When the prima donna soprano is unavailable for performances, it's up to the young soprano Christine to fill in for her role. She's been training with a mysterious angel of music, a phantom who haunts the opera. Thinking that he is her father, she goes along with the lessons. Christine soon realizes that he is not her father and that he's responsible for several of the deaths and mishaps that have taken place in the opera house. Her lover, Raul, gets a little too involved in the whole scheme, and the Phantom, jealous for Christine, attempts to end his life. Christine's compassion for the Phantom sways his judgment, and he lets them go off and be together as the theater burns to the ground.

AUTHOR'S NOTE

The first time I saw *Phantom of the Opera*, the staged version, I walked away extremely confused. The Phantom, to my fifteen-year-old understanding at the time, was forty, Christine—a sixteen-year-old, and no one seemed to act with any kind of rationale.

The sequel staged production, *Love Never Dies,* made even less sense.

Christine, in particular, bugged me. Because she often, in many staged adaptations, just lets things happen to her, and she has little agency. The appeal failed to reach me...until I read the original book for the first time.

And everything suddenly made so much more sense.

The book, for those who haven't read it, varies a great deal from the staged version. But in the book, Christine has far more agency, and I absolutely love it. She constantly tricks the Phantom into releasing her, whenever he kidnaps her, by praising him and flirting with him.

She's very clever. And I wanted to bring a clever Christine to the pages of a book once again.

Something that also caught my eye in both versions of Phantom is this idea of what we see, versus what truly is. In this book, I wanted everyone to have a secret of some sort. And that only when we truly get to know a person, we can understand their intentions.

In the play version, Phantom is a misunderstood person, yearning for love.

In the book, he's a psychopath who murders people.

And in this book, I wanted my version of Christine to struggle with which phantom she's stumbled across. One who had gotten caught up in circumstances outside of his control, or one who held the strings the whole time?

Huge thank you to the readers who accompanied me on this journey. This book intimidated the heck out of me. Having written quite a few middle grades in 2021-2022, it had been a hot second since I'd written a YA book, twice the length of those MGs.

Every book scares me, but I wanted to make sure to capture the intrigue and everything that makes *Phantom of the Opera* so lovable. I do hope that I succeeded in this endeavor.

ACKNOWLEDGEMENTS

Because every book scares me to write, I want to first and foremost thank my Lord and Savior Jesus Christ who gives me the strength to write these in the first place. Thank You, Lord, that You see me—all of me, even the parts I keep secret from others—and choose to love me anyway. This one goes out to You.

To AJ, who leapt at this book concept and supported me full-force all the way. I hope I was able to provide enough swoony moments. I know that even though I write quite a few romances, I can get really shy when it comes to those vulnerable scenes.

To the wonderful editors who worked on this book—whose names I will include once I learn who is assigned this :) —I know I'm the world's worst proofreader when it comes to these things, so thank you for your grace. Thank you to the rest of the Q&F team. It takes a village to raise a book.

To my wonderful agent Tessa. As always, so sorry. I know I throw way too many books at you. At the time of writing this, thank you so much for finding homes for twenty-one of my books. I do hope we can house several more in the future.

To the theater programs I've participated in in the past, especially Taylor University Theatre, which helped me to get my feet wet in the world of opera. Opera and theater, although similar, are different entities in many ways. I enjoyed helping out on productions such as *The Marriage of Figaro*, *Gianni Schicchi*, and the *Pirates of Penzance*.

To the wonderful world of #operatok. Although I did much more research than just scrolling on Tiktok, I promise, thank you so much for bringing the world of opera to life, and contextualizing it for a whole new generation.

To my relentless encouragers. I think now of Jess, Tyler, Trey, David, James, Alyssa, Ellen, Sonya, Nikki, the Pizza Squad, The Cyle Chat, The PWR Chat, and all the other silly group chats I'm a part of. Huge shout out to my family, as well, for supporting me in all writing endeavors. I'm sorry I write way too many books—and you all are having a tough time keeping up with them. I'm having a hard time keeping up with them too.

To my friends and family members who have POTS. Disabilities need to be represented more in fiction, and I've only seen a handful of titles with characters who have this, so I was so excited to introduce another one to the scene.

To music teachers past and present who gave me a good understanding of musical dynamics, breath support, stretching vocal range, and more. Looking at you Mrs. Moore, Dr. Kwan, Miss Tina, Connie, and the numerous other vocal directors in the number of choirs I've been in—I'm afraid I may have lost count.

To my dance instructors in the past who gave me a nine-year understanding of movement. Although I was unable to stick with the craft due to finances, it has shaped my performances and understanding for this book project.

To the many wonderful people who shared about the book upon launching. I think of the cover revealers, reviewers, sharers, and all the lovely people who request this book at their library. What an absolute dream!

And of course, to the wonderful readers. Thank you for sticking with me for another tale—or if this is your first time—welcome, and I sincerely hope you enjoyed the read! You are what makes this performance so, so worth it. Thank you for your encouraging notes, your angry voicemails, messages when I throw plot twists your way, and everything in between.